Kelly's Keys

Joshua Sarver

iUniverse, Inc.
Bloomington

iUniverse books may be ordered through booksellers or by contacting:

iUniverse
1663 Liberty Drive
Bloomington, IN 47403
www.iuniverse.com
1-800-Authors (1-800-288-4677)

Because of the dynamic nature of the Internet, any web addresses or links contained in this book may have changed since publication and may no longer be valid. The views expressed in this work are solely those of the author and do not necessarily reflect the views of the publisher, and the publisher hereby disclaims any responsibility for them.

Any people depicted in stock imagery provided by Thinkstock are models, and such images are being used for illustrative purposes only.

Certain stock imagery © Thinkstock.

ISBN: 978-1-4502-9695-3 (sc)
ISBN: 978-1-4502-9694-6 (hc)
ISBN: 978-1-4502-9693-9 (ebook)

Printed in the United States of America

Library of Congress Control Number: 2011902325

iUniverse rev. date: 02/18/2011

for Kelly,
my children, my family and friends

"I won't let you die, trust me, I've got you." –anonymous EMT

Acknowledgements

To my friends that made this book possible.

Bill Brennen
Donna Dyke
Bryan Huff
Al Lewin
Kari Selinger

Introduction

Many wonderful works of prose attempt to describe the thoughts, feelings and emotions one feels when one true love, that crosses all boundaries of time and distance, enters into their life. This work is somewhat unique and provides a fictional concept of reality, love, loss, life, death and ultimately emotional resurrection.

Each component is necessary to accurately describe the plethora of emotions that bombard the soul when love is experienced in a pure unadulterated form. I wrote this book to describe true love and how it can save your life.

I spent the majority of my life surrounded by death, agony, grief and in rare cases had the opportunity to observe the effects that true love can have on an individual and the miraculous effect it can have on the human soul.

This story is my perception of what could happen, if one were lucky enough to come to the edge of darkness and despair nearing the edge of life and at the last moment be retrieved from the abyss of darkness by the true love only a special woman can give.

My life as a paramedic, responsible for the lives of others, pales in comparison to the love of a woman that against every challenge, barrier and obstacle pushes forward to save the existence of the one she loves.

I hope you enjoy the book.

Joshua

Foreward
by Bill Brennen

My name is Bill, and I am a friend to this story's author. We met while working at a private ambulance service in a small Midwestern town in southern Illinois; both of us being employed in the field for some time, found common ground swapping stories and experiences. As we sat up late at night on our 24 hours shifts, smoking cigarettes and downing pot after pot of coffee, we would talk.

We would discuss all sorts of topics from philosophy, religion, and politics, to obscure movies and books; most of the time though, it was some sort of very dark, morbid humor that only veterans of emergency services could appreciate. This sort of thing is fairly common in our profession. If we couldn't laugh, surely we would go mad. It's a sort of coping mechanism to help deal with the absolute extremes of the job.

A lot of our days would consist of transporting elderly patients to and fro from nursing homes and the ER for garden variety problems that don't necessarily warrant lights and sirens. For the most part, they are mundane and uneventful trips that can be frustrating to the adrenaline junkies that seem attracted to this job.

Then there are the calls that can truly change your life, or at least your perspective of it. Some are an absolute gift; like helping a young mother, bring life into the world in the back of your ambulance. Once in awhile, you may actually get a pulse back from a pulseless patient and watch them leave the hospital in a week or two. These calls reinforce the belief that you are doing some good in the world.

There are others too that will leave you questioning the existence of a higher power. Too many times you will be staring at the horrible consequences of poor judgment, poor living, or just plain bad luck. You are the one thrown into these situations to try and make it better. Despite what network television tries to sell you, not everyone lives another day.

Most, if not all, people drawn to this job want to be a hero in one way shape or form. These bad calls are the ones that slap us in the face and bring us back to reality. They wear on you over the years.

I offer this little glimpse into the world of Emergency Medical Services, as a reference to the character of the author. Through all the years of service, with all its ups and down, Josh was living the text of this book. Over the years, the content of this book and its story were being played out.

Josh is one of the good guys. He's scrappy, sometimes a little scruffy, and a little more educated than the average Joe. Everything he has written in this book has some truth to it. I can attest to this because I heard the story and witnessed the later chapters firsthand.

Josh has written, in a way, his autobiography in the following pages. Most, if not all, the characters in the story could exist in the real world. He has lived an extraordinary life in comparison to what most people would consider normal. I count myself lucky for having met him and calling him a friend.

I would hope that the readers find half the enjoyment in these pages that I have experienced watching the actual events unfold. The old adage, "You can't make this stuff up." holds true.

Bill Brennan

Chapter 1

"Al!"

The paramedic breathed heavily as he clutched the small cellular flip phone in his right hand. His blurry vision began to clear as sweat poured from his body and dripped onto the concrete floor of the two car garage in a small town a few miles south of Springdale, Illinois.

"It's Josh, come get me!" He breathed heavily struggling to speak into the handset.

His lungs, partially paralyzed, were becoming useless and unable to inhale the precious life-sustaining air that surrounded his weakened body. He was nearing unconsciousness. Josh had to force himself to breathe. He had miscalculated. He was supposed to be dead already. He had taken plenty of the drugs, yet something had gone wrong.

"Josh, buddy? Is that you? What happened, huh— wha—?"

Al stammered in shock realizing he was talking to a long-time friend and, from his impression, a very solid strong man in the emergency services profession.

"Yeah, man—I'm dying Al— if you don't hurry! OD—30 tabs of Tramadol—30 mgs each. Nine hours ago, full—"

Josh had to stop talking and force himself to inhale. His view of the garage door was becoming blurry. He wasn't drifting off to sleep like he planned. He was going to die violently. The OD was going wrong. His blood pressure was going crazy, he could feel it. He was going to be fully alert when his lungs gave out. He was going to suffocate! He wished he had stayed in front of the train a week ago and let it splatter him all over the tracks. At least it would be done.

Now, with this escapade, he feared he would end up with brain damage if his lungs didn't start working soon.

"I need 4 mgs of Narcan— bad! Don't call anyone else. Just you and Bryan come and get me!" He said quickly to save what air he had left in his lungs.

"Bryan! It's Josh!" Al screamed as the idea sunk into his head that Josh had tried to kill himself. It is a bad thing when a medic attempts suicide, they usually succeed. Josh was almost there.

"Just fucking go, Al! I know what is going on! I know! Let's go— goddamn it! I talked to him at one!" Bryan screamed in the background as he fumbled to zip his combat boots.

"We are coming, buddy— hang on! We are coming!" Al said quickly, as he dropped the phone to the floor.

"Hurry Al, or I am not gonna be alive when you get here." Josh whispered to himself as he lost his grip on the telephone. Al and Bryan were on their way, but he did not expect them to make it in time.

He began to crawl toward the entry door. He couldn't breathe. His head felt like it was full of sledge hammers that were smashing into his brain. He knew his blood pressure was not right, he expected it to be low. He was wrong. Uncharacteristic of a narcotic overdose, his blood pressure was nearly at stroke level. The drugs had fully metabolized and were racing through his system with a vengeance.

Josh had awakened twice before and actually grinned as the he felt the paralysis beginning in his lungs. All was working according to plan. He became drowsy in 30 minutes, as he expected, after ingesting the pills. He felt his kidneys and intestines stop working, he even smiled with this event; he began to panic when something went wrong—he kept waking up. The drugs met Josh's bloodstream at 1:30 AM. It was now nine or ten in the morning. He should have been dead already, but his body kept fighting and forcing him awake with the severe pain in his head. His body was fighting to survive whether he wanted it to or not.

A paramedic, who was one of the best, was calling his own crew to save his life. The man who had saved many lives in the last seventeen years was now asking someone else for help. Josh regretted that he had failed in the suicide. He wished he had planned better.

He crawled to the door and after several attempts pushed it open. He fell, face-first, onto the patio outside his garage. His vision was becoming feint and his lungs were stiffening. Josh was almost there. The pain was excruciating. He was going to enter hell screaming. He wished he could forget how he came to this dark place; sadly, he could remember every detail in vivid clarity. He hoped he was still alive tomorrow to regret it all.

Josh began to fall asleep as the sirens screamed in the distance. It would not be long before he could not hear them anymore. He wanted this to all be a dream. As his eyes closed he thought," *I wish I was back in Tremane"*.

Seventeen years earlier, a phone rings at 3:00AM in a small apartment in Tremane, Illinois. Tremane was a country town, nearly a hundred miles from St. Louis, Missouri to the east, and six hours south of Chicago. It is a little town of only ten thousand, if you do not count the pets.

It was a place that held little significance in the state identified as the Land of Lincoln. It is an interesting paradox that Illinois, made famous by honest Abe, was home to one of the most famous criminals in history, Al Capone, who operated in one of the most corrupt cities in the country, namely Chicago. Illinois is full of contradictions.

Tremane was a typical agricultural community far removed from city life. Tractors could be seen slowing traffic on roadways during harvest, everyone knew everyone else's business and if they didn't, all they needed to do was get a haircut. In the time it took to have your hair trimmed, you were informed of divorces, marriages, births, deaths and the recent scandals about town. High school football superstars now managed the local tire shop and former prom queens sold insurance. Life was relatively simple and average. Some would say boring.

The phone kept ringing. Josh groaned and uttered a few curses under his breath as he picked up the receiver.

"Uh huh", he muttered from under the blankets.

"Hey, Lil Shit … You got a woman in there?" Johnny's voice emitted from the receiver accompanied by a hint of sarcasm.

"No, if I did, I wouldn't be talking to your sorry ass now would I? What's up?" Josh asked.

"Got one to go to Saint Luke's, Lil Shit, you want it?" Johnny asked.

"Yeah, sure, be there in a minute", he said and hung up the phone.

It was too early. Josh hated being up in the daytime and daylight would be arriving in a couple of hours. He had been a bit nocturnal since he was a little kid. He would fight sleep until the late hours of the evening and then have trouble waking up for school the next morning. He was a night-owl from birth. He loved being up when others were asleep and vice versa. He liked to let the mundane days pass him by and enjoyed being awake in the midnight hours when the odd things that go bump in the night really bumped hard.

He had only been asleep for an hour. He found the night exciting and his job more so. He stayed awake late into the night, even on the nights he was not working. It was odd to refer to his childhood as something in the distant past considering he was only eighteen. In many ways he still acted like a little boy but he had a very grown up job or so he fantasized.

Josh, a.k.a Little Shit, was an emergency medical technician or EMT. He was introduced to the profession by accident. His high school friends bet him a case of beer that he was not "smart enough" to pass the course. He proved them wrong three months later after completing his training program with a respectable *B* in the course. Josh applied for a position at the local hospital and was hired as a per-diem employee. He worked whenever they asked for his help.

He was rarely involved in anything critical since he was rated as an EMT-A. The *A* stood for ambulance, which simply meant that you were allowed to work on a basic life support ambulance or assist Paramedics that worked on an advanced life support unit. The paramedics were the only ones allowed to handle the tough calls. His participation in the department was minimal. He would transport stable patients by ambulance from one hospital to another. He was basically a medical babysitter.

The extent of his medical training was barely more than advanced first aid and CPR. Nonetheless, he fancied himself as a lifesaver on his way to becoming a bonafide hero. In high school his response to the senior question *"What do you want to do with your life?"* was simple, *"Get paid for being a hero!"* He was to say the least, a bit cocky.

His confidence stemmed from necessity and a bit of naivety as well. At five feet five inches tall and one hundred and sixteen pounds he was truly a little shit. Do not let his size fool you. He had a lot of fire burning inside of his small frame.

Josh had already been arrested once in school for pounding on a kid, twice his size, because of the harsh comments the boy had made regarding a girl. Josh managed to damage the bully's teeth with a well placed left jab and multiple right hooks, before being dragged kicking and cursing to the principal's office.

Josh was a scrapper. He had to be to survive. He grew up in the country and learned to live on little and hope for greatness. He was a dreamer. His father and mother were devout Christians. His father was a Pentecostal pastor at one time. His mother was a small framed black-haired woman with a meek personality. He had a poor, but fairly structured, childhood that included church, school and chores in that order.

Joshua was the eldest of two boys. His brother was appropriately named Caleb to complete the pair. Joshua's mother was not happy when Josh discovered the biblical story of Joshua and Caleb and said with excitement in his voice,

"Mom, did you know you named us after two spies that destroyed a city with the help of a hooker?"

He was referring to the deal the two biblical characters made with Rahab, the harlot, to spare her family if she would signal the approaching Israelites when it was the optimal time to attack by waving a scarf out her window. The Israelites destroyed the city but left the source of the signal, Rahab's home unharmed.

He enjoyed the idea of his namesake and often felt like he had some of the talents of the biblical Joshua. He enjoyed being a scrappy character that would fight men but speak softly to women. His mother did not share his zeal as she walked away grumbling something about it being meant as a servant of the Lord not a womanizing con-artist. Facts are facts. Both Joshua's seemed to have this little talent but, that flaw aside, they both tried to be noble despite their little faults.

He hated church, tolerated school and despised chores. He hated the country life and everything about it. His father had little education and bad luck with jobs but always preached that God would provide. He felt his parents were insane for believing in that philosophy. He learned to work by growing up on a scrap of dirt with a few head of hogs, one cow, and ten chickens that his father fancied a farm. He thought it was just a dirt trap. He could not wait to get away from the farm and escape to the big city.

The boy had plans to travel ten states away, never to be heard from again. He made it twelve miles. He always knew he was different from his parents. His brother was more like them. At the age of seventeen he began his "hero-training" while secretly planning to save the world. He was a dreamer.

He tossed the covers away from his naked body and sat on the edge of the bed. He rubbed the sleep out of his eyes and stood up. He surveyed his small empire where he was almighty king. Josh resided in a basement apartment that was put together for him by a two friends from the hospital, Tanner and Susy. Tanner was a radiology technologist that acquired the house as a result of a divorce. Susy was an EMT that worked with Josh.

In exchange for the room, he paid for a third of the rent and utilities. The basement was his little world. Apparently, Tanner and Susy felt that they needed to look out for Josh. He had been living in the hospital call rooms to avoid the farm and, of course, be available to the hospital if tragedy struck and the world needed saving. He romanticized everything.

The trio split the living expenses, and was a fairly cohesive family unit considering they all worked different shifts. Josh enjoyed the inexpensive lifestyle since he was only paid five dollars and five cents per hour.

He inherited a cat from Susy and Tanner that seemed to like to hang out in the basement. A gray Persian named Harry, who thought Josh had the best part of the house. Harry seemed to adopt Josh the same way the girls did. Josh didn't mind the cat. Harry was good company late at night when everyone else was asleep.

He groaned again and stretched. His ribs were always visible when he did. He hated being so small, he would have to fix that. He was lifting weights at the YMCA with Jake and Tony, a couple of amateur bodybuilders that had befriended him. He thought that people helped him due to his charming personality but in reality they were kind and saw how badly he wanted to be someone that everyone admired. In a way Josh was a people pleaser.

The teen took a shower and washed his brown hair which fell just below the collar. He had long hair in high school, just to rebel against his parents, but he had to cut it to get the job. He planned to let it grow again; he liked the "rockstar" look.

He had been working at the hospital since May. It was now October and as the temperature started to drop his experience as a professional lifesaver began to mount, or so he fantasized. Five months is a long time for an eighteen year old.

As he brushed his teeth and looked in the mirror, he gave his best, "*I'm here to help you*" look and grinned. One of those crooked, evil grins that you see from a child when they have chocolate on their face. He was told he looked like *Alex Keaton*, the Michael J. Fox character from the eighties sitcom, *Family Ties*. He didn't think so. He had high cheekbones, dark hair and hazel eyes that would change colors from green to blue, depending on his mood and the clothes he wore.

He was, at best, a cute kid that tried really hard to please. He had a sense of humor about his own silliness that made others laugh. He always had good timing with a joke. One special talent he possessed was the ability to write poetry whenever the mood stuck him. He was never sure how he gained that skill, but he assumed it was from some unknown and probably famous relative.

Josh gathered his uniform out of the dryer. Tanner had just taught him how to do laundry the week before. He was proud that he could do everything on his own, even cook if it involved a microwave.

He put on the blue dress pants and the heather blue polyester uniform shirt. He loved the way it felt. Each time he wore the shirt he would look at the patch on his right shoulder with the words Lafayette County Hospital – Knowledge, Speed, and Concern— that encircled a Star of Life. On his left shoulder he sported the Illinois EMT patch. He was so proud to be an official—something.

The would-be hero strapped on his gear which included: a pair of trauma shears (he had only cut paper with so far), a glove pouch (that had rarely been used), two pair of hemostats (that did not have a scratch), and a shiny black pager that was two months old. He was ready to save the world.

He ran up the stairs with Harry at his heels. He opened the door and took a deep breath as the cool morning wind caressed his face. Josh turned to say a brief farewell to Harry.

"Goodbye Tiger, be back soon, maybe with a treat— stay warm little buddy." He said giving Harry, who was still sitting on the threshold, a scratch behind the ears.

Josh could smell winter coming, the leaves had just started to turn. He knew the coming winter meant slick roads and crashes, all the more opportunity to be a hero.

He opened the door to his tan nineteen eighty-seven Chevrolet S-10 and turned the key. The truck started with a whine. He slammed it into reverse, popped the clutch and careened out of the driveway of the house on Elm Street. He drove quickly to the hospital and parked in the on-call space for ambulance personnel. He felt like a doctor when he did that.

He ran up the ramp and opened the ER door. Sarah was working. He loved to flirt with her although she did not know he was flirting.

"I'm here, he stated as though he was waiting for applause.

"Good—the lady with the abdominal pain is ready, I think", she said nonchalantly.

"Triple A?" He questioned trying to sound medical. The only abdominal condition he could remember was an abdominal aortic aneurysm that would have warranted a helicopter and definitely not his pitiful self.

"Uh… I don't know what that is", Sarah replied, "but they said she hasn't pooped in four days and she won't stay here. She wants to see her doctor in St. Louis for the enema."

He felt the wind die out of his sails. He lowered his head and walked the rest of the way to the ER staff room.

"Hey Little Shit, Eric is bringing the truck around. Are you good to go?" Johnny, the EMS supervisor, said with a grin.

Johnny had taken him under his wing for some reason, he liked the boy. Since Johnny was the boss and considered himself "Big Shit", our little dreamer was, of course, "Little Shit." Johnny was a jovial man with thinning hair and a bit of a belly. He was thick in the shoulders and walked with a bit of a strut. He had been a paramedic for over fifteen years and enjoyed that fact. He liked to teach the newbies and boast a bit about his exploits. He chewed tobacco, coached wrestling and was overly flirtatious with any female in the room.

He was married with two kids, to a very attractive wife who worked as a nurse in the ICU. Josh always thought Johnny was lucky because he had such a beautiful wife. He wondered how you could even look at another female if you were married to a woman in the prime of her life who seemed to become more attractive as each year passed. Josh easily developed crushes on older women. He thought teenage girls were ridiculous. Girls his own age were not attractive to him in the least, no matter what they looked like. He liked women that knew what they wanted. Older women were stunning to Josh; he could barely contain his interest when he spied a beautiful woman in her forties that wore just the right amount of make-up.

Women in mid-life were a challenge and extremely seductive to him. He looked at them with a sense of respect and desire. He rarely spoke to them but he could not help but gaze upon their beautiful faces where each thin line told a story of happiness, sadness or even love. Their deep eyes led to their soul and seemed to share brief flashes of secrets and loves long past. Josh dreamed of a beautiful woman that had class, style, beauty, charm and intelligence. He knew he would never have a chance with such a woman but he held the dream close to his heart never telling anyone for fear they would laugh at him.

Josh tended to place women on a pedestal in his heart. When a woman criticized her self about the thin lines around her eyes, Josh would interject quietly and say,

"Those mean you smile a lot and you are happy to be you. I think they make your eyes look brighter, but that is just my opinion".

He would quickly look at the ground and walk away after speaking in such a way. He often left the woman with a puzzled look and no doubt a flattered smile on her face.

Eric arrived with the cot. He was a backward lanky kid, about twenty years old, that Johnny used to tease about how hot his mother was and how Eric may be his son. Josh always laughed, as he did with most of Johnny's jokes, but Eric did not find humor in the jest.

Josh and Eric moved the cot into the room to find a frail elderly female. She was still sleeping. They gently woke her to inform her that she was going to see her doctor. She smiled softly at her transporters and touched Josh's hand.

"You're cute sweetie", she said in a grandmotherly voice. Josh smiled and said,

"Thank you, you are cute too, I will make sure you have a nice smooth trip to St. Louis."

He turned and glared a bit at Eric. He knew Eric's driving skills left a lot to be desired. Eric looked at the floor as if remembering the reprimand he received the week before from Roy, another paramedic, about driving too fast around corners.

They lifted the woman to the cot, bundled her like a child and strapped the seatbelts snuggly around her. A few moments later Eric and Josh were on there way to St. Louis.

Eric keyed the radio transmitter from the driver's seat and said in a low tone,

"KRS 218, 4 Adam 94"

"Go ahead", Sarah's soft sexy voice whispered through the speaker.

"10-76 to St. Luke's –mileage 126—126", he responded.

"10-4, time out— 0559, KRS 218— clear."

Josh was taking vitals on the patient and smiling. He enjoyed helping people even if they did not know he was helping them. The antique ambulance lumbered down the alley toward Grove Street and Interstate 70.

Josh took the patient's blood pressure again. She smiled and touched his hand for a second time. Her skin was soft like velvet. Her hands were old and showed signs of age but no clues of physical labor. She had no scars, no callousness of skin, and manicured nails. Dark spots of age had begun to cover the once elegant hands of this woman.

She smiled again and closed her eyes. As he watched the smile fade, he wondered what her life was like. She was well-dressed and her hair was styled and in place.

The hum of the engine and the steady rocking to and fro made it hard to stay awake. Most people felt seasick in the back of a moving ambulance but he felt comfortable. It was his world. He wanted to be a hero so badly and this was his laboratory in which to learn. He over-examined his patients, constantly checking heart sounds, lung sounds, and blood pressures. He thought it was best to learn what normal is on the stable patient so he could pick up diagnostic clues faster on those critical patients he hoped to be good enough to care for when he became a paramedic.

He flipped through the history and physical and found under the heading of social status that she had been married to a judge. They were married for sixty years. He wondered what would make someone stay with one person for that long. It must have been real love he mused, harboring a soft smile that was more visible in his thoughts than on his face.

Eric was talking to himself again as he drove. Josh wondered if that was a technique that Eric used to keep himself awake on these long boring transfers, or simply part of a split personality that was only allowed out when he thought no one was looking. Josh didn't care. As long as the truck kept moving and the dirty side stayed down, he was content to watch the judge's wife sleep and make his five dollars per hour doing it.

He yawned and stretched. He hated being up in the daytime. The sun started shining through the back windows. In the early morning hours the sun was too bright and angry. He fancied himself nocturnal and maybe even a bit of a natural vampire. He thought the nocturnal lifestyle added to his self-perceived persona of mystery. In reality he was a simple kid with dreams of being a hero in a world that never asked him to be anything. Blissfully ignorant is a fairly decent description of Josh, the EMT from Tremane, Illinois.

Several hours had passed as the ambulance pulled into the city of St. Louis. Josh moved to the jump seat to look at the muddy river as they crossed the bridge on Interstate 64-40.

St. Luke's West hospital came into view. Josh leaned forward to look at the site. He always liked the hospital. It was pretty and upscale. He checked on his patient once more and gave a rather lengthy but unimportant radio call-in. He always felt important giving patient reports. It made him feel official and in-charge.

Eric pulled into the bay and shut the engine down. Josh opened the back doors as the patient awoke and smiled.

"You're cute, sweetie", she repeated. He wondered if that was the only thing she was capable of saying. He smiled back at the elderly woman as they unloaded her. Josh softly lowered the wheels of the cot to avoid jarring his fragile patient and Eric pressed the entry pad on the ER doors.

The doors opened slowly and the scent of alcohol and betadine wafted through the air. The smell of a hospital that induced nausea in most people was a familiar scent to our young heroes. They spent more of their time in a hospital than at home. The nurses were polite and Josh tried to flirt as much as possible and see if he had any takers. As usual they were all about business and ignored him. The considered him a young, green, throttle-jockey, with too much time on his hands.

They left the patient in the ER with the young nurses and began their trip back home. Eric was driving and Josh was dazing off into the late morning sun. It was close to lunch and Eric was whining about being hungry. Josh agreed to stop since he didn't know how long it would be before he had the opportunity eat again.

He had learned from the veterans that you eat what you can, when you can. You may be up for several days and not have the chance to eat a decent meal until the job is done. Especially if ER is crazy. It had the tendency to get that way. The full moon was the worst. The police and fire department personnel had the same attitude as the ER and EMS crews about the influence of the lunar celestial being and its ability to drive people insane.

Josh would have loved to be the paramedic on a full moon weekend. He relished the thought of being in charge when the proverbial shit hit the fan. He fantasized about barking orders at the scene of a ten car pile up with helicopters flying around like a massive evacuation from Saigon, kicking in doors, shocking a person back to life, delivering a baby, and carrying some scantily clad supermodel out of a burning building; which means, of course, she would be indebted to him forever for his heroism and beg him to marry her on the spot. The boy did have an active imagination.

"We are here." Eric interrupted his dream just as Josh was about to accept to the model's invitation to marry her. People were always stopping him from finishing that daydream.

He groaned as they walked into the restaurant dining room. The supermodel wife would have to wait. She would always be there. He was a stereotypical teenage boy. He was always seeing the world as he wanted it to be despite the harsh cold reality of true life.

He ordered a burger and fries along with coffee. He loved coffee. By now he was already an addict thanks to the summers he spent with his grandfather. His grandfather, Leonard, was a WWII vet that was a machine-gunner during the Normandy invasion. He hit the beach at the Utah location and survived throughout the war. He was very close to Joshua. He taught him how to make wine, corncob pipes and "good coffee", which was too strong for most connoisseurs.

Josh and the old man would play rummy and peanut poker for hours while he told funny stories about the war. Leonard always filtered the horrors he must have experienced during combat to protect his little man from any bad thoughts or potential nightmares. After grandma would go to bed they would watch old black and white comedies and, if they were lucky, a Raquel Welch movie would be showing and they could watch her run from dinosaurs while wearing a fur bikini.

Josh loved his grandfather dearly. He always feared that he would never be such a great man as his grandfather. He was a war hero and Josh knew that if he could just be some kind of hero his grandpa would be proud. The old man was already proud of his grandson and said so everyday, but Josh was thickheaded about things concerning himself. He had to prove everything. He was a stubborn child but loyal to that old man and thought his word was law. At eighteen he still felt the same way.

He drank his sixth cup of coffee and reminded himself that he needed to go see his grandpa soon. Leonard was dying of emphysema and Josh knew it. He had been sick for a while, but Josh always knew his grandpa would pull through and always be there for him. The German army couldn't kill him so why worry about a cough. Grandpa was indestructible and someday Josh would be too.

The drive back was a bit longer than they expected. Traffic on Poplar Street Bridge was in a gridlock due to construction. Eric cursed constantly. Josh laughed at him.

"Go screw yourself!" Eric growled.

"I just may", Josh replied jokingly, "nobody loves me like I do."

He stared out the window as Eric sped back to Tremane. Josh would lose himself in his dreams as he watched the landscape morph into a blur of colors. No one would be waiting for him at home. He knew the only real companion he had was Harry. Josh was a lonely but hopeful kid that had a world of heart to give to a woman if she would simply give him the chance.

Chapter 2

The emergency room was already steady with patient activity in Tremane. The evening rush of people arriving with sore throats, shortness of breath, chest pain and sprained ankles, was in full swing by five o' clock in the evening. Tonya and Lilly were working this particular day.

Tonya was tough. She had been in EMS before and had seen a lifetime's worth of death and grief. She had become cold to most things. Occasionally, a patient would strike a cord in her heart and you would see her soft side, but you had to watch closely because it was gone in an instant.

Tonya was a big girl and she didn't care. She had purple red hair, from too many dye jobs that just never seemed to work right, and a tan. She had a round face and dark eyes. She was an excellent ER nurse and a Trauma Nurse Specialist, TNS for short. She said TNS stood for "Takes No Shit" and she didn't from anyone. She was in a bloodhound rescue program and came to know Lilly.

Lilly was about as round as Tonya and just as tanned. She had platinum blonde hair and was about forty. At one time she was a bombshell, evidenced from past photos, but children, married life, and ER stress had helped her pack on the pounds. She was an avid dog lover and she clicked right away with Tonya when they met in OB some years back. She had a sick sense of humor as well and was just as cold as Tonya.

They were a good match and a hell of an ER crew. The ER buzzer went off signaling a patient was arriving at the registration desk.

Lilly got up first spouting" Great, now we are gonna miss supper! If this doctor would get his ass movin' we could get these people outta here!"

"I will be there in a minute unless they are dying. Shit, all I wanted was supper on time for once!" Tonya barked. Tonya soon entered into room three and began to take the history on the new patient. Lilly stomped around to take vital signs.

Josh and Eric were pulling in to the Quick Stop to get fuel. Josh was on his eighth cup of coffee by now and the sun is starting to descend. He liked the fact that it was getting dark earlier during autumn in southern Illinois. He was more in his element now. He felt energetic. He was borderline slap-happy.

Eric walked inside to pay for the fuel. Josh finished pumping the gas and jumped into the driver's seat. He pulled up to the front door of the convenience store to pick up Eric. He cranked up the radio as Eric belted himself in. Josh never wore a seatbelt. He was just too cool for that. *"Seriously, what police officer is going to pull over an ambulance?"* He thought as he smiled.

He loved getting away with things. No matter how small and insignificant. *AC/DC* was on the radio. He blasted *Highway to Hell* as they darted up Grove Street toward the Eighth Street turn to the hospital. Josh felt so cool and completely in charge of his life.

Eric whined about the noise. Josh smiled and turned the music up louder and began to head-bang while driving. Eric just pouted.

A few moments later they pulled into the ambulance garage. Josh checked the oxygen levels while Eric darted for the hospital doors and the time clock.

Josh finished giving the ambulance a once over and walked out of the garage locking the door behind him. As he sauntered toward the ER door he wondered if Sarah stayed late. He was not sure what he was going to do tonight except hang out in the ER and wait for something good and exciting to happen. He opened the ER door and walked back to the staff room. He heard Tonya explaining a case to the ER doctor.

"Look doc, she is a sweet girl that has just been through a lotta shit lately. She is a police officer, from up north, and she just wants someone to listen. She has been on edge and just needs to relax. It has been really bad up there. Admit her like I ask and don't piss me off; I know where you eat and sleep, savvy?"

Josh had no idea what she was talking about but it sounded juicy. He sat down quietly to eavesdrop pretending to complete his run report which he finished hours ago. The story was just getting good and it gave him an excuse to be nosy.

"Okay, let's admit her for observation for fatigue and just give her a few days to relax." the doctor said reluctantly. Josh stood up and went for the coffee pot. Tonya stood in front of him. "Don't you need to go smoke little shit?" she snarled.

"Uh— I guess. Do I?" He inquired with a puzzled look on his face.

"Yes, you do. I have a patient in room 3 that is here for fatigue", she emphasized the word, "and you need to take her out to smoke and no stupid shit, you hear me?"

"Okay." Josh agreed to go, glad to be helping Tonya whom he idolized.

Josh was used to this. Since he was a smoker, *Marlboro Reds* as a matter of fact, he was always given smoke detail for patients that the ER wanted to keep an eye on. He didn't mind it; it was a chance to have a cigarette and get paid for it, plus she may be nice to look at.

He walked a few steps down the hall and started to speak before looking up.

"Hi, I'm Josh I heard you needed a ciagreee—", his voice trailed off.

Sitting on the cot with her right leg tucked neatly under her left, semi-Indian style, was the most beautiful creature he had ever seen. For once, Josh was speechless.

She was so perfect. Her face was soft and tanned. She had the smoothest skin he had ever seen. Her eyes were a bit swollen from recent tears but they were cinnamon brown and accentuated her auburn hair that fell just passed the shoulders. She was thin, muscular and beautiful.

He could tell she was probably about thirty which drove his heart into his throat that much further. She looked at him with pleading eyes as if to say, "Get me out of here, this was a bad idea."

She said not a word. She just nodded her head and stood up. As he watched her gather her cigarettes (Misty Blues in the white box with stripes down the side), and lighter he nearly tripped over his own feet.

She was about five feet six or seven inches tall with a slender build and the most perfect set of legs he had ever seen. She couldn't have weighed more than one twenty but it was all put together as if God took time to do it by hand. To Josh, she was like a beautiful gift for him to catch a glimpse, if only for a moment.

He swallowed hard as she walked in front of him. He couldn't help but notice her derriere. Her body was firm and toned. He could tell there was lean muscle hiding beneath those snug jeans and that blue polo shirt. She looked like she could have been a dancer the way she walked with light footsteps and perfect balance. She turned to look at him as they walked out the door.

"Here?" she asked.

He immediately knew she was from near the Chicago area. He could hear the hint of a northern Illinois accent in her first word to him. He nodded, afraid to speak for fear his voice may crack or he would sound like a hillbilly. Josh tried to get bigger. He stood as tall as he could and tried to slyly puff out his thin chest, like a rooster on steroids.

As he fumbled for his cigarettes he noticed that his hands were very small and his arms that were way too thin. He knew he couldn't pull off the muscle guy. He hadn't been to the gym enough times with Jake and Tony. He was dumbstruck at her beauty and hoped she did not notice how small he was.

She lit a cigarette, took a puff, exhaled hard and licked her lips a bit as if she was angry and ready to spit nails. She ran her slender hand through her hair and tousled it in frustration. She may have growled a bit or maybe let out a heavy sigh. He couldn't tell. He knew she was upset but he couldn't take his eyes off her.

She looked like she had been active in some aerobics or weight training in the recent past. She had strong well defined shoulders that hid beautiful sinewy muscles beneath the polo. Her stomach was flat and hard which accentuated the perfect breasts above. She was thirty four but her physique rivaled that of any twenty year-old athlete.

Josh could barely remove the wrapper of the new pack of Marlboro's. He fumbled with the package, cursing the invention of cellophane under his breath while she paced and smoked. He wondered if she would run. He half-heartedly hoped she would so he could chase her. He wondered what it would be like to touch her. She was so beautiful.

Her thighs wore the jeans like a second skin. He saw the gentle taper from her hip to her knee and the outline of a strong lower leg that supported her frame. He imagined that even her feet were tanned and pretty. He couldn't stop looking at her. His stomach churned. His lips were dry and the last thing he wanted was the taste of a cigarette in his mouth but to stand next to her he would have swallowed battery acid.

Josh lit up a smoke and inhaled too quickly. He nearly gagged and coughed. He quickly looked to his left at the boiler as if the sight of it was something unique. He did not want her to see his face reddening from the rapid inhalation of smoke. He was afraid to look at her too long. He didn't want her to notice him staring or think he was a creep. He knew she was way out of his league. He could tell since his hands were beginning to sweat and his head started to spin. He was physically dizzy when he looked at her.

He had a plan though; he would lean on the rail to keep himself upright and look over her head at the wall, that way he could appear nonchalant and keep from falling at the same time. Josh thought he was savvy.

When she finally looked into his eyes he almost fell over. She didn't seem to notice or care. He was panicking in his head. He had to say something; something clever and cute or manly. Perceptiveness saved him as he noticed a badge on her left lapel.

"Great! A cop too, now he officially could not take it! God, just take me now!" He thought.

He could not stand this sight and the thought of that exquisite brown body in a uniform was too much for his teenage mind to handle. He was going to implode. She was driving him to the point of unconsciousness without knowing the effect she had on him. She stood there looking at him, waiting for the mute idiot to speak. He took a deep breath, which came out like a shutter, and opened his mouth.

"So... Uhhhh... Cop huh? Where from?" he stammered.

What made this question ridiculous was that he could read the name of the city on the badge right in front of him. He looked at her stomach and pretended not to notice the perfect apple sized breasts above that teased him. He hoped she thought he was staring at the ground.

He felt himself blush as he thought, *"Damn circulatory system overload in response to sexual excitement!"* He was not sure if he had an erection because he hadn't been able to feel his lower half for the last twenty seconds. He was glad the railing was there, it kept old people from falling off the edge and idiot teenage EMT's from crashing into the parking lot when they were staring into the eyes of the most beautiful woman in the world.

He thought, *"Okay, I may vomit now."* Josh had never been so nervous in his life. She was too much, too perfect, too everything. He inhaled again. The smoke burned his lungs.

"Okay, pain is familiar, that will keep me distracted," he thought. He was wrong.

She took a soft puff from the Misty and blew the smoke out. Even her cigarette smelled good to him. It was official; he was cracking up and if he made it out of this conversation, that hadn't started yet, without having a biological accident it would be a miracle.

"Up north, close to the city", she said dryly taking another drag from the Misty.

He gathered his thoughts and was finally ready to belt out something so amazing and memorable she would love him for all time. *Here goes.* He steadied himself.

"Oh" he squeaked *"Damn."* Now he was officially six years old staring at a bikini poster again.

"So what do you do here, you a little security guard or something?" she asked bluntly.

He would have normally been hurt by the "little and security guard" comment but he was glad she was talking to him, although she didn't have much choice.

"Uhhh— no, I am an EMT", he said with no hint of ego. He almost sounded weak and shaky. This worked out well, considering he was weak and shaky. Normally he would go on a tirade about how much danger was involved and the extensive training needed. This of course was bullshit and for some reason he knew she could see right through him.

Those brown eyes and the hair with hints of auburn colors dancing about every other strand, made her look like she had a permanent glow about her. He was smitten with her beauty. She could have slapped him and called him a goofy little leprechaun and he would have grinned and asked if she liked *Lucky Charms* cereal. He tried to speak again.

"No, I am not bright enough to be a security guard and carry keys to outhouse doors. I only qualified for CPR. I hope, if I study hard, they will give me some pepper spray. I hear it tastes great on mashed potatoes." He joked a little.

Then the most amazing sound he had ever heard came from her mouth—laughter.

She nearly choked on cigarette smoke. As she bent over with laughter, tears came to her eyes and this time they were happy tears. He could not believe that his idiot joke about himself struck her so funny.

"Okay, this may work", he mused. I can make her laugh. He decided to try again.

"Yeah," he pulled his pants up well over his navel stuck out his lip, to imitate a tobacco chewer, and faked a hillbilly accent and said,

"hyar EMT's and nurses at this ol' place have theeeee fiiinest health care available. Yessireeee. Hell we have triple bypasses right thar in that ER—it is when a nurse walks by a cabinet three times before she realizes what she wanted in the first place— Quadruple bypasses are for the nurses over sixty. We do liver transplants in the cafeteria; it is when they transplant the liver from a pan to your plate. They do it at noon and five fifteen every day, like clockwork."

She was now rolling with laughter. He kept it up. His nervousness was gone; he was now on stage with an audience of one, the most important one. He was entertaining the woman that would change his life forever. Lady Luck was working her magic and this young man was a pawn in her play.

He continued adding more southern sounds to his voice.

"Why, yes ma'am, we just got right on upscale down hyar now. We even got us one of them new fangled doomahickeys that recharge the heart. It almost voided the warranty on the damn thing. The maintenance crew thought it was a battery charger. Damn near killed 'em both."

"It never fails, shit always happens when one of our guys say, 'hey watch dis'; yup not sure if Glenn will ever pee straight again after that little ordeal." He continued,

"Yea, we hope to get our band-aid station license as soon as we can save up the money for the band-aids. Pharmacy is jest too damn pricey. We are waitin' for the word from the bank 'bout the loan."

She was still laughing as he pretended to spit and strutted about the dock like a peacock on crack. She kept laughing. Finally she sighed and brushed the hair back again. He felt the dizzy coming back. He had to be cool or he would blow it. "You are a piece of work— funny, but a piece of work." She said with a smile.

He could not believe she was smiling at him again. She was looking at him and smiling! Those dark eyes held softness beneath the frustration that she had harbored there just a few moments ago. She was so pretty. Her smile was electric and her eyes twinkled with small stars in the microcosmic universe she held within them.

Josh was smitten by her. She was the answer to his prayers. The supermodel in his mind was obliterated by the sound of her laughter. He could never hope to touch or kiss her, but if she just remembered him that was enough. Even if only for a moment, he wanted to be in her mind.

He calmed down a bit and began to speak normally as he said,

"Are they treating you alright in there?"

"Yeah, I guess. They think I am crazy, just been stressed lately", she mumbled.

He snapped right back.

"Good, if you are crazy then you will be hired shortly. HR hired me and see how that turned out?" He punctuated the joked with a cheesy grin and crossed his eyes. She giggled again.

"Work shit got ya upset?" He asked with an honest softness in his voice.

"Yeah, been a rough few weeks", she said.

"What are you doing all the way down here in this shit-hole town?" He asked.

"My friend Shirley lives here and I needed to get away", she replied sounding distant.

"Well, you came to the right place. We are two miles from the end of the earth; the dragons and sea-monsters sleep at the edge of town, so you are safe" he quipped.

She smiled without laughing.

"So, are you working or just hanging out?" She inquired.

"Both. I just got back from a transfer and they asked me to come and smoke with you", he answered.

"So what do you do, as a kid in this town, for fun?" she asked lighting another cigarette.

"Drink, get in trouble and run from you cops" he replied.

"That sounds about right." She said with a smirk on her face.

"How old are you anyway?" She asked not knowing why she cared.

"Eighteen." He answered too quickly. He regretted it immediately. If he would have waited a few seconds for his brain to react he could have easily lied about his age.

She simply nodded and looked away wishing she hadn't asked.

"You think they are gonna put me away somewhere?" She asked with fear in her voice.

"Nope, Tonya is telling the doc what to do. They are gonna put you upstairs overnight instead of sending you to the looney bin; cause if they do I have to take you and they may keep me instead. Then you could steal the ambulance. See it's just not safe to send you anywhere", he joked.

"Great. Overnight in the hospital", she vented.

"Tell you what, if you want, I will make it more fun for you", he offered.

"And how you going to do that little man?" she questioned.

"I am gonna sneak into your room and make you laugh all night. I will cure you", he boasted, "Only if you want me too", he added.

"Sure. What the hell", she said never expecting him to do it.

"Ma'am in matters like this you have to address the situation appropriately", he said in his best cop voice.

"Sometimes ya gotta say— fuck it!" He stuck out his tongue and crossed his eyes again while doing the peacock strut.

She started laughing all over again. The jokes went on for about twenty minutes. He never asked what she said to the nurses or asked why she was there. He assumed it had something to do with suicide or suicidal thoughts or they wouldn't have been so guarded with her. He didn't care. If she wanted to end her life he would give her reason not to, even if for a little while. He was planning to rescue her and he would do it at any risk. He was falling in love.

"What's your name, so I can find you on the unit tonight", he asked.

"Kelly O'Hara", she answered blinking slowly and looking at the ground.

Tonya opened the door and glared at Josh. He looked at the ground just as Kelly was doing. He knew Tonya was pissed. He had kept Kelly out there too long.

"Miss, we have your room ready", she said hinting for them to come inside.

Kelly walked back in as Tonya lead the way. She turned and looked over her shoulder at Josh who was still standing on the stoop. The look from Kelly lasted longer than he expected; she was trying to tell him something but he did not know what it was. As she turned away he felt his heart sink. The nausea was back. He lit another cigarette to distract his mind. He was afraid he would never get to see her after tonight but devil be damned if he stayed away.

He ran to the back entrance to the ER and checked to make sure his ambulance garage keys fit the lock. He grinned evilly as he heard the familiar click that loosened the door. He knew he could take the back elevators later that night and never go through ER for his sneak attack on the unsuspecting hospital.

Josh could get fired but he didn't care. He could always go back to work at the gas station. He shut the door and turned to leave when he saw Lilly wheeling Kelly to the elevators. The hospital policy stated that patients had to be taken up in a wheelchair even if they could walk.

He looked through the window. Kelly was in a hospital gown now and barely covered with a white sheet. He could see her tanned legs beneath the gown. They were just as pretty as he imagined. He blew her a kiss from the window. She could not see him but that did not matter. He would see her tonight.

He ran across the alleyway and opened the door to his truck. He drove home to Elm Street and began to prepare his plan to cure the wounded Kelly O'Hara. He immediately rushed into the shower and scrubbed until the skin on his body was pink from the forceful washing. He shaved the three hairs on his chin and coated himself with *Stetson*; it was the only cologne he had.

He dried himself and put on his black boxer briefs. He had thrown away all of his tighty-whities after moving in with the girls. They told him that boxer briefs were the sexy thing to wear. He slide on his *Levi 501 Blues*, donned socks and darted out of the bathroom.

He checked the time; he needed to wait until after eleven. It was seven fifteen. He sighed. He would have to wait for four lousy hours before he could see her again. He knew what he could do; go buy something to cheer her up at Fast-Mart. That was perfect!

Chapter 3

To Josh, Fast-Mart was always a one stop shop for everything: food, drink, books, music and romantic props. It was a wonder that Josh ever had a chance with any woman. The beginnings of his life were based on poverty and lack of culture. He thought Fast-Mart was the place to buy anything and for once he had a little money.

Lilly opened the door to room 315. Kelly was perfectly capable of walking but hospital policy prohibited patients walking to their rooms. It must have been their way of controlling the activities of the patients as if they did not have enough control already.

Kelly was not used to being controlled. As a police officer she was responsible for controlling others and their behavior, whether by conversation or force, either way, it didn't matter to her. She viewed her position as a patrol officer as a job and nothing more. She had a high tolerance for stress in most circumstances. As of late, the problems at the Riverday police department had become more than even a strong cop, like Kelly, could bear.

With her mind racing she stood from the wheelchair. Wearing only her hospital gown and white socks made her feel more exposed than ever. Lilly looked at her with kindness in her eyes and said,

"Just have a seat hon', the nurses will be in here in a minute. Do you need anything?"

"No", Kelly replied. She never needed anything from anyone.

Her mind began to race as Lilly left the room. *What was going to happen to her? Would she be able to get past this event and go on with her life?* Millions of questions without any foreseeable answers flooded her mind. She hated being uncertain. In her line of work being uncertain can get you killed. She sat on the edge of the bed. It was hard and uncomfortable. The sick smell of alcohol and bleach filtered through the air. Kelly hated hospitals ever since her grandmother became ill. She could not stand the stench of hospitals.

At least the room had a window. She noticed that the sun had set. Kelly wondered if this was what prisoners felt like, she had never thought of that before. She felt like a prisoner in her own life and now a prisoner of Tremane Hospital.

Society dictates that women should be brought up as pretty little girls in sundresses with flowers in their hair and teddy bears as constant companions. Then they should grow into well versed women with culture and poise that become model mothers, wives and citizen activists in all of the "right" causes. Women are to: feed the hungry, help the poor, protect the children and all of God's creatures, have a career and still have time to cook dinner before five. Human society is delusional.

Kelly grew up raising horses. She lived with her grandmother for most of her life. She was never close to her mother. Her father taught her what he knew before he left and then she was left to fend for herself. Kelly never expected anything from anyone. She was rarely disappointed.

She looked out the window at the night sky. The stars were oddly bright that particular evening. The twinkling of them could be seen despite the reflection of the streetlights in the hospital parking lot. The view of the nearby physician's offices and the ambulance garage disgusted her. Kelly hated everything about hospitals and most of all she loathed needles. The thought of those sharp sterilized pieces of metal, soaked in alcohol, penetrating her skin made her stomach churn. It was going to be a long night.

Room 315 was adjacent to the nurses' desk. Critically ill pediatrics or patients that are a flight risk are admitted there. Kelly was definitely a flight risk. She had already surveyed the scene, which was more of a habit than anything else, on her short ride in the wheelchair. She knew there was a staircase on the left and elevators on the right side of the hallway. The hallway teed at the nurses' desk and dead ended on both ends. Two exit points. From the look of the nurses and their physiques, Kelly was sure escape would not be difficult. The only presenting problem is getting out of the ER. It was locked down after 8:00 PM.

She mused about running passed the nurses and darting down the hall to the stairs. Smiling, she imagined four, fat out-of-shape nurses huffing and dripping with sweat as they chased her down the stairs. Fancying that she sprinted past the registration desk and out the front doors like a gazelle, as the nurses waddled further and further behind her she, nearly giggled.

Kelly was an athlete. She ran track, played softball, volleyball and any other sport she could participate in throughout high school. Her body was still firm and in shape and she knew she could still run like gazelle on those thin muscular thighs despite the Misty habit.

The hours seemed to drag by as nurses and aides muddled about their business of healthcare. She would hear them talk in the hallway about other patients, doctors, their vacation plans and who was sleeping with whom at the hospital. She heard them grumble about the EMTs.

"EMT", she thought. She wondered where that little guy was and what trouble he was getting into. It was ten thirty. She looked at the clock twice hoping she had misread the time. He said he was coming to see her after eleven tonight. She wondered why she even cared. Despite her own wishes she began to feel anxious about whether or not he would show.

"He probably won't", she thought to herself. He was just a kid that was being silly and as with any eighteen year old, his attention span had to be almost as long as that of a fruit fly. She assumed he was probably wearing that polyester blue uniform and trying to win the heart of some teenage girl with stars in her eyes. She shook her head as if trying to remove his face from her memory.

Why would she spend her night worrying about whether or not this kid would make good on his promise?

There are more adult issues here and she should not be drifting off like some goofy teenage kid over some boy with a gift for telling stories and the uncanny ability to make her laugh at the drop of a hat.

Laughter had been foreign to her for the last few months. She missed the ache you get in the pit of your stomach when you have laughed too hard, for too long without taking time to inhale. She giggled again as she thought about his antics on the dock and how silly he acted. Rolling her eyes, she thought, "I bet that little shit is with a girl right now".

A strange feeling came over her at that very instant. Her eyes narrowed to a slit and she involuntarily clenched her jaw. She had felt this before. A controlled mix of anger, disgust and hurt all bundled together into an acidic weight that settled into the pit of her stomach— Jealousy.

Maybe she needed to be admitted since this was the most insane feeling she could have at this moment in her life. He was a kid, nothing more. He was thin, short and just plain goofy. *Why in the world would she be jealous of that?* She couldn't answer her own question so she didn't try.

Kelly turned on the television and mindlessly clicked through the channels. She couldn't tell what was on because even though her eyes viewed every channel her brain chose not to register any of it. She was still thinking about him. Eleven o'clock. "*Where is he?*" She thought as she looked at the door.

The door never moved. The shadow of nurse feet shuffling back and forth was the only indication of human presence on the third floor. Census was low and the floor was quiet. Kelly was patient number three for the hospital.

The only other patients were a husband and wife couple at the other end of the hall. The old lady was diabetic and the husband was a cardiac cripple. When one was admitted the other was usually admitted as well. The family doctor felt it was better that way. Both patients had enough ailments to warrant admission on any given day of the week. They were fine when they were both home to help each other through, but alone each of them was helpless. They needed each other to survive. Kelly did not know them but she would soon learn what it means to need someone so badly that you cannot survive without them at your side.

She turned the television off and rolled onto her left side. Looking out the window she stared at the parking lot. She wished he was here. He could make the time pass as if he controlled the hours with his words.

Eleven ten. He wasn't coming, she knew it. This was the perfect end to a terrible day. She pulled the sheets up toward her neck and readjusted the flat, brick-hard pillow that partially supported her head. Reluctantly she turned the television on again hoping something would pique her interest or at the least help her fall asleep. She stared at the screen not really seeing what was there. She was in a daze not caring if she ever snapped back into reality. Reality was the white walls, stiff sheets and a scratchy blanket. Boredom was the enemy and she chose not to accept her surroundings. It was much better to drift off into random thoughts and forget about the day, the last week, even the last month. Life was too complicated and the last thing she wanted to do was to think about it.

She exhaled deeply feeling her stomach shutter as the air escaped into the atmosphere. Her eyes became heavy. The crying earlier in the day had taken its toll on her eyes. She was sure they looked terrible. She could feel the swelling under her lids and the subtle sting was a constant reminder of what had caused her to breakdown. She hated feeling out of control and she loathed showing emotion in any form. She preferred to hide everything on the inside and deal with life alone. People complicate things and Kelly did not like complicated.

Kelly heard a knock at the door. She was expecting an aide to come and take her blood pressure and temperature.

"Come in", she answered softly.

Her heart jumped into her throat and she felt a wave of heat rush through her body as she heard a familiar voice.

"Damn traffic jams, hyar in Treeemaaannnee, we had two cars waiting to pass a tractor and I was stuck in traffic for three whole minutes. Damn city folks!" Josh said with an unnecessarily overdone hillbilly accent. Kelly bolted upright in bed pulling the covers close to her neck as if she was trying to make herself invisible like a ten year old hiding from the boogey man. She had nowhere to run and he was blocking the only exit.

"I told you I would cure you", he said in a voice too deep for him as he tried to sound suave and sexy. He failed of course, but the attempt was cute.

Josh was holding something in his hand. Flowers. He had brought her flowers. Kelly was really nervous now, this was getting ridiculous. Talking to him was a bad idea. Now he had flowers and way too much cologne. He smelled like he had fallen into a vat of *Stetson*.

"Hi, uh— what's up?" She said shakily, unsure of what was going to happen next.

"I'm here to cure you and since you're already half naked I guess I should get out the twister game. Be right back!" Josh replied as he pretended to bolt out the door.

She shuttered at the thought, she hoped he was not serious. *Was he really this crazy?* She had no way out but deep down her sense of curiosity got the better of her. She wanted to see what he would do next. He sauntered over to the edge of the bed and tossed the flowers at her. They landed on her lap.

"Those are high dollar, cost me eight dollars and ninety nine cents, plus tax, at Fast-Mart. Now you are half naked, covered in flowers, so there is nothing to be upset about; except, that you are trapped in here with a psychotic man that loves to play twister, so when in doubt just say—Fuck it!" Josh said as he crossed his eyes and stuck out his tongue.

She started to laugh. The laugh was what he was waiting for, he could begin his routine. He was on stage and his audience of one was ready to be entertained. He began by discussing his concept of being a kid from the woods. His primary objective was to make her laugh and he succeeded easily.

Josh made fun of the nurses, the doctors and mainly himself. His antics made Kelly laugh to the point of tears. She laughed so loudly at times Josh expected the nurses to come in and kick him out. He loved to hear her laugh. He was developing quite the crush on Kelly O'Hara.

As she expected the time passed quickly. It was nearly two in the morning before he ran out of material. He sighed as he sat in the chair next to her bed. Kelly's eyes were red from the tears she produced from laughing so hard. He looked at her in the hospital gown decorated with some indistinguishable pattern that littered the front. The pocket on the front, designed to hold a telemetry box, gaped just enough he could sneak a view of her naked breast beneath the garment.

The blanket was no longer covering her from the waist up. She was sitting upright and smiling. He was beginning to feel uncomfortable as his desire to touch her was increasing with every passing moment. Her form hidden slightly beneath the sheets was exquisite. His body ached for her. He could smell a hint of her shampoo and perfume. He was having trouble concentrating.

She waited patiently and looked into his eyes ready for act two. It never came. He stood up, hoping she could not see the erection through his jeans, and walked closer toward her. She took a deep breath to prepare for whatever goofy action he may take that would cause her to laugh uncontrollably. Again he surprised her.

"I guess I need to get out of here before the dayshift comes in", he said quietly. She realized then how young he looked. His face was so smooth and unmarked with the lines of age. He had a look of fear on his face, similar to a teenager afraid to be caught by his parents. She knew he was right. She wondered if she would ever see him again.

"Okay", she said reluctantly. "Do you have to work tomorrow?" She blurted out all too desperately.

She regretted speaking the words as soon as they left her mouth. She tried to recover. "Take it easy, thanks for the visit it was fun", she said quickly as if trying to avoid any emotion.

"I am off tomorrow" he replied wanting to say more but the words wouldn't come.

Josh stood there for a moment plotting his next move. He didn't know what to do. She was waiting for something but he had no idea what it could be. He didn't know if he should try to kiss her, shake her hand or just spin on a heel and leave. He took the middle ground and leaned forward. She did not recoil as he moved closer. He kissed her softly on the forehead and said, "Get better."

"I think they will let me out tomorrow and I will probably go back to Shirley's." She remarked, trying to sound lax about it. "I will call her to come and pick me up", she said dryly.

"I could come and get you then drive you home if you want", he offered. He felt like he was begging for any amount of time she would allow him to have with her.

"You would do that?" She asked with a hint of excitement in her voice.

"Sure, maybe even do breakfast, if you want. No one is home at my house and we could rent some comedies and hang out—if you want— but that is up to you", he offered again, trying not to sound too pushy. He didn't want her to think he was a weirdo that was trying to kidnap her and bury her out in the timber.

"Okay, I might call you." She blurted out again. Regretting her quick response, she wondered why he was so attractive to her. He was only eighteen but she really wanted to spend more time with him. She could not understand why he made her feel so alive. *Was it youth or just his personality?* She was so confused. All she knew for sure was that she wanted him to pick her up and spend the day with her.

He wrote his number on a scrap of paper and handed it to her. The hand writing was atrocious but she could make out the numbers. She looked at the paper longer than she needed to because she did not want to look into his eyes. He could see into her heart when their eyes met and that frightened her.

Josh shuffled his feet like the nervous teen that he was and tried to decide how to make a grand exit that would remain in her memory forever. He ran through all of the movies he had ever seen and the heroes he admired, searching for a great way to leave this woman that he wanted so badly. Her hair cascaded down about her shoulders as she looked at the note. He wanted to touch her so badly. His chest was on fire.

He looked at her as long as he could without her noticing his stare. She looked up from the note and smiled a little.

"See you", he said with his voice cracking a bit. "Don't forget to call— I mean if you want to..." his voice trailed off. He nearly fell over the chair while walking backward toward the door. He felt a wave of heat engulf his face as the blood rushed to his forehead. He turned quickly so she would not see him blush. He opened the door and looked back at her one last time. Her face burned into his memory. She smiled softly as he closed the door. He leaned his head against the cool hard wood and sighed. She was the most beautiful woman he had ever seen. He could still smell her shampoo. Or maybe he imagined he could. It didn't matter. He was in love.

Josh walked quickly down the hall hoping to reach the stairs before being spotted by one of the nurses. He opened the door to the stairwell and proceeded to dart down the staircase toward the first floor. The back hallway of the hospital was deserted at this time of night except for the occasional janitor or maintenance man.

The escape was complete as he exited the dock door. Feeling as if he had gotten away with something, he ran to his truck and slid into the driver's side. He started the Chevy and pulled out of the alley and drove toward Elm Street. The truck lurched forward as he shifted into second. He smiled as he pressed on the gas. His heart was lighter than it had ever been, he knew she would call, he just knew it. He wanted to get home to set his alarms: the one on his clock, his pager and his phone. Josh did not want to miss the call from Kelly. He knew she would call, she just had too.

Kelly slid down beneath the sheets. She was exhausted, partially spent from laughter and the remainder of her energy had been depleted from the past few weeks of stress and worry. She felt that, for once, sleep would come easily to her. The evening turned into dawn as Kelly drifted off to a dreamless sleep. The rhythmic beeping of the distant monitors was singing to her like lullabies in the early morning hours. Her breathing deepened as sleep surrounded her like a gentle blanket of peace.

Josh sat down hard on his hide-a-bed in the basement of his house on Elm Street. Harry the cat came to say goodnight with a gentle purr. He stroked the fur of the Persian softly as the purring became louder as Harry curled up on the pillow. Reclining into the uncomfortable mattress Josh's mind began to drift off to memories of Kelly. He wondered if she was asleep yet, he hoped so, she looked very tired. He hoped she would get some rest so she would have enough energy to enjoy the great day he had planned.

He checked all three alarms again and sprawled out over the bed. Harry's purring was the last thing he would hear as he drifted off to sleep.

Chapter 4

Susy and Tanner were in and out of the house during the early morning hours. They were making more noise than usual. Josh had come to the conclusion that women that live together for a long enough period of time begin to experience premenstrual syndrome together. From the noise and the banging of cabinet doors, he assumed that it must be that time of the month for his roommates.

Harry and Josh always hung out in the basement during that time of the month. It was dangerous to be around the girls, being one of the male species and all. He assumed that the girls thought all men were Satan's spawn and it was best to make himself scarce. Josh learned to mark the calendar to remind him of when the cranky fest started and knew when to get the hell out of Dodge.

It was a little after seven when Josh decided to get up. There was little point in trying to sleep after the PMS duo had awakened the dead with all of the banging and cursing. Harry ventured up the stairs to his food bowl which usually meant the coast was clear. Josh trusted Harry so he followed suit; Harry would never go upstairs unless it was safe— animal instinct and all.

Josh shut off his alarms and decided to shower. He planned to skip the cologne this time; it was still soaked into his skin from last night. The thoughts of Kelly still danced in his mind. He was grinning wildly as he stood naked in the bathroom waiting for the shower to heat to boiling temperatures. The reflection in the mirror revealed how truly small he was. His chest was thin and his arms were lanky. He flexed, hoping to make a miracle of muscle occur. No luck. He was still just a skinny kid. He did a quick zit check to see if he had any eruptions planning to ruin his potential date with Kelly. All clear, no pimple meds needed. He was good to go.

After showering quickly he prepared for the telephone call from Kelly. He just knew she had been waiting all night to call him. He was sure of it. Josh patted Harry again and tossed the cat a few treats then sat on the couch. Coffee sounded good. He made a pot drank one cup, then another and still no telephone call.

Josh picked up his keys a few times as if to go somewhere, then put them away and sat down on again the couch. Harry was confused but nonetheless followed Josh to and fro from the couch to the door. Harry thought it was a game that he gladly played.

The telephone rang at five after nine. A familiar female voice with a northern Illinois accent said quietly,

"Come pick me up? I will be at the dock." She asked more than stated.

"I'm on my way", Josh squeaked. He grabbed his keys and ran out the door toward his reliable steed, the old Chevy. Harry stood at the doorway, tail flicking this way and that, cheering his partner in crime onward to seek the lady. Josh always had a flair for the theatrical viewpoint of things, even something as simple as a cat in the doorway. She called. He could have never been happier as he drove toward the hospital as fast as his little truck could take him.

He kept saying over and over, "She called! Goddamn it! She called!"

The ride to the hospital seemed to take forever even though he lived only two miles away. He ran three stop signs and nearly hit an old lady in a Lincoln. He didn't care about that; it wasn't like he was going to get a ticket since he was a hero and all.

Kelly paced on the dock. She was starting to have second thoughts. *What was she doing? What did she expect to happen?* She was not going to have sex with this guy. She was just going to spend a few hours with him to laugh some more and forget about life for a while. *Right?*

He made her feel like a kid and she enjoyed the feeling. She continued to rationalize and talk to herself as she paced and smoked her long-awaited Misty.

She smiled as the tan pickup pulled into the drive. He opened the door and stood as tall as he could. Josh hoped Kelly would imagine him as a knight on a buckskin stallion awaiting the opportunity to take her away from the prison in which she had so wrongly been detained. Josh dreamed way too much. Kelly simply looked down at a cute kid in a beat up truck that was trying to impress her.

Kelly preferred that version better. It was real and true and in some odd way it was wholesome. She walked toward the truck. Josh ran around the truck and chivalrously opened the door for her. He grinned as he bowed and pointed toward the seat. Kelly rolled her eyes and smiled at his overacting. She loved that he did not take himself too seriously. He was a card and she could not, under any circumstance, let this kid get to her. She was sure that it would never happen. He was just an entertaining friend that was there for her at a bad time in her life. Kelly waited as her rescuer bounced into the driver seat.

He had a wide grin that nearly swallowed his face. The dimples in his cheeks accentuated his high cheekbones and when accompanied by a smile made him adorable. Kelly could not fall for this kid. He was just a friend that was all and she would not even touch him.

He leaned over and kissed her on the lips. She kissed him back without realizing that she had done so.

He crossed his eyes and giggled, "Mmm, taste like honey… shall we my dear?" He said in his best upper society voice.

She had made a mistake. *God she kissed him! What was she thinking? That was it; nothing more.* She could not fall for this guy. He was a poor investment he was too young, too unstable, too ungrounded. He was not good for her but he was all she needed at the same time.

Kelly looked at him as he drove. She didn't care where he was taking her and he didn't seem to know anyway. Josh didn't even mention breakfast. He must have forgotten about it. She wasn't hungry and she was way too nervous to eat.

Josh pulled into the drive on Elm Street. He looked about nervously to ensure that the girls were not home. He was safe; Susy was to be away for two days hence the obsessive banging this morning as she packed for her trip to her parents home. Tanner was probably spending the night with a man to be named later.

He opened the door for Kelly who was patiently waiting on the stoop. Josh motioned for her to come inside. Harry met them both as they entered. He gave them the feline greeting by brushing his tail against their legs and tossing out a mew or two of approval. Kelly immediately bent down to pet the cat and Josh immediately looked down her shirt. He was just evil and he knew it.

The thoughts of an eighteen year old kid were at best short sighted. His only concern was how to make her laugh, feel comfortable sitting with him alone in the house, and hopefully to get a kiss or two before she decided she was bored and leave. Josh did not really expect someone like her to be alone with him for too long. Kelly was way out of his league, but he could not stifle the dream of making love to her and holding her in his arms until the sun came up.

A dream was all that he had. He assumed she was not interested in anything truly physical, but he could pretend in his mind that she was. After a few moments thought a rush of fear plagued his senses. *What if she did want to make love to him? Would he disappoint her? Was he good enough? Would she laugh at him? What if he did something wrong?*

He had only been with two other girls in his life. He pretended to be experienced but he knew deep down that he was a rookie in the love department. Josh always acted as if he did not have a care in the world and he could always get the girl. In fact, he was very self conscious around Kelly. With other girls he could really care less; if he got lucky, great, if not he would look elsewhere, but he really wanted to impress Kelly. She was different. Not just because she was older, but there was something special about her as a person. She made him feel like life was a new adventure everyday and he would be such a lucky young man if she asked him to tag along on those adventures.

Thinking too much was always his problem. He had wandered off in his own mind while Kelly was right in front of him paying attention to the cat. Harry darted toward the sofa as if to say, *"Hey, stupid! How about you invite her to sit down? You dumb ass!"* Harry had a way of sending messages of sarcasm in a feline sort of way.

"Come on, lets take a look at the movies I got for us" he said trying not to sound too nervous and without letting his voice crack too much. Kelly reluctantly followed him into the living room. He offered her a drink. He tried to sound disgusted about not having any beer, as if he was such a hardcore drinker and always had it around. He was trying to be grown-up. Kelly said she was fine and did not need anything. He sat next to her on the sofa. She stared blankly at him as if to say, *"And the movie?"*

He sheepishly looked at the television and the black screen that glared defiantly at him. He had forgotten to turn the damn thing on! This was not going to go well if he did not stop acting like such a…such a… teenager!

He knew the only way to save his reputation, and his chance, with her was to play the fool. After making a comment about early onset Alzheimer's, he lurched from the sofa and turned on the television.

"I rented *The Jerk*", he said confidently about the movie starring *Steve Martin*. He hoped that the antics of the comedian would lighten the mood, relieve the tension and most of all make him look more suave and sophisticated in Kelly's eyes. It should be easy to look like a good choice when you compare yourself to Martins' character in the movie.

Kelly smiled just a little and said nothing. Her eyes were dancing as if she had somewhere to go. Josh wondered if she was looking for the exit points to allow her to get away. He had to play it cool and keep her interest. Playing the jester was the safest thing to do. The movie began with the familiar phrase in Martins' monologue, "*I was born a poor black child*." Kelly started to giggle softly and her shoulders relaxed. Josh breathed a sigh of relief; he knew he could count on the actor to carry the load and ease the awkward silence that presented when he ran out of comedic material.

He had ninety-eight minutes to come up with a game plan or something to keep her entertaining the thought of staying with him. The movie would end soon and, if he did not have something very good to say or do, he would have to take her home and she would never speak to him again. He was something of a neurotic idiot when it came to Kelly. He just wanted her to fall madly in love with him and that would be that. This was his fantasy and he preferred to keep it in his head and never let her know how badly he wanted her.

Kelly laughed at the movie and Josh occasionally added comedic anecdotes to add to the fun, but secretly he was watching her breath and fidget on the sofa. He stared at her profile and her thin muscular legs as long as he could without getting caught. She smelled like honeysuckle and her auburn hair flowed down to her shoulders. She even left her sunglasses in the truck, Kelly rarely went anywhere without her shades. She looked pretty and very comfortable sitting next to him.

Josh, on the other hand, was a nervous wreck. He could feel his breathing increase and the temperature in his face skyrocket as he accidentally brushed his hand against her firm thigh. She didn't seem to notice, or if she did, she paid no attention to it. The all too familiar feeling of sexual excitement was beginning to overtake his teenage senses. He was becoming too excited, too fast. He hoped she could not see his obvious interest. He needed to do something quickly.

Pain was the ticket to his salvation. He bit down hard on his bottom lip and hoped the feeling would subside. He did not want her to see him that way. It would be too embarrassing and he could not joke his way out of it. The self inflicted pain helped somewhat, but Josh knew that he had better come up with something better to take his mind off her beautiful female form or he would sever his own lip or have an orgasm the next time she laughed hard and her firm breasts moved even the slightest direction toward him. He was a sexual time bomb and the clock was ticking, plus the movie was nearly over. *"Fourteen minutes to get your act together"*, he thought to himself.

Harry jumped from the sofa to the floor, no doubt planning a run to the litter box, when Josh noticed the TV guide. He quickly turned to the day's date and began to scan the channels quickly. He found a stand-up comedian channel that may buy him some more time. The movie ended and Kelly took a trip to the bathroom. In her absence, he quickly turned the channel to the comedian program and positioned himself in his "coolest" TV watching pose, which consisted of him leaning back on the couch with his left arm over the head rest and his left leg bent on the sofa cushion. It was a pose that mimicked a Playgirl shoot for the developmentally disabled. He was such a kid and he could not make himself more mature in ninety-eight minutes, although he tried.

Kelly returned and sat next to him. Their legs touched. He could feel the heat from her thigh and her scent was intoxicating to him. He wanted to taste her. Instead of kissing her, he opted to take the coward's way out and introduce the comedian. She turned her attention to the Hispanic comedian on the television screen.

Again, Josh had bought some time. The comedian held her attention and made jokes about dogs that want to continually roll on their backs to get your attention when they wish to be petted as if to say, "Hey people, I know you had a bad day, but I need to be petted and to make you feel better take a quick look at my balls!" The comedian repeatedly referenced this routine canine action throughout the skit. "Sometimes you gotta say, Fuck it!" was another tag line he used to sell the show and get laughter from his audience, as well as from Kelly.

Josh decided, after advice from a pre-recorded comedian, that sometimes you have to say *"Fuck it"*. He turned to Kelly, she looked at him; he immediately pressed his lips to hers.

"Fuck it", he said. She smiled. He kissed her again. His feelings were back, but this time he didn't care he was taking his chances. She kissed him hard and he felt her warm tongue lightly caress his own as she probed inside his mouth.

Kelly's eyes were open wide; he could see her pupils dilate with excitement. Her cinnamon eyes pierced his heart and soul, as she tilted her head back while kissing and looking longingly at him. He was caught unaware, her eyes indicated she wanted more but she moved subtly away— acting coy, as if she wanted him to chase her. She leaned backward against the sofa propping herself against the armrest slightly moving her thighs against each other.

Josh's heart began to race. His mouth felt as dry as the Sahara causing him to have trouble swallowing. He felt like his skin was on fire. He could not keep from biting his lip.

Josh could smell her shampoo and the hint of perfume. Kelly wore very little fragrances and her natural aroma was sweet as sugar cane to him. Her lips were pressed tightly together in an attempt to hide her physical interest in him. Josh felt the heat increasing in his chest as his craving for her reached flashpoint. He had to have her but he did not want to frighten her away. Kelly could never be a one-time thing for Josh; he had to have her in his life. He could not reason out or understand why he felt so strongly about a woman and had known for less than a week and knew very little about. There was no way this could be love; love was a tediously long drawn out process that may take years to cultivate, *Right?* He didn't know or didn't care. He wanted her, all of her. He had to be careful and do everything right.

Josh leaned forward cupping her face in his hands while kissing her as softly as he could. She parted her lips ever so slightly to accept his kiss. He tasted her mouth gingerly. Her breathing became deep and deliberate as he kissed her again. She touched his face as he pressed his lips to hers. She was becoming excited, yet afraid to completely give in to her desires.

She wanted him to invite her to bed but at the same time she felt it was a mistake. He was too young and she barely knew him. He was cute, but not what one would consider a man that exuded sexuality. He was barely a man, not much more than a boy— but she wanted him. She felt safe with him; he made her laugh and her heart feel young and free when he touched her. Nothing mattered when she was with him—nothing at all.

Josh stood up taking her hand in his. Kelly looked up quickly, her eyes wide with fear and excitement. *Was this really going to happen? Had he read her thoughts?* She hesitated for an instant as he applied a gentle beckoning pull to her hand. She curled her fingers around his and stood to her feet looking immediately behind her as if she had dropped something. She did this to gather herself for a split second. Kelly was afraid if she looked into his eyes she would collapse into his arms and cry. She wanted to be loved so badly and she hoped this would not be a mistake. At this moment all she was worried about was today; tomorrow was not an issue. Her mind was so conflicted about everything to do with Josh. She found him attractive, funny, warm, caring and even a bit naïve. All of the things that made him Josh— made him perfect for Kelly.

He slowly led the way down the stairs to his small basement apartment constantly looking behind him, partially to ensure she was still there and he wasn't dreaming, and to make sure she did not trip on the steep concrete steps. He hoped she didn't think of his meager residence as a dungeon. She didn't. She would have spent the night in a dungeon, if it meant being with him. She wanted this and much as he did.

Josh embraced her trying to flex as much muscle as he could to seem very strong and virile. She noticed that he was trying hard; she thought it was adorable and she let him pretend. He kissed her again. Josh looked into her face and asked for permission to take her without saying a word. She lifted her eyes to meet his and gave him a coy, *"Yes"*, with only a faint smile. She saw him blush and inhale hard. She could feel him pressing against her. Kelly knew he was aroused by her. She sat on the bed as he kissed her again and followed her to the mattress.

He cupped her head in the palm of one hand while navigating toward her midriff with the other. She shuttered with anticipation as he kissed her neck and softly nipped at her earlobes all the while caressing her bare stomach. He enjoyed feeling the muscles in her abdomen beneath the skin. She was so strong, he could tell she had worked hard most of her life. She was fit and held strength, unknown to most women, within every muscle fiber of her core. He wanted her with every part of his being. He kissed her harder as she accepted his tongue with a light sucking motion. She writhed slightly beneath his weight. Her legs opening ever so slightly to signal her acceptance of him as he touched her with more strength allocated to his hands. She liked the different touches; soft about her face and neck yet strong and firm when he touched her body.

He lifted her shirt and removed her bra, surprisingly, without much difficulty. As most teenage boys he always feared the brassiere; it just had too many clips for easy removal. Kelly reflexively covered her bare breasts with her arms; she was not used to exposing herself with the last hints of daylight filtering through the basement windows and illuminating her naked chest.

Josh kissed her hard on the neck causing her to uncover herself and touch his face with her fingertips. His face was smooth and soft, she liked the creases of his face that appeared only when he laughed then simply faded away soon after the joke had ended. He was not joking now. He was so intent on every move. He looked like he was concentrating. She had never seen him so serious; he looked like he was trying to defuse a bomb at an orphanage. He was cute, just cute. She almost giggled as he struggled to unbutton her jeans since he had done so well with the bra. *"My god, he is starting to sweat!"* she thought noticing a thin trickle of sweat traveling down his cheek. *"He is really stressing about me!"* she thought again.

Finally, the buttons gave way and Kelly arched her hips to help him a little. He assumed it was out of pity, he was embarrassed that he had trouble with the jeans but he could never let her know that he was. He had to play it cool like everything was intentional. Josh slipped out of his clothes easier than he had gotten Kelly out of hers. He leaned forward to her as she embraced him. His erection pressing against her made him groan with anticipation.

Kelly kissed his chest softly as he clenched her hair in his fist. She could feel the warmth from him as she felt herself moisten with anticipation. She kissed him again pressing her tongue deep into his awaiting mouth. He accepted her tongue greedily. Kelly loved the feel of his hairless chest and smooth skin as she raked her nails softly across his body. She felt him harden more as he pressed against her, rhythmically rocking against her making her more excited with every moment.

She arched her back as he kissed her breasts and quickly encircled her erect nipples with his tongue, his hand pulling her panties away exposing her. The panties were white cotton with blue flower designs, nothing exotic; that was not her style. Josh leaned backward to his knees as Kelly opened her legs to allow him to position himself above her. As he stared long and hard at her naked body, she became uncomfortable.

Her insecurity was creeping in.

"What was he looking at?"

"Was she fat?"

"Was she too old?"

Millions of thoughts passed through her mind as she looked at the naked teenager above her. He smiled, leaned forward and began kissing her body again.

He whispered, "I have to taste you". He began to kiss her stomach and caress her inner thighs with his fingers gently moving further down. She felt herself open to accept him. His lips were dangerously close to her opening. She inhaled sharply and pulled at his hair. She had never let anyone kiss her there before and he seemed determined.

Kelly flexed her muscular thighs around his head and arched her back to deter him from his prize. She wanted his mouth, but she was afraid at the same time.

"*What would he do, what would it feel like?*" she questioned in her mind.

While she argued silently with herself she relaxed her grip and Josh took the opportunity to taste her.

He could smell her sex and the wetness between her thighs held her scent nicely. The hint of sweet sweat and the smell of her body nearly drove him to madness. He deliberately inhaled again and closed his eyes. Kelly's thighs were shaking as she grabbed his hair in her fist, trying desperately to pull him back up to her. She wanted him inside her now; she could not wait any longer. Josh would not be denied of her taste. He had made it this far and he had to taste her. Her scent was growing stronger and more acidic as her excitement increased. A small trickle of her fluid dripped to the sheets below her. Josh knew she was ready.

Kelly gave in and relaxed her thighs to accept his mouth around her. Josh caressed her softly, yet firm enough not to tickle, with his lips. Kelly groaned and arched her back. Josh penetrated her with his rigid tongue. She was exquisite! She pressed her pelvis into his greedy mouth. He savored every drop that she would give him. His tongued danced around her inside and out, pulsing around her as he tasted her gifts. She rocked again, now pulling his hair, forcing him deeper into her body.

She was breathing rapidly, wanting to scream and cry at the same time due the emotions ravaging her senses. Her skin was on fire, it was hard to breathe, she couldn't swallow— she needed him to stop, but she could not ask him to do so. She climaxed. He greedily drank from her finishing by kissing her as he ascended to her navel. Kelly shivered in anticipation as she felt him graze her sensitive areas. She convulsed as he entered her body; he was slow and gentle at first, and then as she opened he pressed deeper into her. He felt her soft pubic hair against his own and the wetness from her covered him like honey. She was warm and he nearly lost his control as he thrust inside her.

She kissed him hard. He pulled her hair while lifting her head to his, forehead to forehead they made love. She felt him swell inside her; the heat from his body was unbearable but she never wanted him to stop. His eyes changed color as he looked at her; they were as green as emeralds enhanced by the sweat glistening on his face. He groaned softly, as he buried himself deep inside her. She had never felt as complete as she did at the moment as their bodies joined together in sweat and sex. She climaxed again covering his erection with her release. She lunged onto him. She nearly sat upright and bit him hard on the left shoulder as his hand squeezed her leg hard covering the bird of paradise tattoo she sported on her thigh. He began to moan as his orgasm came.

He flooded her with his warmth; she felt him fill her from deep inside. He continued to thrust harder, pushing himself deep inside her. She writhed hard side to side attempting to feel all of him inside her body. He was touching her hips now, spreading her body open. She gladly accepted the motion, no longer vulnerable; she was giving all of herself to him. She could smell the sex of the two of them filtering through the air of the basement apartment. The scent of her body covered him, she knew he was hers. She had marked him by giving him the most intimate part of her. She allowed him to ravage her body as he wished. She nearly felt guilty when she looked into his face as he continued to penetrate her. He was trying so hard to satisfy her and be sensitive and loving at the same time.

Kelly thought it must have been hard for him to think of all of these things all the while being sexually charged with the thought of loving her. He pressed deep again, she moaned and winced a bit at the rambunctious thrusts of the teenager. She was nearly dizzy, as he climaxed again; he seemed to be so full. She felt part of him trickled from her body as she could not hold all of him inside. She didn't care she wanted all she could hold. She exhaled slowly as his speed decreased and he began to deliberately glide inside and out of her. She relaxed her body to allow all of her senses to experience the changes in him as his energy depleted. He had given everything to her.

Still inside her, he collapsed onto her chest. She embraced him softly; kissing the top of his head as she felt the contractions of his body slowly decrease. She loved the feeling of him inside her. His mouth was a dangerous weapon and she was proud of herself for giving in to his desire; she normally thought that was disgusting and would have never allowed anyone to perform that way for her. He seemed to want her so much and she would not deny his pleasure.

Kelly looked at the ceiling as Josh continued to pant with his head on her chest. She wondered what would happen now. She felt him soften inside her and the remaining mix of their love cool inside her body. She exhaled slowly again. Josh lifted his head and looked into her eyes. He said "*I love you*" without saying a word. She knew she had him— heart and soul.

Kelly tuned to her side as Josh fell to his back beside her. She placed her head on his chest deciding at that moment that she would not think anymore until morning. This evening was about feeling and nothing else. She wanted to feel love, compassion and trust, and that was all she wanted. It was all she needed and, at that moment in time, Josh was the only one that could give it to her.

Josh was spent. He could barely speak and he knew his voice would crack, so he tried to be strong and silent. His thin body was covered in sweat and remnants of the fluid Kelly had so generously cover him with during lovemaking. He loved her smell. He never wanted to wash her scent away, never. He was in love with her. Emotions were so high in his brain he wanted to cry. He could not, of course, that would not be manly. He had to hold it together and he did so by holding her tightly as she rested her head on his chest. Her red hair flowed across his chest and part of her face as she gently rubbed his chest with her fingers. Each time she touched him it felt like lightning striking him to the very core. He wanted her again, but his body needed time to recuperate. He was satisfied but always greedy for Kelly.

"What would it be like to make love to her every night and see her every morning, naked and in bed with me?" he thought wishfully.

Nothing else in the world could ever matter as long as she was next to him. He looked at Kelly from the corner of his eye not wanting to move and disturb her. Her eyes were closed and she was breathing heavily. She was falling asleep at peace next to him. He was in heaven. Josh had satisfied Kelly O'Hara, or at least he hoped he did.

He felt her hot thigh cover his as she pressed in closer for warmth and sleep. She was going to stay. He grinned and bit his lip again. The breathing of the two lovers began to synchronize and their chests inhaled the cool air together. He had never felt so alive and in love in his entire, although brief, life. Her naked body next to him cooled quickly giving him cause to cover them both with the old comforter that Susy had given him. He was lying on a second hand hide-a-bed in a basement apartment in a one horse town, in mid-western Illinois, and for a brief period of time he felt like the wealthiest man in the world. He had just made love to Kelly and she was not indicating that she ever wanted to leave.

Maybe he was fantasizing but he did not care. He let himself live the fantasy as he listened to her breathing deepen. She was falling asleep and he was holding her tightly, as if she would disappear into thin air and he would awake from this dreamful bliss in a nightmare full of horrors. The only fear he had at this moment was losing her.

Kelly's hand fell from his chest to his stomach. She was asleep. She looked angelic as the reflection of dim light highlighted her face and her scarlet hair. He loved her. Josh began to smile as his eyes closed and the thoughts of waking next to her filled his mind. He fell asleep quickly full of hope contentment and love. He was in a real relationship he knew she loved him her eyes and body said so, it had to be fact.

Harry pounced down the stairs and quickly found his perch on the back of the bed. Harry looked curiously at the couple lying silently in embrace. He blinked his eyes slowly, thinking. He seemed to know something—something he could never tell. Harry liked Kelly, her scent was pleasant and she had an air of kindness toward animals. She petted him first so he knew she was good but there was something that she was hiding; a human fear that only and animal could sense. Harry lowered his head in sadness as he watched her sleep. He wished he could speak; Josh needed to know that Kelly was afraid of something. Josh was his friend that always shared his food and movies with Harry. For once, he wished he was human…he could help them by telling Josh what he sensed, but alas Harry was still a cat.

Harry curled up on his perch and closed his eyes and as kitten dreams began to fill his head, he resigned himself to the fact that life would turn as it may and he was helpless to stop it. For now, let them sleep, let them sleep. Harry drifted off and the purring set in for the night.

Chapter 5

The sun set quickly in Tremane that evening, a signal that winter was rapidly approaching. A year full of coldness and harsh winds were merely physical afflictions to the couple that could in no way prepare for the personal emptiness to come.

Josh held Kelly tighter and whispered in his subconscious, "*I love you Kelly, no matter what happens, I love you and I always will.*" Harry seemed to hear the unconscious thought as he awoke abruptly and sat bolt upright. He hated being a cat. The keen sense of awareness was annoying, however the independence was nice. He mused, just for tonight he would sleep next to the humans. He crawled silently, with feline feet, onto the bed next to Kelly. He hoped he was wrong about what he was sensing as he looked at her with his oval eyes. Harry fell into an uneasy sleep and silently he drifted off without the usual purr of contentment.

The bell on the alarm clock sounded with a deafening ring. Josh moved onto his side, calmly flipped the lever to silence the mechanical beast and promptly rolled back to Kelly's naked body. He held her and smiled. Harry opened one eye from his curled up position at the foot of the bed checking to make sure the two lovers were still there and it had not been a dream, then slowly closed it again returning to slumber.

Kelly moved into Josh's arms and made a slight moaning sound of contentment. It looked like it was going to be a comfortable lazy day after such an interesting night. The couple slept, with Josh's chest against the warm, smooth skin of Kelly's naked back. Kelly loved to feel his warmth. He was quite the little evening inferno that kept her warm. She was prone to coldness and she enjoyed the feeling of gentle heat that his body projected in the late hours of the night. It made her feel safe, secure and even loved.

She had fallen asleep easily, after their night of lovemaking, which was odd for her. On trips she always hated sleeping in a strange bed. Hotels, a friends house, or even homes of her family members always made her feel uncomfortable at night and sleeping in a strange place was always difficult. She did not have that issue when lying next to him even if it was on an old, second hand hide-a-bed in a basement apartment.

Soon a second annoying noise interrupted their blissful sleep. The shrill sound of an emergency medical services voice pager echoed through the basement, followed by Claude's voice. Claude was a paramedic that worked with Josh at the hospital. He had been in EMS since he was about twenty two, he was now nearly forty. He was an excellent paramedic with trauma and anything that required methodical thinking. If there was a protocol for something, Claude new what it was and he always…always followed it, often to a fault. Claude's father was an accountant that worked for a corporate agency, somewhere near Elgin, Illinois, for most of Claude's childhood. Claude was actually born in Russia, but was a naturalized citizen of the United States. In the late fifties, Claude's father had been sent to Russia to work for the company for an extended period of time. Of course, he had taken his new bride along with him.

A few years later Claude was born. He was home-schooled and taught only English and was rarely allowed to interact with other children. His parents wanted him to be fully Americanized by the time he arrived in the United State at the age of five. Apparently, his father did not want his child to have any exposure to the Russian culture during his stay. It may have been due to the Cold War era mentality that considered Russia a communist threat. Claude's father would not have his son becoming a "*Red*" under any circumstances. To avoid this, he simply kept Claude at home with his mother making American meals, reading American books and becoming an American while living in Russia.

The result of this upbringing was Claude's socially backward nature or so everyone thought. Josh always respected Claude because of his kindness, dry sense of humor and to be honest Josh always felt sorry for Claude. Rumor had it, from some of the nurses aides Claude had dated, that he was very well endowed. Josh always giggled at the irony of the concept that Claude, who was not the ultimate picture of "coolness" with his one-hundred-eighty-pound-five-foot-seven inch frame and dark hair, parted sloppily to the side, coupled with a dark black mustache and the way he always rubbed the joints on his mandible when he spoke—no doubt to ensure they were working properly, was hung like a racehorse and had no idea what to do with it.

Claude was very intelligent, but socially awkward. That simple fact made him interesting to Josh and the few that really understood Claude. Josh always rooted for the underdog, as cliché as that may be. He always wanted Claude to do well and receive a little credit for the hard working, loyal individual he was. He worried about everyone and always sought to mediate and keep peace amongst the den of rattlesnakes that ER can be on a bad day. Claude's peacekeeping attempts usually got him in hot water. For Claude it was true that no good deed goes unpunished.

The pager hissed with the sound of radio static and Claude's dry voice booming over the speaker,

"Josh, it's me Claude and if you don't get up they are going to can your butt, you'll lose your money and they will take away your truck! Now get up and get in here! See ya buddy." Josh could hear giggles in the background as the pager went silent, save a few timed beeping reminders to indicate the device needed to be reset.

"Oh Shit! Kelly I am late. I have to work today! I completely forgot about it. I am such an idiot!" he shouted bolting out of bed, his bare bottom streaking to the dresser to get his uniform. Kelly sat up quickly as the blanket slide softly to her waist exposing her beautiful torso. Josh stopped dead in his tracks with his clothes half-donned and darted back to her to kiss her firmly and quickly on the lips.

Kelly rubbed her eyes and silently began to put her clothes on, starting with her jeans.

"I will walk up town and call Shirley to come pick me up", she said very softly with a hint of hurt in her voice. She was beginning to think this was it; he had her for a night and now she was in his way and he would dump her off on the street to save his five dollar an hour job, so he could pretend to be a hero.

This was perfect, exactly how she was afraid it would turn out; all men are the same and this punk was worse. He was eighteen and already learning how to be inconsiderate after he got what he wanted. He had her body and now he was done with her. She wasn't even angry with him she just assumed it would happen as it always does. She was furious with herself even though she wasn't awake enough to show it. She should have went back to Shirley's and left the thought of this goofy kid as a smile on her face that only she would understand and that would have been that.

Josh stopped again; fully dressed in the uniform that was two sizes too big and walked back to Kelly as if he had heard her thoughts.

"I do believe, that will not happen my dear. I am going to drive you to Shirley's, albeit at a rapid rate of speed, I shall take my lover back to her castle and after I fend of a dragon or two and rescue a planet or galaxy, I shall return to pick up the fair maiden, as the sun sets this evening", he boasted as he traversed the basement floor to hold her face in his hands again. He loved being dramatic with a side order of bullshit.

Kelly was floored. This did not fit her preconceived notion and now she had to re-evaluate and respond. That meant he wanted to see her tonight and maybe more often which could mean that he wanted a relationship and a regular thing. *This could not happen, he was supposed to be a one night thing— what was he doing!*

"Wait a second", she thought *"I just made a complete mental circle and disagreed with myself in the twenty seconds it took me to put my pants on— over what I thought a young man was going to do and he did the complete opposite!"*

"He may be just trying to save himself" she pondered for a moment.

She said, "That's okay— really it's no big deal. I will call Shirley. I don't want you to get in trouble at work."

That should do it, now he had an out and Kelly was back to her opinion of what he was going to do; Josh would fit the mold she had carved for him and all would be well with the world and Kelly could go home and regret ever sleeping with him. The universe was now in balance again.

Until Josh spoke. He always has a way of blowing up her pre-planned universe with his words and more so—his actions.

"Ha, yeah right, you just made wonderful love to me, you are tired and now cold" he began.

He was right too Kelly was freezing, standing there in her white sock feet with her jeans on but not buttoned and without a shirt, which she was having trouble locating. It must have been tossed under the damn bed.

He continued, "I am taking you home, fuck the job. It's just Claude and Mick; they will just give me shit about it but that is it. I will not get fired and I don't care anyway. I am taking you home and coming back to get you tonight, if you want me too," he smiled wildly, baring his straight teeth that were as big as the Cheshire cat's would have been before disappearing.

Kelly immediately started looking for her shirt which was of course tangled up in a mess of blankets.

"Are you sure?" She questioned not waiting for an answer to continue dressing, "She lives quite a ways out of town?" She was still giving him an out.

"Yep, I will live. It is just a job", he lied. He loved working there, but he was not going to bail on her for that job. If he got canned he would go to work at a gas station and try again somewhere else, hopefully with Kelly in tow.

The couple ran up the stairs and jumped into the little Chevy truck then drove toward the west end of town with gravel flying as they left the drive. The truck groaned and jerked as Josh slammed through the gears as quickly as he could. He hoped Kelly didn't become frightened of his maniac driving.

She was not frightened at all. She was a bit stunned that he wanted to see her again tonight and he was risking his beloved job to get her home safe. Now she had a bigger problem, *What if he was planning on this being more than a brief thing?* She could not help but think of it, even though she wanted to avoid the thought. Kelly could not keep arguing with herself over this guy. She said very little on the ride to Shirley's which was, by Josh's estimation, just far enough out in the country to get him good and fired.

The trip to Shirley's was about eight miles out of Tremane on the roads that had to hold the record for the biggest potholes, sharpest turns and deadly gravel in Lafayette County. Josh prayed his little truck would make it there and back. He thanked God he had fuel in the tank and spare tires; a flat and out of gas would have been just his luck. He felt he could have gone to the moon in the time it took to get there.

He was having his own issues. Josh wanted to romance her through the day, make her feel like he was the greatest lover since *Casanova* and make her fall madly in love with him; He wanted her to eat chocolate and drink wine, then make love to him all day then run along the beach into the sunset together as the movie camera in his head faded to black. Instead, he basically tossed her half dressed into a beat-up truck to drive like an idiot to take her home, though ten cow pastures and a gravel road. He felt more like John Wayne in *True Grit* instead of *Casanova*. Even when Josh was acting like a moron, he fancied himself a movie star in some form or another. It was a delusional defense mechanism he had developed.

"So", he said as he saw the driveway of Shirley's home come into view, "can I pick you up after work?" he said trying to sound suave as he missed third gear and ground the hell out of the transmission gears which caused him to wince mid-sentence.

"I will call ahead if you give me your number", he asked sheepishly while frantically driving and looking for a pen.

Kelly did not hesitate. She spat out the numbers so quickly he had to ask again to make sure he got them right. He wrote them on his pack of Marlboros and stuffed them back into his pocket. Kelly realized as they pulled into the drive that he had only removed his hand from her jean covered thigh long enough to shift gears. He had driven this entire trip frantically with one hand, just to touch her as long as he could. She nearly cried at the thought. "*He is really falling for me*", she thought.

As the truck screeched to a halt with gravel flying and dust exploding into the air he leaned over and kissed her hard on the lips again.

"I will call as soon as I get off work. I will be here about eight", he said nearly out of breath. Kelly opened the door and quickly stepped out of the truck onto the driveway.

Josh blew her a kiss, ground some more gears, nearly backed into a tree and turned his truck toward town to go save the world. Kelly stood there alone in the driveway as the dust settled around her collecting in her hair and throat. The tickle in her throat that had become a lump wasn't the dust, it was her aching heart. She was missing him already.

She turned to walk toward the house. She knew Shirley was not up yet and if she was Kelly wasn't in the mood to talk to her. Her mind began running in circles again with a thousand "*What ifs*", "*Why did I's*" and a few "*What am I doings*", but she didn't care. She would see what happened tonight. He would call; she already knew it in her heart. She could not lump him in with all of the rest. He was too innocent, too trusting and he tried so damn hard.

He could use some more weight but other than that, he was perfect for Kelly at this time in her life. She needed simple, honest and open. Josh was all of those things even though he always tried to pretend to be something else in order to impress her. What he did not know, was that he had already made his mark on her heart without knowing it by just being himself; the honest crazy kid that had dreams of saving the world with hopes of one day becoming a hero.

The woman turned one last time to look down the road toward the dust clouds of where his truck had been. The last specks of dirt had settled and all that was left of Josh was the tire tracks in the dirt and the faint smell of him still lingering on her skin and in her hair. She inhaled deeply to savor the smell of his body. She began to recall all of the events in the previous night's lovemaking session. He didn't do everything right, but he was close—really damn close. That thought sent a shutter through Kelly's body with as much force as a bolt of lightning striking a power station. *Could she be falling for him too?* It was too soon to tell and she needed coffee and a Misty. She hoped he made it to work without any more trouble.

"I am sooooo fucked!" Josh said aloud in the cab of the S-10 as he finally hit pavement. He ran every stop sign in town as he darted down Grove toward Eighth Street and the hospital. He was still thinking about Kelly and how much trouble he was going to be in for being late. He could still taste her in his mouth and he missed her already. It was 7:30 and he was supposed to report for work thirty minutes ago. He wanted to go back to her but he had to have a job.

How else could he get a place for them to live?

The thought never crossed his young mind that she had to go back home to Riverday. He was way too shortsighted for that. He was in love and all that mattered was Kelly O'Hara— nothing else.

The truck came to a screeching halt accompanied by smoke rolling from beneath the fenders. The pungent smell of scorched brake pads filled the air. Josh slammed the door and ran past the boilers, up the ramp, through the back door, past the elevators to the time clock. He punched in his identification numbers, since he had forgotten his name tag, and walked quickly to ER.

He was thinking about her the entire time. As he ran past the boiler (his distraction when he didn't know what to say to her as they chatted on the dock), as he ran up the ramp (where he nearly fell while looking at her), the hand rail he touched (that supported his weight when his knees buckled as he looked into her eyes for the very first time), the back door (where he spied on her being taken up to her room and where he first caught a glimpse of her naked tanned thigh), the elevators (that took her away from him), and finally ER # 3 (where he had first seen her face and lost his powers of speech).

Kelly was everywhere he looked. He loved it. He could be reminded of her every time he went to work. He decided at that moment that he would never leave the hospital, unless Kelly asked him to of course. He loved seeing her in everything he did. Josh felt like she was watching him and he had to impress her more with every action. He tried wholeheartedly to do just that.

"You had a woman with you didn't ya Little Shit!" Johnny bellowed, as Mick feverishly filled out his time sheet and scooted out the door.

"Yes I did. I am so sorry I am late— I took her home." Josh said rapidly.

"Little Shit got laid. I'll be goddamned. Next thing you know the nurses will be able to hit a vein when they start IV's and the world will end shortly after!" Johnny joked.

"Don't be late anymore Little Shit or Mick will have a stroke, then I will have to write it up and you know I don't like to do that— makes management think I follow orders and I don't want to ruin my reputation", Johnny said only half-seriously.

"I won't. Big Shit, I won't. I'm sorry", Josh stammered but secretly he knew he would be late everyday, if Kelly wanted him to be.

Johnny begged and pleaded intermittently throughout the day for more details about Josh's love interest. Josh gave him very few. He knew how Johnny was and it was a hell of a good juicy story for him to spread around the hospital.

"Susy, said you came to visit some chic that was admitted here. Little Shit, you got balls. I will give you that, just like me. Meet a chic on the dock, talk to her on the floor and take her home the next day. You got the beginnings of some talent kid; just don't get caught." Johnny said admiringly of the young man's good fortune.

Josh was stunned and silent. Susy must have seen him sneak in and that bitch from the floor must have narc'd on him.

"Damn fuckers, why don't they mind their own business!" he belted out to Johnny.

"Because they don't have a life and your adventures must be more entertaining, at least this week; look at it this way you were just a kid last week that took transfers, now you are a stud banging a hot older chic. That means there must be something interesting about you. The girls will be trying to figure out what it is. The door is wide open for you buddy, just go get what you want. It happened to all of us when we were your age. It's just your turn. Long term care and Med-Surg are already betting on which chic is gonna try you out." Johnny said, as if explaining a math equation.

"Not interested." Josh said dryly walking out to the dock with Johnny close behind.

The sun was unusually warm for October. Josh felt the heat strike his face when he walked out on the dock to light a cigarette. Johnny promptly packed a pinch of tobacco into his lower lip, spit on the sidewalk and continued, "True love eh", he said with sarcasm in his voice and an evil glint in his eye.

"Maybe" Josh replied

"We will see Little Shit. We will see. Mark my words, the first one never sticks around" he said looking away as if lost in a memory.

"She ain't my first", Josh stated with vinegar in his words.

"I mean the first love, not first sexual encounter— there is a difference", Johnny snapped.

Josh realized what Johnny meant. Josh nodded in confirmation. The day seemed to drag on for hours; no calls and very few ER patients. Josh and Johnny talked, laughed and joked most of the day. Although Johnny was a good friend, partner and his stories were always funny, Josh kept looking at the time and waiting for the day to end. He had Eric cover call that night so he could be with Kelly again with no interruptions.

6:45 pm. Josh was pacing. He had smoked a pack of cigarettes and drank three pots of coffee throughout the day. His lungs were on fire and his brain was a wreck. He needed to see her so badly it hurt. The longest fifteen minutes of his life passed and he picked up the phone and dialed.

"Kelly", he asked to the woman on the other end of the phone.

"No hang on a second", it was Shirley. He heard her call for Kelly loudly in the background.

"Hello", the hint of an accent from Chicago was the sweetest sound he could ever hear as Kelly spoke the greeting.

"Hey, it's me. Can I still come get you at 7:30?" He asked. His heart couldn't take the extra thirty minutes to wait until eight.

"Yeah, sure I will be ready", Kelly said quickly as if the faster she spoke the faster time would pass.

"On my way", Josh said and hung up the phone. The conversation sounded like a CIA agent talking to a contact instead of two lovers setting up a date.

Josh drove home to Elm Street, patted Harry on the head as he ran through the door and straight into the shower. He stripped and scrubbed his body so briskly he was pink again when he exited the shower. His metal S-10 horse waited for him in the driveway. He was backing up before the driver's door was even shut. He drove as quickly as he could to the west end of town.

What seemed to take ten days, to travel eight miles, passed and the end was in site. He saw Shirley's house and the front door. He slammed the truck into third and sped toward his prize. He tried to knock on the door, though Kelly was already opening it. He caught a glimpse of Shirley in the background; she was eyeballing him as he left with Kelly. Shirley was a thin moderately attractive woman but she was no match for Kelly in the looks or body department.

Josh grinned with guilty pleasure as Kelly sat next to him in the truck. He leaned toward her and kissed her gently this time. He had to make up for this morning. Honeysuckle again. He loved her scent and the taste of her lips. He asked her if she was hungry, she declined food and simply stared at his profile with love in her eyes as Josh drove them back to Elm Street.

Harry was sitting on the kitchen table when they arrived. He greeted Kelly with a purr and a whip of his tail then pounced to the floor. He was glad she was back. Josh and Kelly sat close holding hands on the sofa watching comedy and laughing together. They made idle comments about the act, but they did not have a personal conversation of any substance during the show.

Kelly was not sure what to say and Josh was in no better shape to delve into his heartfelt emotions. He was afraid he would scare her away.

She was worried about tomorrow. She had to leave and she didn't have the heart to remind him. Josh began kissing Kelly. She seemed to melt into him this time—no chasing. She was willing to be with him and he felt it. He grasped her hands and led her again to his basement apartment.

She sat on the bed looking up at him as he removed his shirt. He leaned forward she met him halfway and they kissed. Kelly helped him with her bra this time and soon they were again in each others' arms.

Josh was erect and his body was heating up quickly. He covered Kelly with his body as she opened her thighs to accept him. He was inside her again and the rush of emotion nearly brought him to tears. She kept looking into his eyes as he loved her. Occasionally her eyes would widen and she would bite her lip when he over-stimulated her. They kissed hard as she reached climax with a whimper; he soon followed suit and looked into her cinnamon eyes as he filled her inside.

She quickly pulled him by the neck and embraced him forcefully not letting him move. She wanted to cry, but she could not let him see her do so. If she did, he would start talking and if he started talking, she would never leave. She had to go home. She had to and it had to be tomorrow.

"Josh", Kelly said with her lips near his.

"I have to go home tomorrow", she whispered.

"I know, but then what?" He asked as his face dropped. He did not want her to answer.

"You can come visit maybe", she said not knowing if that would take place.

"Okay", he said and began kissing her neck. He did not want to think about tomorrow. Just being with her tonight was all that he wanted. They made love again and fell quickly to sleep.

Chapter 6

"Goddamn it!" Susy shrieked after stubbing her toe on the basement steps. She was carrying a laundry basket down to the utility room

Harry scampered under the bed and Josh sat bolt upright. Susy was far too motherly for his liking. Kelly quickly hid under the blankets. Susy locked eyes with Josh and sent the signal with her eyes that only a woman can. It was a clear message; *"Get her out of our house!"*

"Fuck you! I pay rent!" was the vengeful eye-to-eye response Josh sent to Susy in a way that only a man can send it. Susy stomped up the stairs and soon after the distant whispering between her, Mara her girlfriend, and Tanner began.

"I better go", Kelly said and quickly began to get dressed. Josh was going to argue but he did not want Kelly to hear anything the ragging bitches had to say about them. Again Josh and Kelly left the house on Elm Street and drove back to Shirley's. Not many words were spoken on the way.

Josh was sick to his stomach; he did not want her to go. He rationalized that he would soon see her again, but he found no solace in his thoughts.

"Give me your phone number and work number and I will call you when I get home", Kelly said as they pulled into the drive. Josh wrote it very carefully in a scrap of paper and handed it to her with shaking hands.

She kissed him quickly, exited the truck and walked toward Shirley's front door never looking back. Josh stared as long as he dared, then slowly drove down the drive not stirring as much as a wisp of dust as he moved away. He feared that he may have let go of the beautiful Kelly O'Hara, maybe for the last time in his life. Josh consoled himself briefly with a cigarette and a lie. He lied to himself that it would all work out and she would stick around and all would be well. Life always worked out for him. He felt he was lucky and life was good to him.

The road to Tremane seemed to be five hundred miles long. The job would be there in the morning as usual but for now he just wanted to avoid Susy and Tanner. He was not in the mood for a lecture and the drama that they were no doubt plotting to discuss with him as soon as he came home. It was an odd thing, he pondered as he took another deep drag from the Marlboro inhaling the smoke into his lungs, that the people that have very little going on in their lives, the victims of routine, the boring, the unattached and the going-to-bes, are always obsessed with getting involved with people that always have adventure in their lives.

Usually these people are uninvited guests that offer unrequested advice and opinions. Josh felt these people must have this phrase running through their head all the time,

"If I can't create my own excitement, I am going to stick my nose in your business, criticize you and secretly be jealous of your life at the same time."

The smoke burned his lungs but he didn't care. He just drove. His mind was empty of thoughts. He did not want to think about Kelly, if he did not think about it, all would be fine. He still had the mind of an eighteen year-old and the *"wait and see"* philosophy. Raines' sounded like a good place to go. He hadn't been there in a while and his friends would be glad to see him. They were always there sitting at the turnaround next to Carl's General Store, since most of them had still not found work since graduating high school. They were a pretty good group of kids but they liked alcohol more than searching for work. Josh always knew he could have a good time and forget about Kelly and the thought that she might never come back, thanks to Susy and her damn PMS attitude.

Route 140 ended as Josh entered the edge of Tremane. He traveled through town and eventually turned onto Kennedy Avenue. He continued north toward the small town of Raines.

It did not take long for Josh to meet up with his old crew and it took even less time for him to get drunk. He drank beer and cheap whiskey until he vomited. He acted foolish with his friends and tried to drink the thought of Kelly leaving away. He did not think about it much when he was drinking, the alcohol had an unusual effect on Josh he went from pleasantly buzzed to completely trashed in a matter of hours.

One of his more well-versed friends always said,

"It was not the amount of drink we ingested; it was the sheer velocity in which it was consumed, that led to our intoxicated state."

Josh enjoyed his friends but every month or so that he worked as an EMT, the similarities, interests and attitudes between he and hid friends seemed to become more and more disjointed. His friends did not really admire him; he was still just Josh to them. They looked at him as the show-off at the party. He was still the guy that was either making everyone laugh or passing out from having way too much fun. He had one way to do everything—all or nothing. Josh did not really understand the concept of moderation.

He passed out in the back of his friend's truck that night. It was a good thing there was an old horse blanket back there and the truck was covered with a camper shell or the young idiot would have frozen to death. It was getting cold early this year and it looked like it was going to be an angry winter in Illinois.

The sun and the need for a biological function awoke Josh in plenty of time to get back to work. It was 5 AM and the October sun was unusually bright as if God was trying to punish him for the excessive alcohol intake by inducing a migraine into his hung-over brain with each piercing ray of the unforgiving sun.

The truck bed creaked as Josh sat up. The noise seemed to be amplified and caused Josh to reflexively grasp his aching forehead in an attempt to massage away the pain that felt like needles scraping his brain and shards of glass scratching the back of his eyes. Cheap whiskey always did that to him. He didn't care. After an episode of severe nausea and a few dry heaves, the boy decided to try to make it home. As he walked passed the truck he saw Don curled up in the front seat with Melissa, a cute tanned brunette with a cheerleader body and the brains of a fruit fly. She was wrapped around Don for warmth and her naked thigh was draped over his waist. Josh knew she was naked under what was left of the blanket.

His first thought was, "*Well, at least he got laid. I hope he used a condom, if she gets pregnant he is screwed for life.*"

Don looked up from the truck seat as he heard Josh start the S-10. He gave the thumbs up sign as Josh waived farewell. Don lowered his head to rest on the hips of the naked teenage girl still asleep in his truck.

Every bump in the rode drove the needles further into Josh's brain. He hated hangovers. The ride was long considering he had to stop twice in a twelve mile trip to vomit again. He smelled like he had fallen into a vat of corn mash and his mouth tasted like acid. He was sick, but he was still going to work. It was just pain and it would go away eventually, like everything bad in his life. He just ignored it and it would go away. He drove into Tremane and proceeded to Elm Street. Harry was sitting on the counter when Josh passed through the kitchen to the bathroom. The cat gave his greeting with a soft mew and a flick of his tail.

Josh said. "Hey Harry, yea it was a bad night. Glad I don't do that every day." Harry answered with a longer mew as if he agreed with the statement.

The shower felt good as the hot water flowed over his thin frame. He stood with his head hung down and his eyes shut from pain. As his thoughts began to clear, he realized that Kelly was leaving if not already gone. He felt the nausea coming back. It had to be the alcohol. The feeling passed and he began the ritual of brush—gargle—brush— gargle, then brush again to hopefully eliminate the smell of whiskey that still lingered on his breath from the night before. Satisfied that he had removed the hint of alcohol consumption from his body, he walked to the basement wrapped in a towel to retrieve his uniform. He always told Susy that he felt like a superhero when he wore it. Today, he felt like a hung-over teen that just wanted to sleep.

He dressed and drove to work at the hospital. He arrived on time and walked into the ER.

He poured a cup of black coffee and began to sip quietly without speaking to anyone. He was not in the mood.

"You look like shit", Mick said, "Guess you were out late with that chic you met here huh? Wear your ass out did she?" Mick said jovially hoping for details.

"No", Josh whispered quietly.

"Oh, sorry man…. happens to the best of us, except me of course" he remarked with a hint of sarcasm and maybe a bit of empathy." "Truck's good to go. I am out of this shithole", he snapped as he walked out of the room.

Roy came in and sat down. Roy was a pompous ass that thought he was the most intelligent medic in the world and no one could hang the moon correctly to suit Roy. Especially new EMT's like Josh. He loved gossiping like the nurses and acting like he was better than everyone else.

"Mornin' Joshy!" Roy said with an exceptionally loud voice. He could tell Josh was hung-over.

"Out late last night", he questioned.

"Yea", Josh snapped. "I am going to go check the truck"

Josh made it through the day with few calls and a quiet day in the ER. He would be glad when he went to nights. He hated working days;

the people were soccer moms and wannabe politicians and he hated management. He always thought their rules got in the way of patient care. He wanted to work the night shift because the people were more fun and all of the exciting tragedies happened at night, or so he thought.

At seven in the evening, he went back to his house on Elm Street and watched television after taking a handful of ibuprofen to kill the headache that reminded him not to drink whiskey anymore. Harry was exceptionally attentive to him that night; he sat curled in a ball with his head on Josh's lap. Comedy shows were not funny without Kelly there. Everything reminded him of her presence. The television, the sofa, the cat and even his bed, the sheets still carried her smell.

He gave up on television and just sat quietly. As he prepared to retire for the evening, the telephone rang.

"Hello", he said half interested.

"It's me", a familiar voice with a Chicagoan accent whispered through the speaker

"Hey you," he exclaimed with excitement in his voice despite the headache.

"I made it home okay and you asked me to call," Kelly said with a grin in her voice as if she was pretending to be doing him a favor. She had thought about him all day but she would never let him know that.

"When can I see you again? Are you ever coming back?" he blurted with impatience regretting the words as soon as they came out of his mouth.

"I don't know. I have to work and I won't be off until Thanksgiving", she said with a hint of sadness in her voice.

"Maybe you could come up?" she offered

"Damn right I will! I can leave anytime not a problem. Tell me where to go. I need your number. Should I stay with you or do I need a hotel? How long can I stay? Do you need anything? When can I come? What dates? What is your address?" He rambled like a senile old man talking to himself.

"Slow down there cowboy. How about November 24th and stay a day or two?" she answered.

"I will be there!" He exclaimed while thrusting his arm in the air as if he had just scored the winning touch down in at the Superdome on Superbowl Sunday.

Kelly laughed at his enthusiasm. Josh had to play it cool now he did not want her to think he was desperate for her attention, although he was and could barely contain himself. Harry bounced from the sofa and jumped to the counter next to Josh and did a little celebration by stretching and rolling on his back; he hoped for a belly rub to boot. Josh obliged and patted and scratched Harry's furry belly.

The conversation continued for an hour with Josh performing his stand up routine with whatever material he could come up with to make her laugh. He loved to hear her laugh. It was infectious. His heart was warm and he smiled until his face hurt when he spoke to her. She was truly a wonderful woman that had stolen his heart. He was smitten with Kelly. If he really told her how crazy he was about her she would probably think he was a psychotic stalker, so he had to play it down a bit. He was not very good at it.

The call ended with directions and drawn out goodbye as Josh waited until she hung up first to replace the telephone on the receiver. Immediately after the call, he ran to his truck and sped to the hospital. He had to request time off immediately.

He unlocked the back door to the hospital and trotted down to ER. He was grinning like never before. His hang-over was gone and he had a date in a few weeks with the woman of his dreams and all he had to do was work at a great place until then. Life was good, until he saw Susy.

"I have a bone to pick with you young man!" She barked as she met him in the hall.

"Outside", she ordered pointing to the door. She stomped her five—seven, one—hundred— eighty pound frame to the dock door, the same place where Josh first spoke to Kelly.

Susy was the sister of one of Josh's best friends. Susy's mother was the ER director and Susy had been working as an EMT with Josh. They were inseparable during the first few months that he worked there. They always hung out together, discussed dreams and relationships and at times cried on each other's shoulders.

Susy never had any luck with love and people often thought she was sleeping with Josh. It was not true. Susy had recently, after several tearful road trips in the dead of the night bearing her soul and conflictions to Josh. Finally, she had admitted she was gay. She had met a woman on the medical unit and had fallen in love.

Josh was always her support system and he always cared for her. She taught him how to be an EMT and mothered him constantly even though she was his elder by only four years. Josh looked up to Susy and wanted to protect her. She was his boss' daughter, his best friend's sister and his mentor. He always wanted to be part of her life and would visit ER on his nights off to hang out with Susy.

When Susy decided to tell her mother that she was gay, she asked Josh to help. He agreed, not knowing what to do but simply sit there in case Velma, Susy's mother, had a heart attack. He could at least perform CPR. Susy told her mother she had something important to tell her. She began with Josh sitting faithfully at her side.

Susy began with a shaky voice, "Mom I have fallen in love with someone."

"You two are getting married! I am so happy it is him!" She exclaimed with the wrong assumption. Josh bowed his head and stared at the floor.

"No mom, it is someone …" she paused and took a deep breath, "of the same sex."

Velma began to sob. She started asking all of the questions you would expect about how she could have done things better as a mom, was she gone too much, etcetera, etcetera. Josh just sat there, being moral support and a bump on a log. He was then charged with telling her brother, Brandon, his best friend that Susy was gay. He took a bottle of bourbon to Raines completing the task and stayed with Brandon until they both passed out. He loved Susy like a sister and he was about to get an ass chewing.

He already had a cigarette out when they reached the dock and the lashing began.

"What the fuck are you doing bringing a strange woman in our house and to top it all off it was a patient! A goddamn patient. Tonya told me that she knew you were up to something, you little shit! She was a cop too! Damn it you know when those fuckin' cops snap that they can kill you! Look, I understand that she had some bad shit go down and I feel bad too, we rely on cops and they take shit home on their shoulders, just like we do and I know it can get to be too much, but goddamn she could have killed us in our sleep!" Susy ranted.

"Shut the fuck up, Shut the fuck up, you are more fucked up in the head than she could ever be, she was scared! Now you can go to hell! I thought you were my friend and I care about Kelly and you can go fuck yourself! I pay rent and I can do as I choose, you are not my mother and if you check, bitch, I didn't listen to her either", he fired back

"Maybe you should calm down", she said trying to be mature and failing miserably.

"I am going back in there and requesting time off to go see her over Thanksgiving, if I don't come back, tell Harry bye and throw my shit away!" He screamed.

"And your job?" she asked

"Fuck you and…. and….. my job. It is my life", he stammered and stomped through the ER entrance slamming the door behind. Susy stood alone dumbfounded, he had never screamed at her before.

After the time sheets were completed Josh left the building and sped out of the ER driveway with gravel flying. He was already planning on moving away to live with Kelly, if she would have him. He had nothing which made moving easy. He could haul everything he owned in one trip in his little truck. He could always find a job and live with Kelly and take care of her and make her laugh every night and even learn to cook if she wanted him to; he would do anything to be with her and Thanksgiving could not come soon enough.

The next few weeks dragged by and Josh was becoming more irritable as the days passed.

He worked constantly to exhaust himself and then he would sleep as long as his body could take it. He was trying to make the days pass by quickly and avoid everyone, especially Susy. He lived at work and slept in the basement with Harry standing guard. He was a recluse counting the hours until he could see Kelly.

A few days before his long-awaited trip, Kelly called in tears, "Can I come down?" she sobbed as Josh answered the phone.

"Are you okay? What is wrong? Did someone hurt you? Want me to come get you?" he began rambling again.

"No… I am okay. I just want to see you. I need you now. Can I come?" she begged.

"Yes, leave right now! I will get us a place. Call when you are in town and I will come and get you and take you to a nice hotel and you can stay until I find a place", he said rambling and planning it out in his head. If he would have repeated the word *and* once more, he would have been declared an official literary idiot.

"Okay, I will leave now. It will take about four hours. I will call when I am in town." She whispered with her voice shaking.

"Okay, go now!" He instructed and hung up the phone. Josh ran three stop signs to get to the Resting Inn in town. He paid cash and reserved a room for Kelly. He ran the same three stop signs on the way back to Elm

Street. He ran into the house and called Kelly back to make sure she was gone. No answer. Good. She was on her way.

He sat by the phone with a cup of coffee and Harry. They both waited for the phone to ring. He calculated the trip in is head and where she could be at any moment. He did this over and over until he began to drive himself insane. He paced, he tried to watch television, he cleaned, he cursed at what or whoever may have hurt her. He would kill them if they touched her. He had guns at his dad's place and he was a good shot with a rifle. Many insane scenarios ran through his tortured impatient teenage mind.

Harry paced too. He was nervous because Josh was nervous. The phone rang with a short burst. Josh answered before the ring was complete. It was Kelly.

"Where are you? I will be there quick. That was fast!" he said smiling at the thought he could see her in a few moments.

"I am back at home." She said dryly

"What!" he exclaimed

"I couldn't leave my dogs; there is not anyone here to take care of them. I am fine, I just overreacted", she said.

"Bring them! They can stay at my Dad's!" he begged. He could tell by the silence that she wasn't coming. He had to calm down; he did not want to push.

"You still want me to come this week?" He asked not sure if he wanted an answer

"Yes, please come, I will see you then….Bye", she finished the call.

The click was like a gunshot in his head. After a small tantrum, Josh drove back to the hotel and canceled the room and of course lost his deposit. He didn't care it was only money. He went home and went to bed. He rested but did not sleep. He hoped things were okay, he knew it had to be about her job.

The next night at work he wrote a letter to Kelly. He joked and wrote silly poetry about how much he missed her and hated her stupid boss, but he kept it light. He wanted to make her laugh and make sure she would not become sad or depressed. Since his penmanship was atrocious he wanted to type the letter for her. One problem was that he had never typed before. He used two fingers and the "hunt and peck" technique, it took him three hours to type a single page letter. He expressed mailed it the next day.

November 24th arrived and Josh left Tremane at 7 am. One hour into the trip, a rainstorm arrived suddenly causing truckers to pull off the side of the road. Josh kept driving blindly through the rain and hail. A thunderstorm was not going to keep Josh from his Kelly. He would drive through hell to see her and the devil rain was not even a challenge. He was going to see her even if it killed him.

He arrived at Kelly's home around noon. She greeted him with a hug and a kiss on the cheek. She looked beautiful in her tight jeans and a black tank top with glitter on the front. Josh wanted her so bad he could barely contain himself. She brought him in and gave him some coffee. They talked and laughed and he made jokes about the trip and the rain. They sat for a long time and chatted at the table then she invited him to go to dinner at Pepe's restaurant.

At dinner, he chattered excitedly while Kelly listened. She could tell he was nervous. She thought it was because he had driven so far from home and was in Dalton City, so close to Chicago. He had to call for directions from a pay phone when he finally made it to the city. He was very lost and she could hear the nervousness in his voice as she gave him directions to her home. What she didn't know was that Josh was not nervous about the drive or the city but the simple act of eating in front of her made him very nervous. He was so afraid he would make a mess and not seem to be suave. He envisioned dumping an entire plate of Mexican food into his lap, so he barely ate anything.

After dinner they walked to Kelly's car, a blue Honda Accord, and were approached by a thin black man asking for money. Kelly told him to go fuck himself and mumbled something about drug addicts. The police department had made her hard toward the plight of humanity. She had nearly been killed by drug dealers, crack addicts and gangbangers. Josh was shocked to see the hard and cold side of Kelly. She had learned to defend herself very well during her time as a police officer. The ride back to Kelly's was surreal. Josh continued to talk nervously, while Kelly listened and occasionally laughed. He continued to wonder what was bothering her but he was too afraid to pry for fear she may loose interest and tell him to go home.

Kelly pulled into the driveway and shut off the engine. She looked at Josh as if to tell him something. This time he patiently waited in silence. The words never came. She invited him in to sit in the living room and watch television. He noticed the police car model encased in glass on her entertainment center. He made a comment about the car and how nice her place was and it was so much better than his apartment. Josh complimented her and her life every time an opportunity presented itself.

Something had to be bothering Kelly. He fully expected her to run into his arms, kiss him wildly and drag him into the bedroom and make love like they had before. It did not happen that way. She was pleasant but distant, as if her mind was somewhere else. He had to try much harder to make her laugh and she stared at the television for long periods in silence. Josh made hints that he was tired since he worked all night and may need to "crash soon" as the afternoon turned into evening. Kelly showed him the bedroom and said he could sleep anytime and she would join him later. He was devastated with her lack of enthusiasm, but he tried hard not to show it.

Kelly was lounging on the sofa across the room from the chair where Josh was seated. He went over to sit next to her and maybe try to get a kiss or two. She let him touch her thigh and he eventually he kissed her, she was distant and nearly pulled away. She looked into his eyes with that same look she had in the car. She was hiding something and he knew it. He felt tense for the first time around her; the feeling was more than typical teenage nerves. He couldn't take it any longer, he had to ask. He prayed silently that it wasn't something he did that made her lose interest in him.

"What is wrong?" he asked with hurt in his eyes.

"Nothing baby, just some work on my mind, why don't you get a nap and I will be in there in a few." She instructed.

"Okay, guess you don't want to think about it, I understand", he replied as he stood and reluctantly walked to the bedroom. He undressed. Josh pulled the blanket down and lay down on his back. He stared at the ceiling for what seemed like hours. Finally, Kelly arrived and shut the bedroom door. She took off her pants leaving the shirt in place. Josh rolled onto his side propping his head on his shoulder to watch her undress.

She looked over her shoulder at him and gave him a partial smile. She was not herself, not his Kelly. He wanted to know what was wrong; but her secret was her secret and he respected secrets. Kelly sat on the edge of the bed and took a deep breath as if she was preparing herself for something. It was the kind of inhalation you could not hear, but could see by the way her shoulders lifted and lowered. She slid into the bed and turned away from Josh into the fetal position.

The ceiling was laughing at him as he stared into the miniscule cracks in the paint that were only visible to the naked eye if you strained hard and squinted. Josh had completely given in to the situation. He was confused about being there, yet did not want to be anywhere else. Thoughts were doing battle in his brain. He wanted to make love to her, but he wanted to know what was troubling her more. Kelly was not herself she had a completely different demeanor; her posture had changed. She was rigid and tense. Her shoulders were tight and she carried them high as though someone was holding a knife at her back. Her jaw was clenched like she was trying to hold something inside with vigor and purpose. She was hurting and Josh knew it. It made him sick to his stomach. He was helpless to fix her mysterious dilemma of the mind.

Josh rolled to his side and wrapped his arm around her naked body pressing close to her. For once, he was not sexually excited at the sight of her. He was distraught and afraid she was repulsed by him and could not understand how this could have happened. It had only been a few months.

In his teenage mind the best option was to go for broke and see if he could blow the lid off of the situation. He would attempt to kiss her and if she responded he would make love to her and that would make her feel safe, then she would lie next to him, cry, share her soul and he would console her as she fell deeper in love with him due to his extreme sensitivity. All would be well with the world. He was, as usual, wrong.

Josh placed his palm on Kelly's left shoulder pulling her gently toward him. She responded and looked so deeply into his eyes that it forced him look downward to avoid her stare. Her breasts were barely visible through the tee and Josh preferred to look there instead of her eyes. He was afraid that she would see his fear. She always could look into his soul.

She kissed him first. It was a soft and hurried kiss as she pulled him close to her body. Josh responded to her touches and was easily aroused by her. She could drive him mad with a single touch of her hand. He caressed her smooth brown skin and stared into her face to ask permission with his eyes to proceed. He felt awkward and lost in his own actions. Josh wanted to tell her how badly he wanted to make love to her, but not at the risk of losing her love for the sake of sex.

Kelly answered with a deep hard kiss. As she rested her head on the pillow, her eyes told him a story, "*Go ahead lover, take me as you wish, love me; but let me keep my secrets. Accept what I give and love me. I need silent love with no questions or analysis, just bring our bodies together young one; for my heart is breaking and this may be the last time we love, so love me well, love me well.*" Kelly held back tears as Josh softly kissed her neck. She embraced him with all the strength she could gather.

Her body temperature was hot and her breathing was deep. She seemed to be fighting back the emotions that were tearing her apart internally. She reached climax with Josh and exhaled hard while kissing him on the forehead. Josh withdrew from her body and sat back on his heels looking at her beautiful body, her skin reddened from the weight of him on her torso. Her thighs were still open and her eyes curious seeking his next action. She remained open offering herself to him if he chose. She wanted to please him and love him, but she knew in her heart she would never see him again.

Josh gently lay down beside her and kissed her shoulder. Kelly kissed him full on the lips and touched his cheek. "You okay?" she asked fearing the answer.

"Yeah, I'm just tired beautiful, it has been a long time since I slept", he lied. He knew this answer would suffice to avoid complicating an already complex situation. The tension was so thick in the room it felt like a blanket of dread looming above them. He knew it was over and he was afraid to admit it. He did not know why and he desperately wanted to know what he had done to push her away. He needed to ask. He wanted to ask—He didn't.

He held her tightly and kissed her neck and face hard fighting back the tears. God help him if she saw him cry. Josh took the easy way out of the situation as most teenage boys would. He did what they do, he fell asleep holding Kelly hoping it was all a misunderstanding on his part and life would be wonderful when the sun rose the next morning. A typical teenager is excellent at avoiding situations that require mature thought and action. In this case Josh was no different. He pretended life was fine and he lied to himself as his last moments of consciousness drifted away into the night.

Kelly lay beside the young man adjusting her breathing to avoid waking her sleeping lover. She was terrified of the morning. Thoughts roared through her head so loudly she imagined he could actually hear them if the volume in her head increased a single decibel. She did not want him to know what was going to happen. She wanted him to have one last night dreaming a blissful boy's dream that the life he created in his mind was still intact.

Several hours had passed and Kelly quietly moved away from Josh's sleeping body. She sat on the bed; arms folded hoping she could let him go easily. She was falling for him and she could not let that happen. He was too young and had plans of saving the world and many teenage dreams that she remembered all too clearly from her youth. She wanted to protect his dreams feeling the pain of her own dreams that had been shattered by life and all that accompanies it.

Kelly was in trouble at work and in the process of being railroaded by the good-ol-boy police department mentality. She had been involved with a police chief's brother and things had turned sour; the famed "boys in blue" were looking to get even. He had become abusive and she would not tolerate it any longer. It became physical at times and there was no excuse for putting up with violence in a relationship. She knew it was going to get bad and she was in for a world of persecution and trauma. Josh could never know.

He was small and at times over estimated his qualities as a man. He could not compete with the manipulations of thirty year old men with badges and pistols that they could use at will. She played the scenario in her head.

Josh would become enraged with them for hurting Kelly. She would try to calm him down; he would leave abruptly and look for his target, no doubt driving directly to the police department. He would scream and yell and try to put fear into the man, who would laugh at him and have him arrested and probably beaten. He would be railroaded in court on trumped up charges and sent to prison for what ever they length the just felt he deserved. Then they would come after Kelly. It was a no-win situation for her and would be even worse for Josh. He was the young clueless boy that was dangerously in love.

Kelly had to protect him from himself and she would, no matter how much it would hurt either one of them. She walked to the kitchen and sat at the table. Her mind calmed as the hours passed and she came to the resolution that Josh would be okay. He was an attractive young man that would do well with the ladies and had a bright future ahead of him. She looked out the window with hatred of where life had placed her. She hated this town and all of the people in it. All she wanted was peace and it never happened when she was with any man, except Josh. She rationalized that this was because he was still innocent of heart and had no pretences about himself. He was grateful for her attention and would do anything to keep it. This flattered her, but her maturity forced her to realize that her dream of happiness was just that, a dream. She could not find any logical way to make this work.

If she ran away with him, they would find her. It would be better if she faced the situation alone. No matter what happened to her she had to protect Josh. She loved him for all he was and more importantly, for all that he was about to be.

Kelly quietly crept into her bedroom. Josh was breathing deeply, lost in sleep. He was sprawled across the bed like a cat stretching in the morning. She stared at his nubile thin body and his sharp features. No lines on the face, his hands were gently resting near his cheek, his lips pursed ever so slightly as if he was kissing in his sleep. Kelly hoped he was dreaming of her. She prayed he would continue to dream of her or at the least remember her as a woman that loved him when he was young.

Her skin touched his as she found a small spot on the bed to rest next to him. He reflexively rolled away allowing her more space to sleep. She could tell he was not used to sleeping with anyone. He always slept alone, aside from Harry the cat guarding the foot of the bed ready to pounce on any would-be intruder. He was such a child. In his sleep his youthful appearance overwhelmed her. She felt guilty for bringing him into her mixed up life.

She could not help herself; it was his eyes that possessed her soul with each look. She memorized all of his expressions and burned them deep into her memory. She remembered the he had written her a letter after she left Tremane. He even tried to make her laugh in prose and poetry. She planned to keep it to remember him. She kept everything from him in a small box that would be hidden from the world.

It was the box of her dreams; a Pandora's Box, if you will, that would surely cause his world to crumble if she opened it. She would guard it and always remember the young man that loved her for her and nothing else. Kelly wanted to build a life with Josh and as sleep finally approached she allowed herself to whisper in the twilight of consciousness,

"I love you Josh, forgive me", she breathed closing her eyes listening as the deep steady breathing of the young man next to her sang her to sleep and covered her with the peaceful feeling only created by a mother's lullaby.

Chapter 7

Josh woke at nine in the morning. The sun was shining brightly though the split between the curtains striking him perfectly in the face. Josh hated the sun in the morning. It was too bright and hot for his taste. He always felt bad in the morning. He loved waking up in the evening when the sun was down and it was cool outside. The night always gave him energy and he often thought he may have been more vampire than human. He grinned at the thought of being Dracula as he stretched and looked about the room for any sign of Kelly.

Dracula had it great as far as Josh was concerned. He was wealthy, hung out late at night, had superpowers, and he got to bite pretty women on the neck and they loved him for it. Being Dracula had to be the ultimate evil. Josh let out a giggle at the thought, "*Blah, I vant to suck your blood!*" He sat up smiling as he relished his own joke.

He smelled coffee. Kelly must be in the kitchen. He was glad to have gotten some sleep. The twelve hour shift followed by a four hour drive was tiring and he was grateful for a comfy bed and Kelly's body next to him made it perfect. He was feeling wonderful; he woke up a bit more and remembered what he was thinking before he had fallen asleep. His mood quickly took a downturn. He dressed quickly and walked into the kitchen.

Kelly was sitting at the kitchen table sipping coffee from a yellow cup. She was looking out the window lost in her thoughts when Josh appeared in the doorway of the kitchen. She looked up at him and set her cup down. Her eyes gave him the message he dreaded.

It was time for him to go.

"Would you like some coffee?" She asked.

"Sure", he replied not wanting to start his nervous chatter. He planned to be as silent as possible and avoid speaking the unthinkable thoughts that he harbored about Kelly wanting him out of her life. Kelly's eyes held worry deep within them. She would not tell him abruptly that he should leave; she knew he could read her all too well and it was best that she not speak the words.

She poured the steaming black liquid into the cup and smiled softly at Josh who smiled in return. They were playing a game. He knew what she wanted and she refused to tell him it was true. The end result would be that this moment would be the last that they would ever share. Josh and Kelly sat in silence and sipped the coffee.

"Would you take this letter to Shirley for me?" Kelly asked handing Josh a letter in a plain white envelope, "It will save me a stamp. I have a few other things for her if you don't mind dropping them off."

She gave him a small bag of things. He sat them next to the letter on the table. He guessed this was the hint it was time for him to go. Josh hated the thought of Kelly experiencing any pain, so he decided to make it easier on her. He would act as though he was in a rush to get back to Tremane, thus eliminating the need for her to have to tell him to leave.

"Well, looks like I better be heading back home. I am on call at seven," he lied. He was off for three more days.

"Yeah, I figured you would need to be getting back, I bet you have family plans for Thanksgiving." She lied as well to continue the game.

"I will be working then, but I will go to my mom's after work. She always has a big meal and family over", he lied again. "I will get this to Shirley tonight for you", he promised.

"Okay, guess I will see you later. Send me a letter or call if you like. If I'm not home, I will call you back when I can get in. I have a lot of work to do before the holidays. It always gets crazy around here with family coming in", she lied again.

Kelly was worried that she may not even have a job and had no plans for family over the holiday; she thought it would be a good way to ease into falling out of his life. She hoped that he would get busy and forget about her. She imagined that it would not take long considering the attention span of such a young man.

Josh knew what she was indicating and he let her lie. She looked so pretty and innocent when she tried to lie to him. He couldn't help but smile, she seemed to care enough about him to avoid hurting his feelings.

Josh made the exit quick. It was just like a removing a band-aid from a wound, the quicker it is done the less it hurts. He picked up the letter and the bag and leaned forward to kiss Kelly. She pushed herself reflexively into his kiss and embraced him hard, fighting back tears. "Take care of yourself and be careful on that ambulance."

"Always, baby, always", he lied again.

Kelly walked him to the door embracing him quickly as he turned to look at her once more.

"Goodbye, Kelly I will call or write soon, I love you." He told the truth this time.

Kelly nodded and turned away, she had to in order to avoid the tears. He bounced from the step and opened the door to his truck. She turned back one last time and waved slightly with her hand near her mouth, as a little girl would wave goodbye to a best friend moving away. She looked so young and small like a little girl with a broken heart. Kelly would soon be alone as Josh waved back from the truck.

The sound of the whining engine of the Chevy pulling out of her driveway was the most painful sound she had ever experienced. It hurt her ears. She watched from the doorway until the truck was no longer in sight and sound of the engine was inaudible. Josh was gone.

Leaving Dalton City was easier for Josh than getting there had been. He did not care if he got lost. He had nowhere to be and he was in no hurry to get there. His mind was racing as he navigated through the city streets toward the interstate. All he wanted was to find a highway that lead south. South was home and he had enough of the northern portion of Illinois. The north meant pain and anguish. For once in his life, Josh just wanted to go home.

He was not looking forward to the long drive home. Josh hated a long drive which was odd considering he was driving an ambulance most of the time. He drove for a few moments seemingly lost in his own thoughts. He was surprised at how quickly he saw the sign to the Interstate.

Interstate 57 South was the route home. Three hours and change would lead him back to the life he had before he met Kelly. He continued to participate in denial as he lit his third Marlboro and inhaled deeply. The damn sun was striking him like a laser beam to the temple as he drove toward Effingham. He hated the sun more today than ever. He wished he could spend his life in the quiet of the darkness and avoid the fiery ball in the sky that always hurt his eyes and burned his skin.

Josh would blame everything, including a star millions of miles away, for the way he was feeling. He drove for two hours looking at the letter lying next to him on the seat. He wondered what it said. *"Why would she send it with him unless she wanted him to read it, right?"* He thought.

He could not take the suspense any longer he found the nearest rest stop and pull off the highway.

He quickly grabbed the letter and opened it, careful not to tear the edges. He remembered gently unwrapping Christmas presents in this way as a small child. Josh and his brother would always open the gifts carefully a few days before Christmas to see what was inside. It was easy since his mother and father left them alone during the day to work jobs for meager salaries and Josh was good at covering his tracks when performing the taboo of opening gifts before Christmas. He taught his brother Caleb the same trick.

"Be gentle with the edges, take your time and always listen for the beginning of a tear. If you hear a tear, then stop and reevaluate." Josh would say to his sibling as he demonstrated the proper way to open a wrapped gift. He was analytical even as a ten year-old.

He pulled the handwritten letter out the envelope and opened it carefully. It was written in blue ink. Kelly always printed in big letters that were easy to read. She rarely used cursive. He began to read with his heart pounding in his chest as though he was invading her privacy and about to get caught.

He was invading her privacy, but she would never know. Maybe she expected him to read it and it was a silent way for her to tell him the truth that was too painful to put into words. He rationalized that this must have been her plan and he was following through on what she really wanted him to do.

Josh was good at lying to himself to justify his actions. He had done this all of his life and it usually got him into trouble; occasionally it got him out of hot water as well. He was a sly one when he wanted to be.

He took a deep breath and looked at the words blinking a few times to adjust his eyes to counter the wicked glare of the sun that danced across the pages of the bright white paper. The rays of the fiery ball that penetrated the atmosphere were rhythmically interrupted by the passing trucks at the rest stop causing the brightness to vary greatly like a psychedelic pattern across the page. *Why was it so hard to focus on the glare of the page?* It seemed that the gods were trying to obscure his vision in some celestial way.

Josh was determined to read this letter. He put the letter in his lap and put the truck into reverse and turned the vehicle toward the rest top building using the nearest semi truck to block the evil rays of the burning sun. *The gods be damned* was Josh's thought as he tried again to see the words on the page. It read,

> *"Hi Shirley,*
>
> *Hope all is well with you and Bill. I am sending you this letter to get some things off my chest……..."* it began with a few words regarding Kelly's situation which Josh promptly ignored. He wanted to see if she mentioned anything about him. He continued to read until he found what he was looking for in the note. It read,

> *"That kid came up to see me this week. I really like him a lot, but he is so young and I have so much going on right now that I think it is best if I don't see him anymore. I just don't think it would work out. He would do anything I asked him to, but I really don't know him all that well and we met at a really bad time in my life. I have to get some shit straight up here and I don't think it would be good for him or me. I don't know why I am telling you this, but I had to tell someone and I sure as hell can't bear to tell him. It would break his little heart and I can't stand to do that. I hope he goes on with his life and remembers me sometimes, but I don't think he is ready or right for me now."*

At that moment Josh knew what a gunshot wound to the chest must have felt like. He let the letter drop to his lap and he slammed his head against the sliding back window of his truck. He felt this sick sensation in his stomach. The kind of burn you have before you vomit but you just cannot convince yourself to throw up. He wanted to walk out into the highway close his eyes and be splattered by the next vehicle passing by that was moving at seventy miles per hour with a fatigued driver at the wheel.

"Fuck!" he screamed in the truck pounding his fists against the steering wheel. "Goddamn it what did I do wrong!" He screamed aloud.

"Was I too fucking nice?" He questioned.

"Was I not good enough in bed?" He asked no one.

"Was my poetry stupid?" He growled.

"Why the fuck did she want me to drive up here if that was all she wanted? She could have done this over the phone!" He exclaimed aloud.

He verbalized all of these questions as if he would get an answer from the gods he had cursed only moments ago. The gods did not answer. He cried with all that he was; he sobbed alone in the truck all the while the sun was still trying diligently to penetrate the trailer to get to him and shed life giving light into his tortured dark soul. He sat there for an hour crying and heaving, not caring if he vomited on himself. He cared about nothing. Shock had set in.

He looked into the picnic area of the rest stop and saw a small child sitting in the grass pulling at the weeds. His eyes were blurry with tears making it difficult to see clearly. He blinked three times and his vision cleared. The child was a little boy with shorts and a tee shirt carelessly pulling at the grass as though he was hoping to find a hidden treasure beneath the sod.

He took a deep breath and sniffed while wiping the moisture from his nose. He hated to cry; it made your nose run and gave you headaches.

The child looked up as a young blonde woman approached. Apparently she was the mother. She bent over to pick up the boy. Josh noticed she was wearing a short skirt that accentuated her thin thighs and firm posterior. The skirt rose up enough to expose her just a bit too much as she struggled under the weight of the child. Her legs flexing as she lifted him to her chest would have been a pretty sight to any teenage boy. She spoke to the child and turned to walk away.

The boy looked at Josh as they passed. The woman paid Josh no mind. The boy smiled devilishly as though he had gotten away with something. Josh smirked back forcing a half crooked smile that caused the only line in his face to deepen. He thought for a moment after the two had passed by;

"Okay, she doesn't want you, you can still live with that, I guess", he whispered to himself.

"She would be better off without you anyway", he thought as he pitied himself just a bit. He felt he deserved a little self-pity.

"Now what are you going to do? You have a job and no responsibility. You can do or be whatever you want, so what is it?" He said aloud to himself, as if he was ready to make a life altering decision at a rest-stop somewhere south of Chicago.

He pondered for a moment and decided it was time to take a walk, have a smoke and maybe a soda. He walked into the rest-stop building and found a soda machine.

Josh put a dollar into the slot and pressed the selection. He opened the beverage took a sip and walked out into the blinding sun. He walked to the spot in the grassy area where the boy had been. He sat cross-legged in the same spot where the pulled up grass had left a bare spot. He began to pluck at the weeds as the boy had done before. He wished someone would come and carry him away too. It never happened. The rest stop was as empty as his heart.

The only noise to be heard was the distant sound of trucks on the interstate passing with a loud rumble that shook the ground. He sat and thought for quite some time. He finally came to a decision. He would do what he should have done a long time ago. Wake up and be what he wanted to be, a hero that was untouchable by everything and everyone.

"Look out for number one. To thine own self be true, etcetera, etcetera", he vowed.

He would never again put his heart on a plate for someone to carve up like a Thanksgiving turkey.

He blamed himself. He had a great time with Kelly and the sex was the kind of experience that stories are written about. A beautiful older woman that loved a young man and gave her body to him for pleasure then let him go in his own way to seek out adventure and live his life with her forever in etched in his memory.

He loved to lie to himself and he was very good at the act. He assumed he blew his chances by becoming attached. He began to think he had been naive all along. She was in no mood for a long term thing and he did not even know what a long term "thing" was. It was better this way. She would always have her little evil secret and he had the pleasure of knowing that he was once loved by a beautiful woman. It was perfect this way.

He lied some more; he was on a roll as he pulled more and more weeds from the earth.

All he had to do now was become the best paramedic on the planet, have as much sex as humanly possible and be the heartbreaker that women pined over when he left them out of boredom. It would be a great life! After he turned twenty one he would drink the whiskey that he could not afford in high school and take on the world. He would live the life of a rockstar to the best of his ability.

"Fuck it!" He shouted for no one to hear. He stood up dramatically as though he was about to render a soliloquy to an invisible audience. Ritualistically, in defiance of the sun, clutching a handful of grass he softly spoke,

"I love you Kelly, but you are right. I will always remember you and I will always remember your smell and the taste of your skin, but I have to go and I will always remember you."

Josh had a flare for the dramatic, but he meant every word he said and before leaving the rest stop that day, he already had a plan. It was simple. Have sex with as many women as possible, drink until he could not take it anymore and hurt every woman that ever thought of loving him and lie, oh God, would he lie. It would be easy. He had a skill that would hit most women right in the chest. His weapons—Words.

He would write poetry to make weak-hearted women cry and fall in love with him. He would use every sexual skill he learned to make women want him and when he lost interest, he would cheat and move on to the next victim while leaving a trail of broken hearts in his wake. He loved to flatter himself with his imagined talents. He believed himself.

To seal the ritual he tossed the grass into the wind as though he was a priest christening the vows. The wind carried the grass toward the parking lot in a less than dramatic fashion, which made the poorly thought out oath that much more of a joke. He walked toward his truck with disciplined steps opened the door, refolded the letter, sealed it and tossed it into the bag. He depressed the clutch forcefully, turned the key and revved the engine. Soon he was speeding down the highway listening to his cassettes of *AC/DC* and *Aerosmith*. He planned to get drunk and maybe get laid tonight if at all possible and it did not matter who it was with or where he would end up.

The sun was behind the clouds now and he was driving south at eighty miles per hour, he held his arm out the window and extended his middle finger at the sun screaming,

"Fuck you buddy, I won't be seeing you unless I have to consider me Dracula, baby", as the sounds of *AC/DC's Highway to Hell* blasted out of the stereo.

He was not sure what he meant by the insane statement. It started with the name. Everyone at the ambulance service had a nickname and he decided on his own. He would put in for nights as soon as he got back and he would do what Dracula did. Manipulate everyone for his own gain. It may be fun and he did not care what happened.

He decided he would go to Don's tonight and see what trouble he could get into. Don always had booze and he would see if the girls were up for some drunkenness. The sad thing about being an eighteen year-old is that the mind moves at warp speed, but conscious thought and planning is somewhat retarded by the influx of hormones and the lack of maturity. Josh was no different. He was hurt and he decided the best thing to do was take it out on himself and whoever else happened to cross his path that particular night.

The drive to Tremane passed by quickly, apparently the police were on an extended coffee break allowing the young teen to drive with wreckless abandon through the highways high speeds.

The sun was starting to set as he exited the interstate into the town of Tremane. He made an immediate right and continued for twelve more miles into Raines. He should have probably called Kelly to let her know that he made it home safely. He rationalized that it did not matter anymore since she had let him go and probably did not care anyway. He had plans and it was going to be a wild night if he had anything to do with it.

He arrived at Don's house just in time. Three girls from Tremane had just pulled into the driveway. Angela, Julie and Sandy were getting out of blue Mercury Capri as Josh came to a stop with a lurch, resulting from popping the clutch, letting the truck die and roll perfectly next to their car effectively blocking the driveway.

"Joshie Baby, what is up you lil' bastard!" Angela screamed as she ran toward him her six foot tall frame sprinting through the grass. She was very tall and he loved to watch her run.

Angela gave him a hug as he slid from the truck seat trying to look cool. Angela was a strawberry blonde that had long slender legs and a pretty face, but not many brains to complete the package. Her crew consisted of Sandy, a dark skinned beauty with a Latino appearance and frizzy hair. She was short and looked minute next to Angela. Julie rounded out the trio. She was a blond bombshell of medium height with the look of a young porn star with thick pink lips and a very toothy grin that shined when she smiled. She had a tropical tan year-round from an apparent lifetime membership to the tanning salon.

They were always together and ready for a party. Josh's friends had nicknamed the trio; Legs, Lips and Hair, respective to their appearance. They were not afraid to drink or get naked. This redeeming quality made them a sure-fire invite to any party that the Raines boys had. Josh always wondered why they never partied in their home town. Tremane had football players and in Raines, they were just country boys.

He assumed they left town often to add to their mystic and give them something to hold over the Tremane boys' heads during the school lunch conversations. He imagined they talked about how they hated the local guys and had to go to Raines to have a good time.

He preferred mature women that knew what they were doing and had no pretences or played head games. Women in their late twenties or early thirties were more comfortable in their own skin and had no time for games. Josh held onto Angela as she wiggled next to him. He thought of Kelly. She would never act like this. He faked interest in seeing Angela and the girls. He sauntered up to Don, who had appeared on the porch with three cases of beer and a few bottles of bourbon.

"How much do I owe ya, for a case and a bottle?" He asked Don while lighting a Marlboro.

"Ten bucks man, consider the rest me payin ya back for the poetry you wrote for Melissa. She was all over it and in an hour I was all over her. Remember last week?"

Josh slapped Don's extended hand and nodded. He gave Don a ten and grabbed a case and a bottle the dark liquor. He set the beer in the back of his truck and opened the bottle. The first drink was always the roughest; it tasted like lighter fluid and burned his throat. He had learned to inhale through his nose to decrease the burn, it was a needed technique used by true bourbon drinkers.

Josh swallowed three times with a gulping noise.

"Damn boy! Rough week out there savin' dirtbags?" Don exclaimed as he noticed the intensity of Josh's drinking.

"Na, just don't wanna think, just wanna be numb man, just wanna be numb." Josh replied looking away toward the north.

"Want me to make you feel better, poor baby." Angela joked as she held her fist laterally to her face and pushed her cheek out with her tongue rapidly to indicate oral sex.

"Na babe, I could not handle your naked ass tonight, but I will get drunk with ya, and hold Don down while you molest his skinny ass", he retorted.

"Damn skippy!" Don giggled.

"Not if I get him. I gonna do him tonight", an already drunk Sandy said from the car window she was hanging out of at the moment; her frizzy hair covering her face.

"Looks like we are popular, shall we head to the cabin?" Don asked.

"I'm good with it", Josh said dryly. "Are the rest of the crew there already?" He asked.

"Yep, Durbin, Ass, Mo-Mo and Payne are there with a few chicks from Pana. I am bringing the last load and going to pick up Stokes" he said.

"You go on, I will go get Stokes", Josh said.

He gave Angela a peck on the cheek and opened the door to the truck. After shifting a few gears, he was on his way to pick up his friend. A few years earlier Josh had taken the rap for Stokes and was arrested for battery after a misunderstanding in a parking lot that led to a fight and one unconscious teenager. Stokes always appreciated it. Josh was arrested and Stokes always felt guilty. Stokes had a record and Josh was clean, so it made sense for him to take the rap. At least they thought it did. It was a few years ago when Josh was barely seventeen. They had remained friends even after Josh started working at the hospital. It bothered Josh that he was starting to lose touch with his high school friends and he blamed it on the job, or maybe maturity, he did not know which.

Stokes was ready when he arrived at the small house on the northwest side of town. Within minutes they were enroute to the cabin owned by a young fellow named Durbin.

It was an old hunting cabin turned teenage party palace. The party was in full swing by the time they arrived. Josh pulled the truck into the grass and shut off the engine. Stokes exited and raised a bottle into the air and hooted like a rockstar arriving at a backstage party. Sandy already had her top off and was dancing in front of Don. Josh assumed it was a lap dance but it looked more like a controlled seizure. She did have a nice body, but as with her associates—no brains. He supposed that did not matter, it was just a sex thing anyway— just sex.

Stokes handed Josh a bottle which he gladly accepted and began to drink. He finished it in a few swallows and opened a beer. He sat near Ass, whose real name was Mike, and tapped knuckles with him in greeting. The girls were getting drunk and the Pana girls were starting to join in the fun. Sex was going to happen for someone tonight somehow. It looked like the beginning of a pagan orgy around the fire as the young nimble bodies of the girls danced around the flames, partially dressed and gyrating to the *Prince* song, "*Pussy Control*" that blared from the speakers Durbin's Ford F-250 pickup.

Josh watched for a while, but oddly enough, the drinks were much more interesting. He wanted to see how much he could ingest without passing out. Alcohol asked for nothing and made him numb which was exactly what he needed tonight. He did not think of Kelly, as he watched the girls run and giggle and loose bits of clothes here and there.

He would be embarrassed of his friends if Kelly was around. He knew the girls had to be plastered since the autumn air was not affecting their desire to get naked. He assumed the fire was hot enough and the booze made them feel warm enough to strip.

He continued to drink heavily throughout the night. He did not mention Kelly to any of his friends as the night wore on. Mike noticed that Josh was quiet and asked,

"What's wrong bro, plenty of pussy out there running around, you don't seem like yourself, you sick?" He asked with as much concern as he dared show.

"Na, just in a mood to get fucked up." Josh answered.

"Bad calls huh? I bet that sucks, all the blood and stuff, well bud we can definitely get ya fucked up, we are trained professionals. See, look at Durbin over there he is the president of Club Alcoholica", Mike said using the *Metallica* reference and pointing at the truck where Durbin was standing in his head, with a cowboy hat still in place, drinking beer from a bong.

"That's why I am here stud, that's why I am here", Josh replied patting Mike on the shoulder. "Ass, shall we toast to all the pussy that got away and all of the hearts we have yet to break?" Josh said as he raised the *Old Milwaukee* can to the sky.

"True that brother, true that!" Mike said in agreement lifting his *Hardee's Moose* cup filled with Whiskey and Coke to the sky.

"To Pussy!" they both shouted earning a hoots and applause from the audience gathered around Durbin's truck watching the beer bonging sideshow.

Josh and Mike stayed by the fire drinking in silence while the party went on around them. Mike had just lost a girlfriend and was drowning his sorrows and Josh had just lost Kelly. They never spoke about their woman troubles to each other, but they understood the pain they were feeling. The boys did all they knew how to do, drink and try to forget.

Josh finished his beers throughout the night vomited twice and passed out by the fire. Lips and Legs crawled up next to him for warmth and passed out as well. Don tossed a sleeping bag over them as he led the naked Sandy off to the truck for sex. Mike was face down in the dirt with a bottle of Jack still clutched in his hand.

The life of a wannabe rockstar began like this and many days and nights would end in similar fashion for Josh. He was no longer "Little Shit" for all practical purposes he felt more like Dracula, a cold heartless thing that merely existed, not ever really living.

A few hours away in Dalton, Kelly stared out the front door of her home with the same yellow cup in her hand. She was hoping soon she would hear the whine of the engine from a broken down Chevy truck pulling into her drive. The sound never came. She knew he was gone and she would never see him again.

"Be safe little man— be safe and say goodbye to Harry for me", she whispered to herself as she closed the door on the city and her life with Josh. It was over and she would never forget how much he made her laugh and how much she truly wanted to love him.

Chapter 8

Josh opened his eyes with a grimace. He could smell perfume and stale beer. He heard the distant sound of Legs vomiting in the bushes behind Don's Chevy Silverado. As his eyes began to focus he located the source of the perfume smell. Lips was asleep with her head on his legs. Her warm body felt good next to him in the cool air of the early morning.

She was still wearing her jeans, but her shirt had long since disappeared. He could see her black brassiere was still in place cradling her breasts a bit too tightly for comfort. He always thought Lips could have been a porn star. She had the look for it. She was blonde, tanned and had pouty lips and not a hair on her body except on her head. Lips was eager to remove her clothes and she loved to dance and wiggle her endowments to frustrate the boys. From what he knew about her, she loved sex and would do things that most girls her age would never contemplate. He was surprised she slept next to him that night. He thought for a moment they may have had sex; then he realized he still had his pants on and her jeans were still buttoned.

He slowly cupped Lips' head in his hand and slid his thin thigh from beneath her hoping not to wake her. Josh noticed how pretty she was in the sunlight as he lay her head down on the sleeping bag and covered her again. He realized that no one would ever take her serious and she would always be the party girl that you dropped off at the end of the night.

"Someone should love you Lips" he uttered under his breath as he walked toward the truck.

Legs continued to vomit violently in the bushes. Josh walked over to her. His head was throbbing with the pain of a thousand cannons firing into his skull while the infernal sun pierced his eyes like lasers from God. He hated the sun more today than ever.

"You okay Legs?" He whispered in a soft voice his throat dry from the alcohol.

"Yea, just lemme get this out." She gasped. "Gonna need a lil hair of the dog baby"

Legs dry heaved twice more then stood upright brushing her hair from her face.

"Do you know where my panties are? I'm cold", she asked holding her shoulders and bouncing on her toes a little.

Josh suddenly realized she was naked from the waist down. He must be hung over to miss that. She had a small Z shaped birthmark on the left side of her pubic area he thought it looked like a lightning bolt which was appropriate for her; Legs was as fast moving as a lightning bolt with everything; sex, booze, and cars. She was just plain fast.

He looked at the ground and immediately saw a red thong covered in mud. He picked it up and held it in the air.

"Don't think these are gonna warm you up much but your jeans are on the back of the truck. I saw them there a while ago", he said with genuine concern in his voice.

She pointed at the truck and Josh nodded. She sprinted to the vehicle and began donning her jeans in hopes that it would blunt the chilly morning breeze. Josh followed her with her mud covered panties still in his hand.

"You still want these? They will wash." He said dryly.

"Yea, they cost me 20 bucks" she said taking them from his hand and rolling them into a ball. "Hey did we fuck last night? I thought it may have been you since we were playin' grab ass and all", she blurted.

"No, I was in the sleepin' bag with Lips. Too damn drunk I guess. I think it was you and Mike, he replied.

"Oh. Okay that's fine. I'm on the pill and Mike doesn't have anything. Where is Ass anyway?" She said nonchalantly as she embraced herself to protect herself from the cold.

Josh pointed toward Mike. "Over there he isn't wearing any pants either. He's still passed out."

"Okay" she said as she lit a cigarette. "You didn't bang Lips huh? She said she would fuck if you wanted" she said inhaling on the Salem light.

"Guess I would have, but I dunno was just in the mood to drink." He said not really understanding his own statement.

Angela inhaled on the cigarette again and said,

"Hey, tell Ass when he wakes up if he calls me this week and we go out, he can have me again if he wants. I am getting out of here I gotta get my mom's car back. See ya", she said flipping the spent cigarette onto the ground. Josh waved half-heartedly as Legs slowly pulled onto the highway in her maroon Honda.

The next time he would see her she would be covered in blood. Josh had to identify her a year later after a car crash. Her face was unrecognizable as he pulled her limp body from the smoking wreckage. In the morgue, he recognized her birthmark and identified her. Legs was one of the many friends Josh had retrieved from crashed cars as a result of accidents he witnessed as a paramedic. He didn't eat for a week after seeing her mangled body. His friends were dying and he was responsible for trying to save them. He hated the personal part of his job.

Josh started to walk to his truck when Lips woke up.

"Hey cowboy!" she exclaimed. She sat up and her breasts nearly fell out of the brassiere. "You leavin?" I'm still cold!"

"Yea, I gotta be on call in a few hours. Can give you a ride back to Tremane if you want, Legs already left." Josh replied.

" 'kay", she said bouncing up from the sleeping bag. Lips never seemed to have a hang over. She wiggled into her tee shirt and skipped over to Josh as he opened the passenger side door for her.

"Such a gentleman" she said sweetly cocking her head to one side, the stereotypical blonde movement. "I am really gonna have to do you someday, your cute!" She smiled and wrinkled her nose.

"Maybe later babe, I feel like shit", he said truthfully as he slammed the door.

Josh drove and Lips chatted incessantly during the twelve mile trip to Tremane. He politely acknowledged her conversation as if he was really interested in her job at the video store. He pulled into the drive on Burtschi Street and brought the S-10 to a slow halt.

Lips slid next to him and gave his leg a hard squeeze and kissed him softly on the neck, then whispered, "Thanks baby, if you want, call." She waved and bounced in a little girl short of way toward the door. Josh waved back and backed out of the drive. He liked Lips. He knew she was a little off and for some reason he felt sorry for her. She was so pretty, but she did not have a brain in her head and someone was gong to hurt her really bad. He just knew it.

She was safe at home and he had a splitting headache. All he wanted now was to get some shut eye. He would worry about Lips later. The trip back to Elm Street seemed to take forever. He opened the door to the small house and was immediately met by Harry. His feline questioning eyes seemed to pierce Josh's heart. Thoughts of Kelly came flooding back.

"Fuck", he growled as he stomped down the steps like a child having a tantrum. An act he immediately regretted as the pain in his head increased ten-fold. He took of his clothes. The cool basement air felt good to him in contrast to the fiery blast of the furnace that he experienced in the kitchen. Tanner and Susy kept the upstairs hot most of the time. He attributed it to hormone rushes. He liked the cool air. He must have really been a vampire considering his preferences for cool dark places.

He sat on the hide-a-bed breathing deeply. Harry joined him in his usual spot. Josh lay back and groaned covering his aching head with his forearm. He inhaled again hoping to catch a hint of Kelly's scent, but all he discovered was the feint hint of moisture from the basement walls. She was gone and he knew it. He drifted off to sleep with Harry standing guard.

The alarm sounded at six fifteen. Josh slowly opened his eyes. His headache was gone but his eyes felt like they were coated in sandpaper. He blinked furiously to gain focus. It was dark already, the signal of winter approaching. Josh didn't mind it meant less sunlight to hurt his eyes.

He sat up and stretched. Covering his face with his hands he began to talk to Harry, who was stretching as well.

"She is not coming back", he said nearly in tears. He hated that she was the last thing he thought of when he went to sleep and the first thing he thought of when he woke up. He did not know why she had affected him so much. He could have stayed with Lips or even Legs. They were young and willing but it didn't matter they weren't Kelly.

He slowly ambled up the stairs with uniform in hand. Harry bouncing up the steps behind him as any good bodyguard would. Josh showered and dressed for work. He didn't want to go but he didn't have anything else in his life and it was a distraction. Harry waited for his goodbye pat on the head; Josh obliged and added a good natured scratch to the ears as a bonus for his feline friend. He filled the food dish and left for the hospital.

Johnny met him at door.

"Hey Little Shit, I gotta split, but I just wanted to let you know I wrote the letter of recommendation for the Intermediate class in Effingham. You instructor will be getting a copy in the mail. Good luck Little Shit and don't let me down. You are the youngest lil' bastard I have recommended, so don't fuck it up. By the way sign up for all the shifts you want, Jeff got into nursing school. Next month we will put you on full-time with Bannett" he said while walking away with his hand in the air.

"Thanks." Josh mumbled too softly for Johnny to hear.

The night was uneventful and the evil sun arose as predicted. Josh kept to himself most of the night while Claude read EMS magazines, his lips moving as he read. He left work without speaking to anyone. He slammed the door of his truck and stared at the ramp, the boiler, the back door and the handrail at the rear entrance of the hospital. Everything reminded him of Kelly, even his own truck.

One more reminder appeared as he looked into the seat. The letter to Shirley was still in the seat. It was a bit crumpled from where Lips had sat on it the morning before, but it was still intact. For some self-destructive reason he decided to read it again to make sure he had read it correctly the first time. Maybe there was hope. The words were the same and so was the pain. He re-sealed the envelope and began the drive to Shirley's house.

Shirley came to the door with a surprised look on her face. Josh handed her the letter. "It's from Kelly" he said quietly trying to keep from vomiting. He did not wait for a response. He turned and walked quickly to his truck.

The next eight months were busy for the little EMT. He finished Intermediate school and passed his exam for licensure with a ninety-two percent. The three trips each week to Effingham, plus four twelve hour shifts per week in Tremane had left him little time for sleep, much less anything else. It kept him busy and for a while he had not thought of Kelly. The ramp was just a ramp and the back door was only the way to the time-clock.

He lied to himself about this every day. He had also picked up an unhealthy habit. He ate very little. He had lost ten pound that didn't have to lose in the first place. He was barely strong enough to lift the cot. It was fortunate his new partner was over three hundred pounds and strong. He had lost his ability to sleep for more than two or three hours at a time. He was truly beginning to look like the walking dead. Food had lost all of its taste when he came back from Kelly's. As the months passed, his body adjusted and food nearly made him sick.

Susy even asked him once if he had an AIDS test yet. She was always curt with her opinions. He had several tests for HIV, due to cuts he sustained from car accidents or accidental needle sticks from careless nurses that did not pick up after themselves. He was somewhat healthy, just not interested in food or sleep. He read and worked—that was all.

Susy took him out to celebrate his EMT –Intermediate licensure. He was now nineteen. He had celebrated his birthday in January alone. He did not answer the telephone when his mother called four times. He did not feel like talking. He did not feel like doing anything but working. Josh had even earned his new found nickname and persona of Dracula. He was becoming an expert in starting difficult IV's and drawing blood from patients with invisible veins. One of the nurses called him, "Little Dracula" because he could get blood from anyone. He liked it. Even Johnny stopped calling him "Little Shit".

The winter had come and gone as well as the spring and the pain from the loss of Kelly had started to fade. It had been replaced by a sense of numbness that he became accustomed to in his soul. He was quiet and sometimes cold. His coworkers considered his attitude maturity; he considered it apathy but either way it benefitted him at the hospital.

As life became routine and Josh began to excel at his new found skills in advanced emergency life support he expected nothing to change. As usual he was wrong. July was hotter than normal in nineteen—ninety—four and it was about to get hotter.

Chapter 9

It was eight o'clock in the evening on July twenty—ninth, nineteen—ninety— four. Josh was working with Claude. The ER had been empty since six and no ambulance calls came in. The coffee pot was burning causing an acidic stench throughout the ER. Josh decided to make a fresh pot. Mary would be in soon. Mary was an old ex-Army nurse and Josh's first true mentor. She had a special bond with the young man and they worked well together. His knowledge of new cardiac protocols made her feel secure and her years of experience helped her teach him how to be an excellent medic and think on his feet, plus they both loved coffee and cigarettes.

Mary's experience in trauma from WWII helped her settle into emergency medicine and Josh loved to hear her stories. He had a fondness for her that probably stemmed from his relationship with his grandfather. Josh always respected the veterans that served in the war to end all wars.

Georgia was the evening nurse that night. She was covering for Tonya, who was in Missouri rescuing greyhounds; she had since expanded her dog rescuing efforts from bloodhounds to greyhounds as of late.

Georgia was a blonde nurse that may have been a bombshell in her younger years, but time and several children had caused her to expand quite a bit in the derriere. She was an operating room nurse that occasionally covered ER. She hated it. It was not controlled and she felt that mass casualty would befall her on the evening shift. All bad things happen at night, or so she believed. She clung to the medics like a cocklebur on a trouser leg. The medics were her saviors from the grim reaper looking to ruin her career. To say the least, Georgia was a bit anxietal about working ER.

Josh poured the water into the pot as the ER buzzer sounded. Georgia bolted up from the table with a start, dropping her Cosmo magazine on the floor. Josh grinned at her actions.

"I got it", she said as she whisked around the corner. Josh continued to make the coffee while Claude read to himself with his lips moving rapidly.

"JOOOOSHHHH! Get in here now! We don't deliver babies here!" Georgia screamed with shear panic in her voice. Josh ran out of the ER staff room with Claude two steps behind. As he ran three steps and turned toward the ER door to the frightened Georgia, his heart stopped and his face dropped with the sight he beheld.

He was staring eye to eye with a very pregnant Kelly O'Hara, who was clutching her abdomen and obviously in excruciating pain. Through the pain of the impending delivery her eyes sent one message to him,

"FUCK! It had to be you!"

Josh could not speak. He stood in complete and utter shock. He wanted to scream, cry, vomit and shit himself all at the same time.

"Dammit! Let's get her into room two. Claude, get the goddamn doctor's ass up!" Georgia screamed.

Claude pivoted on his heel and ran to the phone his heavy boots thudding down the hallway. Josh and Georgia helped Kelly toward room number two. Kelly said nothing.

"Josh get me a gown, we have to get her pants off!" Georgia barked.

Josh opened the door to the linen cabinet with shaking hands. He fumbled with the damn strings. Georgia was busy stripping Kelly.

He looked up into Kelly's swollen, barely recognizable face and immediately thought;

"*Oh fuck, is this my child, oh fuck, count the months is this close? Oh shit, it is close enough! Am I about to deliver my own kid! Fuck!*" He quietly freaked out in his own mind and felt the pain in his stomach come back with a vengeance.

"*I need to talk to her alone, but I'm betting this is a bad time*", he thought, amazed at his own idiocy.

"Claude!" Georgia bellowed as she ran out of the room to find the doctor, "Get the ambulance, we have to get her to Central. Josh, start an IV now!"

Kelly was flat on her back panting heavily and gritting her teeth through the pain. Josh fumbled frantically to set up the IV lock and gather a needle. Kelly said nothing.

As he crouched to his knees next to her and applied the tourniquet with unsteady hands he looked up into her cinnamon eyes that were filling with tears.

He wanted to ask if this child was his but he could not bear to speak the words. His famous Kelly was hurting and he wanted to take the pain away more than satisfy his own selfish need for an answer.

"Kelly, how are you doing right now? Talk to me." He said with genuine concern masked within a shaky voice.

"How the fuck do you think I'm doing? It hurts goddamn!" She had tears streaming down her face as she screamed at him. Josh became focused, very fast. He looked at the vein in her left hand. He knew he would not miss; he could not miss, for all that is true about love, to whomever he called God, he prayed, *Do not let me miss!*

He punctured her brown skin with the eighteen gauge IV catheter and breathed a sigh of relief as he saw the dark red blood fill the flash chamber. He was in. Josh threaded the catheter through the vein and flushed it with saline. As he applied the tape to secure the line and he stayed on his knees holding her hand long after the procedure was finished. He rubbed her skin gently with his thumb. His heart was on fire.

Kelly looked down at him between contractions as he whispered, "Kelly is this baby…"

She interrupted, "No! Don't worry about it! Just get me out of here!"

Their conversation was interrupted when the doctor arrived. The physician promptly ran Josh out of the room. Kelly's water had broken and she was dilated to a six. They still had time, but not much.

Josh remained in the hall and passed equipment through the curtain to Georgi as Claude prepared the cot.

"Looks like I need to take this one. We may be delivering a little one enroute, buddy", Claude said in his usual monotone voice. Josh felt like someone had just shot him at point blank range. He fought to hold back the vomit. He was trying his best to look like he was in control. He was losing his mind on the inside, but the ER crew could never know of his relationship to her or he would not be allowed to drive. It would be considered inappropriate and dangerous. He had to make his face tell lies. He did well.

Within moments Josh and Claude entered the room to transfer Kelly. Claude was moping around in his usual methodical manner effectively pissing off the entire ER staff, not to mention Kelly. She kept looking at Josh, her eyes begging him to take the pain away and most importantly keep it together and stay quiet. He received the message and said nothing.

The two EMT's, loaded Kelly into the back of the oldest and fastest gas engine ambulance that Tremane had in the fleet. Claude clambered into back with Kelly who was loaded backwards on the cot with her head at the foot end and her feet toward the jumpseat in the event that she gave birth on the way.

"Goddamn, if Claude delivers this kid I am going to lose it, he should not be looking at her!" Josh whispered through clenched teeth as he slammed the back doors, not customarily asking Claude if he was ready. Josh was going to drive like he had never driven before and to hell with what Claude had to say.

He leaped into the driver's seat and pulled the gearshift into drive. *Fast and soft, fast and soft* were the only two words on his mind. He had to get her to Central, some thirty four miles away, before the baby came and do it without bouncing her all over the cot. He knew he could do it. He exited the hospital parking lot quickly and carefully as he heard Claude began his robotic assessment,

"Ma'am are ya havin any trouble breathin?" He asked in a dry voice no doubt touching his mandibles to make sure they were working. He always did this when he was nervous. Josh did not hear Kelly's response. He could only hear the engine groan as he reached speeds of over one hundred miles per hour. He was glad that traffic was light on the highway.

Josh's mind raced. He counted months. He remembered her laugh, Harry the cat, the jokes, making love, the letter and the night in the hospital room. It all came flooding back and his fear nearly caused him to run off the road.

"God, don't kill her! If you die it doesn't matter and fuck Claude; but this baby and Kelly have to make it! Dammit Claude knock her out with drugs, take the pain away!" He said in a violent whisper, as he squeezed the steering wheel with all of his strength causing his knuckles to whiten under the pressure.

He knew you cannot sedate a woman in labor it could kill the baby, but Josh's mind was not clear, he was afraid for Kelly and he blamed himself. This had to be his baby.

Why would she not tell him? Why did she send him away?

These were questions that only Kelly could answer and she was not able or chose not to share the answers. He had to keep driving and drive hard. Eighteen minutes into the trip, Josh had made it twenty four miles— ten to go. Josh was successfully maintaining a speed of one hundred miles per hour for most of the trip. The truck would do more but he could not risk it with Kelly. One blow out and they were all dead, especially the baby.

Josh was highly alert to everything; deer, cars, holes in the road. His vision and hearing were acute and he felt superhuman. He was experiencing adrenaline overload. His heart was pounding, his mouth was dry, his stomach was dead to the nausea, he was in fight or flight mode. Josh had to fly for Kelly and fight off every human emotion that was flooding into his brain.

Josh noticed the ambulance began to shift a signal that he had learned over the last year that meant things were going wrong. When the ambulance rocks ever so slightly that means the medic is up and moving quickly. That means something is wrong or about to become life threatening with the patient. Josh's heart sank as he pushed the accelerator to the floor. The speedometer was no longer registering anything; the needle had passed the 120 mark.

"Josh looked in the rearview mirror to see Claude coming toward him quickly. Claude fell into the front of the ambulance and said, "Uhh… Josh you better get us there, if she shits we are fucked!" I kept askin' her if she was havin' any trouble breathin' and… uhhh… she stopped answerin' me."

Josh stood on up on the accelerator as if that was going to help push the truck to Central hospital a second faster. Claude went back to Kelly as Josh sped though traffic, blaring sirens and honking the air horn. He knew the baby is coming and nothing is going to stop it in the back of an ambulance; he would be damned if Claude was going to deliver what may be his child. *Fuck that!*

Twenty four minutes after leaving Tremane Josh slammed the shifter of Four Adam Seventeen into park at the ER doors of Central hospital. As he opened the back doors, he could hear Kelly crying. He would have rather been eaten alive by fire ants than to hear her cry.

He was a helpless, worthless piece of teenage crap in his mind. If he was smarter, he could have done something with drugs to alleviate the pain and make the sure the baby was safe at the same time. He was not, he was just a stupid teenager or so he thought. He berated himself all the way to the OB unit as he pulled the cot, Kelly and Claude with all the strength he could muster. Claude simply hung on to the cot as Josh pulled all of them and the hundred pound stretcher down the hall at a dead run. He was pulling like a draft horse and Claude could barely keep up the pace.

When they arrived at the unit the nurses were waiting. Josh needed to talk to Kelly but he had to get Claude out of the way. He went into the hall, while Claude was droning on about her breathing and vitals to the nurse, and took the regulator off the oxygen tank then removed the seal, inserted it into his mouth and bit down hard until the plastic gave way. Josh reinstalled the regulator and turned it to the ON position. The expected hiss of leaking oxygen was music to his ears. This should keep Claude busy for twenty minutes while he tried to talk to Kelly.

His plan was to stay in the room and send Claude to fix the oxygen tank and as the nurses ran to and fro, he would talk to her privately. His plan worked.

The last nurse had left the room for a moment asking the lingering EMT to stay with the patient while she retrieved the delivery cart and called the doctor. He could hear Claude clanging with the oxygen tank. He was safe and could speak quietly to the suffering Kelly.

He approached the bedside taking her hand in his; she gripped his fingers hard. Her hand was hot and covered in sweat from the stress of labor. She looked pale despite the tan and her brown eyes were full of anguish and tears. He felt tears coming to his eyes as he clenched his jaw and swallowed hard.

"Kelly, am I the father?" He asked sheepishly with a boyish whimper in his voice.

She paused her panting which took all the strength she had in her body, to reply,

"No Josh, it is someone else. It is not you, okay? How many times do I have to tell you?"

"Is he coming then?" Josh asked as if he really believed her, which he didn't.

"No. Look you would not understand, just go, okay? All you have to do is go, thank you for getting me here so fast but you can't do anything else. I am fine. I don't need you…." she paused to pant,

"Oh god it hurts", she whimpered.

Josh squeezed her hand in sympathy. He wanted to kiss her and hold her. He wanted to remove her pain. He could only watch as she gathered herself to speak again.

"Just go Josh, okay, it will be better. I am okay now. I don't need you here. It will be fine, Just go." She became quiet again to suffer in silence.

"I will call tomorrow", he said with his heart breaking and tears entering his eyes.

"Okay?" She said forcing his hand away from hers. She turned her head and with gritted teeth motioned for him to leave. Josh wanted to stay and refused to move until the nurse arrived.

"Thank you, you can go. It is going to happen very fast. She is dilated to an eight. You guys did a great job. Call in the morning if you like and we will let you know how it went." The nurse said as she prepared a syringe of medication. Josh slowly turned and walked away from Kelly for the second time in his life.

He said nothing on the ride home. Claude snored in the passenger seat. Josh hated his life, he hated who he was and he hated everyone, except Kelly. He was boy until that night. He was now a bitter angry young man and somebody was going to pay for it.

By the time they arrived at the ER door Mary was outside smoking. Josh joined her.

"The mom and baby are doing fine—can't say the same for Georgi. She is still doing paperwork and shaking like a cat shittin' tacks", Mary said in a raspy voice created from years of smoking Virginia Slims.

Josh waited until six am to make the call. The nurses transferred his call to Kelly's room. She answered. Her northern accent was the sweetest sound he had ever heard.

"Hi." She said.

"Hi Kelly, are you okay?" Josh asked.

"Yes, much better. Thank you for everything, you are always there for me" she said with warmth in her voice.

"And the baby?" he inquired

"She is a beautiful baby girl. She looks like me her name is Meaghan and she is perfect—just perfect." She boasted as only a mother can.

"And the father?" he asked hoping she would say it was him.

"Look, I don't need him, okay? I need you to understand, just let it go. Okay?"

"Um, okay are you sure she is n…." he tried to say.

"Yes, I am sure okay? She is not yours. I wish she was but things change. I am sorry but go live your life. Do what you need to do, be the hero you want to be. I will take good care of my girl." She said with what sounded like controlled breathing as if fighting back tears.

"Can I do anything? If you need anything I can't…" he tried to finish.

"No, just go, I will call you some time. I gotta go. The nurse is in here", she lied.

The click of the phone sounded like another gunshot. Josh slowly hung up the receiver and put his head on the desk and exhaled hard. Johnny came in within moments.

"Hey Little Dracula, heard you did a good job! What's the next adventure in your world? You damn near earned a stork pin!" He said proudly.

"Drink ….Johnny, just drink and work. Nothing else matters. Get me into medic class in January or I quit. And by the way tell Jaida if that little blonde wants to play, I will but I don't want any teenage bullshit out of her alright?

"Whoa buddy, somebody has an agenda. Are you all right? " He asked somewhat shocked at the new attitude of his prodigy.

"Never been better, it's like you said; run hard, fight hard and fuck harder right!" he snarled.

"That's my boy! I will tell her and I will page you when I do. Don't scare her too bad, you little blood suckin' vampire!" He laughed as Josh stormed out of the ER waving like Johnny usually did.

Claude looked up from his newspaper at Johnny and said, "You shouldn't encourage him, something is wrong with him. I think that call messed him up a bit".

"Na, Little Shit will be alright, but god help whoever he decides to take his anger out on, he is a volatile little bastard. That's why I like him!" Johnny joked.

Josh drove to Barb's Liquor and walked in with intent in his steps. He was still in uniform and brazenly grabbed a bottle of Jim Beam and six pack of Bud Light. He slammed a fifty down on the counter. The cashier never even asked for an ID. She simply gave him his change and bagged the whiskey. He was drinking before he shifted into second gear on the way to Elm Street. His path was uncertain but what ever path he chose was going to be hard and fast. Life was just a ride and he planned to accelerate it as fast as possible just like he had done with the ambulance a little over twelve hours before.

He did not think of Kelly while he drank. He only thought of anger and rage and what it would take for him to be the best of all of the medics he knew and how to laugh in their faces when he superseded them.

"Harry, I officially do not give a fuck!" He said to the cat as he swallowed the bourbon straight from the bottle.

Harry sat helplessly watching as Josh drank and stared at the basement wall. For the first time in his young life he was able to finish an entire fifth of whiskey before passing out. The next day would bring a man back to Tremane hospital that none had ever expected to arrive. He was well on his way to a life he had never dreamed of or even wanted, but it was a life he would create.

Kelly looked out the window of Central hospital with the warm pink Meaghan snuggled close to her chest. She thought of Josh and where he was and if he was doing the right things. She knew he loved her and in her heart she loved him too. Kelly knew his intentions were noble, but he could not deal with what entanglements she had in her life. She had to let him go.

Meaghan cooed in her sleep as she nestled deeper into Kelly's chest for warmth.

"Your daddy saved us tonight and someday, maybe someday I will tell you about him and how he was a true hero; at least to me he is and always will be. I love you pretty girl."

Kelly looked up as the nurse came in.

"Honey, you doin' okay? She is a sweet baby", she said as she peered at Meaghan sleeping quietly in her mother's arms.

Kelly nodded and smiled are she caressed Meaghan's still wrinkled forehead.

"Who is Josh, honey? You need me to make a call for you?" She asked with concern in her voice. "You asked for him when you were coming out of sedation."

Kelly felt her heart drop and her face follow suit. She felt tears coming. She bit her lip to fend them off.

"No, it is okay. I don't need anything", she said quickly. She did not remember calling for anyone. All she remembered was hearing the doctor mention that the cord was wrapping around the baby's neck and he was going to have to cut it. Kelly felt him insert the forceps and she reflexively kicked him in the chest like a mustang with a bad attitude. She could not help it. He recovered after a few curses and continued his work, none too gently with Kelly after that little episode.

"Okay honey, I will be back in an hour or so to get the little one for a while to give you some time to rest." The nurse left quietly and closed the door. Kelly and Meaghan were alone again. She looked into her baby's face and saw the nose and eyes that would haunt her for some time. Meaghan looked like her father, too much, way too much.

"They said you were going to be a boy", Kelly said softly as she held Meaghan close.

"I guess you are full of surprises", she said with a grin and nearly a giggle as she remembered pushing the nurse away screaming, "I had a boy! Where is my boy?"

Sedation did not agree with Kelly. She finally accepted the fact that Meaghan was her daughter. As she looked closer at the infant she could see more of Josh with every glance.

She wondered if she was imagining what she saw as one would when they want something so badly that their eyes play tricks on them. Kelly shook her head and began to try to put the thought out of her mind. It was too much to bear and she, as always, would bear it alone. At least she had her grandmother. She would know what to do, but she could never tell the old woman about Josh.

Chapter 10

Kelly's grandmother was a strong woman in every way. The woman and her husband had taken care of Kelly since she was three months old. She was not the typical coddling grandmother. She was a young girl during the depression; life was hard and to survive you had to become hard as well. She married young and her husband spent most of his life on a tanker for *Standard Oil* and came home for holidays and vacations, other than that Kelly rarely saw her grandfather.

She remembered, once when she was in fifth grade, her grandfather had come home for a vacation around Halloween and it was time to put up the scary decorations on the roof. Kelly offered to help. Her grandmother Virginia, or Grandma Honey as she was called, had earned the nickname since she called all of the children "honey" when she was caring for them, had a ladder leaning against the roof. Kelly began to climb the ladder and as she reached the halfway point she had a sick feeling of dread overcome her. She stopped abruptly.

"What's wrong?" Grandma Honey asked.

"I don't wanna go up there", Kelly said with fear in her shaking voice.

"Well, get down then goddammit, I ain't got all night to put up these sons of bitches", she shouted holding an arm full of decorations.

She was far from as sweet as her name indicated. She was tough and hard, loved horse racing and would curse like a sailor when her horse was losing. She drank beer and smoked, but only when she watched the races or maybe when the Cardinals would play. She was all about horses and baseball; she hated people but loved horses. Even though when the horse she had just bet on was coming in slow she would call it a worthless lazy bastard as smoke rolled out of her nose.

Kelly climbed further up the ladder and scrambled her thin gangly teenage form onto the roof. Grandma honey was already halfway up the ladder when Kelly heard the scraping sound of the ladder sliding across the shingles. Kelly tried to grab it despite the weight, but she was too late. Her grandmother fell to the flat patio rocks below and a pool of thick dark blood covered her silver hair.

Kelly screamed for her grandfather and began crying loudly. Her grandfather rushed to Honey's side and carried her into the house. He forgot about Kelly who was trapped on the roof without the ladder. It took twenty minutes before the neighbor put up the ladder for Kelly to climb down. She was up there all alone fearful for her grandmother and terrified of falling. Since that day she has been deathly afraid of heights.

Young Kelly ran into the living room, with eyes swollen from tears shaking uncontrollably, to see her grandmother holding a bloody towel on the back of her head. Her grandfather forced Honey to go to the emergency room for stitches. Honey hated needles and that day she had to suffer through the stitches that left a permanent scar on her head and neck.

Kelly inherited the fear of needles especially dental needles. Her grandmother would bribe her to go with promises, which she kept, to let Kelly ride horses afterward. She would patiently sit in the car for hours while Kelly rode free as the wind on her horse. Honey always took great care of Kelly. It was rare that she ever hugged her, but Kelly knew how much the old woman loved her. Once Kelly was with her in a store and spied some jewelry she liked, Honey discovered she did not have enough for the purchase so Kelly sorrowfully said she did not really need it and it was okay. Honey would not have it that way, so she simply stuffed it in her purse and walked out with Kelly trotting to keep up. Her rationale was they wouldn't miss it and apparently they didn't. Honey had, on more than one occasion, to put the fear of God into a few teachers as well. George was one of Kelly's teachers who had been teasing her about her northern accent and Kelly abruptly told him to 'Shove it!' He grabbed her forcefully by the arm to punish her. Kelly ran home to her grandmother and told her about the incident. Honey said nothing but her face was glowing red with anger.

The next day she arrived at school and walked into the classroom, pointing a thin finger at the teacher and shouted,

"You, out in the hallway, I want to talk to you!" She snarled.

She promptly called him every name in the book and promised, with God as her witness, if he laid a hand on Kelly again she would rip his arms off and beat him to death with the bloody stumps.

The entire school was talking about it by lunch hour. Honey hated her daughter, Kelly's mother, who was absent for most of Kelly's life. Kelly's father was in prison until she was fourteen and Honey seemed to like him better than Kelly's mother, Candy. She invited him to visit Kelly after he was released but he never showed up. Honey and her husband were the only family Kelly ever had. She rarely argued with her grandmother she loved her too much for that. Honey bought Kelly a barrel horse and a trailer to start showing horses. Kelly had an old saddle that was nearing the end of its life. Once after a spat between Honey and Kelly the old woman left in a huff and returned later in the evening and told Kelly to go get something out of the car. It was a brand new saddle!

As Honey aged and Kelly began to show horses more often; Honey would toss Kelly the keys to the vehicle and say, "Be careful", even though Kelly was only fourteen and had no driver's license. Kelly could drive anything, her grand parents had taught her to drive everything from tractors to horses. Cars were no problem at all for the young ruffian. Speaking of a Ruffian, a famous racehorse that broke down on the track during a match race with Foolish Pleasure, during her race was the only time Kelly ever saw tears in the old woman's eyes. Honey simply walked out of the room. They never watched another race together after that day.

Kelly was arrested once for attending a party that was raided. Honey took her time bailing her out.

On the ride home Kelly was squirming in her seat expecting the same wrath that Honey had shown the schoolteacher. Honey simply said, "I hope you learned your lesson" and that was all she said.

This was not the first time Honey had let Kelly off easy. Kelly started smoking and thought she could get away without the old warrior knowing about it. Imagine her surprise when Honey came home and tossed a carton of Marlboro's on the bed next to Kelly and said, "I think those are the ones you smoke. If I catch you smoking them uptown, I will kick your ass!"

Kelly's grandfather never had the option of retiring; he died of lung cancer when Kelly was fifteen. Kelly remained in Raines where they had been living since Kelly was in sixth grade, while Honey went up north to the hospital where Kelly's grandfather was being treated. Kelly had not seen her grandfather in five months. She had the chance for one visit. She began to smile as she saw him walking toward her down the long, dimly lit hospital corridor. Her smile faded quickly as she saw his gaunt waiflike form come closer to her. He did not look human to her.

He was no longer the strong man he had been. Overcome with shock, the teenager sat abruptly on the floor of the hospital hall and began to sob. He died a week later. At his funeral Honey shed not one tear, although in her room later that night Kelly could hear her quietly crying. She never let her grandmother know that she had heard her shedding tears.

After the death of Kelly's grandfather Honey moved in with Candy, Kelly's estranged mother. Kelly always hated being in the same house with her mother. They would get into fistfights and Honey would have to break them up. Kelly began to drink a bit and experiment with drugs. She even tried to run away to Raines, but Honey's friends in Raines would always find Kelly at their old vacant house and send her back on a bus.

One day Kelly returned from walking uptown to see her clothes in the parking lot and her mother on a rampage. Her grandmother was loading up the car and preparing to leave. Honey was going to Florida to live with her mother, Kelly's great grandmother. Honey could not take the fifteen year old with her. Kelly was alone again. She called the only person she could, her brother. He set it up for Kelly to stay with his friend's parents in their basement. Kelly quit school and began doing drugs and drinking.

Shortly afterward she became pregnant with her first child, Jennifer. She stopped drinking and doing drugs and left Jennifer's father to go live with her grandmother, who had recently moved from Florida to Park Forrest. She was renting a townhouse that her brother, Kelly's uncle, had recently vacated. Once again Kelly was back with Honey and a new baby, Jennifer.

Honey told Kelly that she would take care of Jennifer for her and she should do whatever she needed to do to get her life straightened out. Kelly took the opportunity and moved to Tremane and rented a house with her girlfriend Shirley. Kelly would visit her aging grandmother and Jennifer when she could, but she started with drugs and alcohol again. She moved back and forth for years and finally at the age of twenty one she decided to stop the drugs and drinking. She moved to Sim Village and began working at the Police Department.

When Kelly told her grandmother that she was pregnant with Meaghan, the old woman was furious. Kelly never told her about Josh; that would have been too much for Honey to handle. Kelly was ecstatic about being pregnant with Josh's child; she did not feel this way about her first pregnancy. She was much more equipped to handle this alone, or so she thought. At a month of age, Meaghan developed a severe case of colic and Kelly was up for days pacing with the infant with her little dog diligently following her. She had physically worn a path in the carpet of her small rental house in Tremane by the time she called Honey. She was exhausted and sobbing over the telephone.

Honey drove to Tremane and took Meaghan then told Kelly to go to bed. The old woman began the pacing for the night with the colicky child while Kelly slept in the next room.

Honey was always there for Kelly. She loved her more than anyone else ever had, except for a scrawny clueless teenager who was trying to be her hero. Kelly moved from Tremane back to the north with her grandmother. Again it was Kelly and Honey, now with a new baby Meaghan. Jennifer had already begun working and going to college. Kelly was still trying to find her own way.

The one bright spot in Kelly's life was the holidays. Christmas was her favorite holiday and Honey shared her enthusiasm. As Honey reached her late seventies, her mind began to show signs of age. She would call Kelly into the living room and curse at the television and scream,

"I can't understand a goddamn word they are saying."

Kelly informed her that she had the language set to Spanish and adjust the television for the old woman.

Another time when Honey was in her eighties, she was watching golfing on television at one moment then a few hours later she was watching skeet shooting. Kelly asked, "Grandma Honey, what are you watching?"

Nonchalantly Honey replied, "I don't know they are shooting golfers."

Honey was beginning to develop dementia quickly. Over the next few years Kelly cared for her aging grandmother often cleaning her after biological accidents.

"I hoped you would never have to clean me like this, Kelly" Honey would say nearly in tears.

"You changed my dirty diapers. I don't mind." Kelly replied honestly.

As the dementia worsened Honey began to wander and fall often. Kelly refused to put her in a nursing home. The aged woman had run-ins with cat who was trying to eat his meal on a shelf where his food dish was located and Honey, feeling it was inappropriate, grabbed him by the tail and tossed him across the floor then immediately forgot about it. Kelly was almost as surprised as the cat. The dog fared no better. Honey tossed a soda can at the animal then immediately got up to pick up the can.

Kelly shrieked "What are you doing?"

"Oh, just picking up", Honey replied. Kelly could not help but laugh. She had to laugh to keep from crying at the thought grandmother's mind deteriorating.

As Honey's condition worsened, she would escape to the outside and try to sit with the horses that Kelly had managed to buy. Honey would routinely fall near the pasture. Kelly would have to call an ambulance and Honey would give the medics hell. She had a broken wrist from a fall and still managed to walk to the ambulance. She refused to let the medics help her. She was admitted to the hospital shortly after the fall.

Her behavior was worse in the hospital. Honey was vicious to the nurses. She developed MRSA and was not able to go home with Kelly. Kelly again refused to admit her to a nursing home. Honey began to develop bedsores as the infection spread. The doctors wanted to perform surgery on a bedsore that had developed on Honey's back and they promised Kelly that her grandmother could go home with her as soon as she recovered from the surgery. Kelly reluctantly signed the forms for surgery. The procedure was scheduled for nine am the following day.

Kelly worked all night at the police department the night before Honey's surgery, causing her to oversleep a bit on the day of the surgery. She arrived at ten. Fortunately, the nurses at the hospital were running behind in procedures and she had the opportunity to see her grandmother before the surgery. Kelly was wearing a yellow police jacket that looked a lot like Honey's favorite jacket from home. It was Honey's prized possession and she would not lend it to anyone. In her sedated state she tried to pull the jacket from Kelly.

When she returned from surgery she was severely sedated and Kelly grasped her hand. Kelly was surprised that no one checked her grandmother's vitals when she returned. Her hand felt cold. A respiratory therapist arrived and placed a pulse oximetery on Honey's finger. Kelly heard the beeps of the heart rate monitor on the device slow and then become silent. The clueless therapist said,

"Let me switch fingers. I had problem with this thing last time and I need to give her a breathing treatment", he mumbled. He failed to notice that Honey was not breathing.

Kelly snapped and screamed, "She is dead you idiot! Go get the nurse!"

Kelly was alone and Honey was gone.

Chapter 11

Josh opened his eyes. He felt like he had shaved glass in his head. He was covered in sweat from the fitful drunken night's sleep. He sat shirtless on the edge of the bed. His vision was beginning to clear as he stared at the heather blue uniform shirt lying crumpled on the basement floor.

The Lafayette County patch on the left shoulder sported a blue star of life symbol surrounded by the words, "Knowledge, Speed, and Concern". He thought to himself,

"I don't know anything, I have no speed and I definitely do not give a fuck and screw concern."

Harry bounded down the stairs as if he knew Josh was up. He pounced on the bed next to Josh and looked peacefully into Josh's bloodshot eyes. Josh patted the cat on the head,

"Harry, it was a hell of a ride for a few months but I guess it is you and me again." He whispered afraid to raise his voice too much due to the whiskey headache. After gathering himself he decided to take a shower to wash off the stench of a twenty four hour date with whiskey. The hot water felt good.

He meandered around the house nursing his hangover with ibuprofen and an energy drink. He learned that the electrolytes in the drink and the anti-inflammatory properties of the pills seemed to help with whiskey hangovers. This bit of knowledge would serve him well in the years to come.

The day was uneventful and Josh spent most of it in a fog of shock, pain and heartbreak. Harry even kept his distance as though he knew Josh wished to suffer alone.

As the night fell Josh began to feel better and decided he could actually tolerate some television. No one else was home and he did not feel like going out or drinking for that matter. He turned on the television which still reminded him of Kelly sitting beside him laughing nearly a year ago.

Trumpets sounded from the television. An old black and white film was just beginning. Josh had considered getting drunk again, but tonight he was not in the mood and the thought of more bourbon made his stomach churn.

"It's *Cyrano!*" A voice from the screen whispered. *Cyrano De Bergerac,* a nineteen—fifty movie starring *Jose' Ferrer* and *Mala Powers* was beginning. Josh enjoyed swashbuckling movies and always thought that the old movies reflected a simpler time. He liked the satire, wit and generally good acting that was present in this type of cinema.

His interest in the movie grew as the story progressed. He sat upright on the sofa as the plot unfolded. Cyrano was an intelligent soldier in the French army in the fifteen or sixteenth century; Josh could never remember which he just knew it was a long time ago. Cyrano was deadly with a sword and struck fear in the hearts of any challenger.

He was a romantic individual with the ability to use words to woo the hearts of any woman; however, he was cursed with the disfigurement of an abnormally large nose which gave him a comical appearance. It is well-known that Cyrano loved Roxanne, the most beautiful woman in all of France, and always presented himself as a friend and protector but never had the courage to ask for her love. He went so far as to write poetry for the dim-witted, but handsome, Christian to present to Roxanne. Cyrano knew Roxanne loved Christian and he wanted her happiness more than his own therefore he played the game; instructing Christian in the ways of romance and continually writing to Roxanne under the guise of Christian to win her heart for the other man. It is a heartbreaking story that ends with Roxanne realizing, only after his death, that Cyrano was truly the man she loved for his soul and not his appearance. It was the tragic comedy plotline that appealed to Josh.

By the end of the movie Cyrano was Josh's new hero. He related to the wounded romantic warrior that could not be harmed by men, but devastated by the love he held for a woman that he felt he could not win because of his disfigurement. Josh felt like Cyrano, a warrior poet cursed by his youth and Kelly was the fair Roxanne that he could never win.

Josh always had a flair for the dramatic and often took theatrical performances to heart. He did his best to emulate cinema in real life. This was his method of escape from reality. His attitude, coupled with alcohol, could make for a very dangerous combination. Life does not imitate art, but Josh always felt that it should. He was no longer happy with himself and who he was, so he decided he would simply become someone else. The best place to begin was on the job and in what was left of his personal life.

Josh arrived at the hospital with a plan to begin his new lease on life. He spoke to no one unless he had to and spent the entire night focusing on taking care of the ER patients that trickled in and during the off times he completed his application for paramedic school.

Sam was his partner that night and said very little, he was too worried about some issue between him and his eighteen year old boyfriend. Sam never openly admitted that he was gay, but everyone knew that he was and just accepted it. It was not much of a mystery that a forty five year old man that lived with an eighteen year old kid he rescued from East St. Louis had to involve some kind of relationship, no doubt sexual, which made sense since Sam was not the humanitarian or philanthropic type.

Josh was glad to be working with Sam, instead of Claude. Sam was at least comfortable with silence and privacy. Claude tried to hard to be social which irritated Josh. The paramedic application and cover letter was complete by the early morning when Johnny came in to work.

"Johnny, here is my application. Send it off." Josh instructed.

"I am not playing" he said with a stare, "I can be good and you know it."

"No doubt Dracula, by the way you earned that name after you got an IV on that dehydrated six month old. By the way Jaida and that lil' blonde wants you to come visit at the nursing home tonight." Johnny said with an evil grin and more seriousness in his eyes than Josh liked to see.

Josh always liked Jaida. She was a thin, tanned, beautiful natural blonde with a bubbly personality. He always thought she was attractive but he never approached her. She was just a friend.

"What is this Barbie doll's name that I am meeting?" Josh asked halfheartedly.

"Terri. She told Jaida she wanted you to give her mouth to mouth. She saw you doing CPR on that old lady a few weeks ago and apparently you made her tingle a bit", Johnny said truthfully.

Josh nodded in acknowledgement and walked out the door. He went home and fell asleep quickly as the day passed by. Josh was beginning to enjoy the idea of being nocturnal. The traffic, although Tremane never had much, was lighter at night, he did not have to wait in line anywhere and he could avoid the general public as much as possible. He rose from his slumber about eleven o'clock in the evening. He gathered himself and with a sigh left for the nursing home.

Berrywood nursing home looked like an old insane asylum. The darkness of night only added to the creepiness of the old single story building nestled between and muffler shop and the abandoned, dilapidated old shoe factory on route 140. One could only access the home for the aged and dying by driving down the alley that was barely wide enough for the little S-10 to edge through.

Josh was dressed in street clothes and did not really care about his appearance as he pressed the buzzer on the back door. He would know within sixty seconds if this girl was worth wasting any time on. If she did not appeal to him he would just walk out.

Jaida answered the door with a matchmaker grin on her face.

"Hi Josh. She is nervous as hell. I think it is funny. She has been fixing her hair every five minutes. I though you were coming an hour ago?" Jaida asked inquisitively.

"Had some shit to do. Sorry bout that. She's a CNA right?" Josh replied.

"Yeah, come on in" she said waving a moth away from her face that was trying to admit itself to the nursing home.

Josh walked down the hall toward the nurses' desk with Jaida. He partially wished she had invited him there to see her. He pushed the thought out of his mind for time. He could always think about her later and how the white nursing uniform hugged her firmed derriere quite nicely. Josh was only looking at women's bodies, never caring about their hearts, none since Kelly.

Jaida circled the nurses' desk as Josh leaned forward resting his elbows on the counter. She picked up the intercom and pressed "PAGE" on the keypad.

"Terri report to the nursing desk for CPR instruction!" She said trying to sound official and avoid laughing. Josh grinned a little at the joke and fiddled with a pencil lying on the counter.

Terri exited a patient room with an armful of dirty linen. She tossed them carelessly into the hamper on her way to the nursing desk. She was blushing already as Jaida confidently plopped into the chair.

"See, I told ya I would get your man here and here he is. All I had to do was call Johnny, that perverted old bastard, and next thing ya know I got a stud here for ya. Now you can quite whining", Jaida said pretending to be irritated with the entire ordeal.

" Hi Terri, My name is Josh and I am a professional CPR instructor and I understand you are in need of mouth to mouth resuscitation", Josh announced in his official EMT voice.

Terri's face turned bright red as she turned away and pointed at Jaida who was now laughing hysterically.

"You bitch!" Terri snapped as she pointed her index finger accusingly at the laughing nurse. She turned quickly to Josh who was now sporting a sly grin on his face and doing his best to stare deep enough into her eyes to make her uncomfortable.

"Hi, so how do you know Jaida?" Terri asked, trying to return some normalcy to the conversation.

"She is a friend of Susy's. I room with Susy and Tanner on Elm Street." He said.

Josh continued to make jokes and small talk with Terri and Jaida for the next hour. As he prepared to leave he asked Terri to breakfast at Hardees after she finished her shift. She readily accepted and blushed once again. Josh smiled and said he would meet her there at seven thirty.

He left the nursing home abruptly, as any good hero would, and promptly went back to Elm Street. He had no real interest in Terri she was young and Josh preferred older women and Terri was way too young for his taste nonetheless he would meet her for coffee and see what happened.

Josh moved into a small apartment, away from Tanner and Susy, a few months after his first date with Terri. He was still angry with Susy for the way she had treated Kelly and when Mara, Susy's portly lesbian lover, moved in he could not handle the thought of living with three women in the same house.

Josh and Terri began seeing each other soon after their first date. Susy and Johnny would tease Josh about Terri getting pregnant and how the world did not need another "mini Dracula" running around. Josh responded by saying with vigor,

"I'm not having any snot-nosed kids in my life. I would shoot myself first!"

Josh had become selfish as the months passed and his new philosophy was work, drink and have sex, just as he said he would. Work was always top priority. He broke off many dates with Terri to work and would often sign up for extra shifts to avoid seeing her, if he was not in the mood to put up with her teenage view of life. By nineteen he had already seen several people die and nearly lost his own life in an ambulance crash. He was becoming cynical at a rapid rate and women were more of interference to his plan than a pleasure.

His view of life had become very narrow. Women were great for sex as long as they did not want anymore than that and if they did he would break it off. He nearly broke it off with Terri on several occasions, but then the hormones would kick in they would have spend the night together and be back together again. Life was about to change again for Josh. It happened on an idle day about six o'clock in the morning. The ER phone ran and Josh answered. It was Terri on the other line.

"I need to talk to you. I am on my way up there" she said with shakiness in her voice.

"Okay, what is wrong?" He asked pretending to care.

"I will tell you when I get there" she said and hung up.

Josh placed the phone on the receiver without any thought about what the problem may be. He figured it was usually something stupid, such as a friend of Terri's saying something about her she didn't like, or a fight with her dad, or something else insignificant.

Josh walked out to the dock to meet her. He saw her white car pull into the drive. She exited the vehicle without turning off the engine and ran up the steps and embraced him hard nearly knocking him over from the unexpected impact.

"I'm late!" She whispered in his ear.

"Late for what?" Josh asked stupidly, expecting her to mean work and hurriedly get to the point of what was really wrong. He wanted to get this over with quickly.

"My period", she said quietly looking at Josh like a deer looks at a coyote.

Josh felt his stomach drop and his knees weaken. He had always wondered how he would address this issue as it occurred. He did exactly the opposite of what he had planned. Josh simply said nothing.

"Come over tonight after work and we will figure this out", he said as he held up his palm toward her signaling that further discussion was unnecessary. She nodded and promptly walked back to her car. Josh walked back to the ER staff room and retrieved a cup of six hour old coffee. He swallowed it without wincing at the bitter taste of the rancid liquid.

Josh was not in shock or afraid, he simply had to deal with the pregnancy. It no longer mattered if he was happy about it or not. He hated his life and this would just add to his pattern of bad luck. He really did not care either way, he felt his life was destined to be miserable and true to form, it was officially becoming shit.

It took over a year for the child to be born. Terri's initial pregnancy scare was a false alarm. Josh attempted to do the right thing and proposed when he thought Terri was pregnant. After he realized she wasn't Josh did not back out of the marriage, although he could have. Josh's first child arrived and he named her Alexis.

Alexis was brought into the world on a cool March day. She was born in a conventional hospital bed. Terri received pain medication and Josh was there every moment.

Alexis had fiery red hair that rested as a soft tuft on the top of her infant head. She had a strawberry birthmark on her cheek as well. Josh nearly had a panic attack when, as Alexis was nearly ready to enter the world, he noticed *Rush Limbaugh* was on television. He would not have it and quickly changed the channel to the *Three Stooges*. Josh had his standards and he would rather have Alexis arrive in a world surrounding her with laughter. Terri was giggling and a bit drugged up as the doctor said, "Look, she has such beautiful red hair!"

"I can't see!" Terri shrieked with excitement as she craned her neck forward.

"Look in my glasses, at the reflection", the physician replied as she continued the delivery.

Alexis was cleaned and warmed and as the doctors worked on her mother, Josh stared into his daughter's sleepy eyes for the first time. He had tears in his.

"You are my little Irish one, kiddo. I will always protect you. I promise. I'm your Dad." He said as he choked on the words.

Terri and Alexis were allowed to go home the next morning. Josh held Alexis as tight as he could as he carried her to the car that was prepared with a car seat and supplies for Alexis. He had never driven so careful. Josh was now a father and life would change, but he would change more than he ever imagined. He had chosen the name Alexis for a reason. He always wanted his daughter, after he discovered he was having a daughter, to be tough, independent, wealthy, and cruel if needed and never have to depend on a man for anything.

He chose Alexis as the name in honor of the cruel and wicked Alexis from television's *Dynasty. Alexis Carrington* ruled the world and he wanted nothing less for his daughter and God in heaven could not protect man or beast that would dare harm her. Josh continued his mental flare for the theatrical, and in this case he was just being honest about his love for Alexis.

Josh and Terri were only married for three years. Alexis was two when Josh divorced Terri. Josh had lost interest in Terri and had begun wandering. He opted to just divorce and get it over with for the sake of everyone. Terri was not compatible with Josh and in her words, "No one else was either!"

Josh moved back in with his parents for about a month. He would pick up Alexis on the weekends. They would sit on the porch and talk about airplanes and things. Alexis was very bright and could speak like an adult at the age of two. Josh never used baby words with her. He held her when she was hurt, although he did not coddle her, and Alexis began growing up faster in her mind than other children her age. She walked at ten months of age and could speak in complete sentences at eighteen months. She slept all night long and rarely cried. She was growing up exactly how Josh had planned. Fast.

Josh would work all week, pick up Alexis and go out after she fell asleep. His parents watched over her while he was out. Within a month Josh had found a new female target. Josh needed out of his parent's place and he did not care how he did it. This woman was very interested in Josh. He considered that a good thing, since he had gained nearly fifty pounds from living with his parents and eating through the pregnancy with his first wife.

Alexis met her for the first time and immediately after seeing her she said,

"Daddy, I don't trust her. I think she lies" the child said with her green eyes blinking innocently at her father. Josh hugged her and said,

"I believe you. I believe you", he said truthfully, "But I will take care of it okay? You live with your mom anyway and I will be with you on the weekends and you will not have to see her if you don't want to, Okay?"

"Okay Daddy, its okay", she hugged Josh's neck with all of the strength her little arms could gather.

Within a year, Josh and the woman Meridith were married. Josh eventually gained full custody of Alexis. Josh had forgotten that he promised Alexis she would not have to stay if she did not want to do so, however, the little girl did not have much choice. He had broken his promise for the first time in his daughter's young life. Alexis knew this but at nearly four years of age she decided not to remind him. She knew he was wrong but Alexis truly loved her Daddy and would suffer through anything just to be near him.

Josh and Meridith were doomed from the start. She was in her mid-forties and Josh was barely twenty five. He still had the immature sense that he controlled others simply at will. Meridith let him think this.

Between the two it was a game of cat-and-mouse with who could manipulate the other most. Josh thought he was winning when he signed the closing paperwork for the modular home on St. Cloud Street in Tremane.

The first year of the marriage was filled with arguments and screaming matches over, money, furniture, and anything.

Alexis was not doing well with the relationship either. Meridith would always make cloaked remarks about how important it was to remain thin. Alexis dreaded dinner time. Alexis loved carbohydrates and though not particularly healthy foods, she did not over-eat. She inherited the love of potatoes, fries, bread and pasta from her mother. She enjoyed fruits but considered vegetables nearly poison and would not touch them. Alexis simply ate little, remained thin and moped most of the time. The only enjoyment she had was when she had precious moments alone with Josh. He very seldom took time away from the ambulance service to stay with her, but when he did it was a great event in the child's eyes.

Josh planned to accompany Alexis on a trip to the zoo with her first grade class. The little girl was glowing with excitement about her trip with her father. Alexis was always considerate about her time with her father and she would say things like,

"Daddy, I know we can't stay too long but I only want one thing— that's all just one thing".

She asked for very little in her life. She just wanted her father and what minute amount of time he could spare.

The zoo trip was no different. She only wanted to see the elephants. Nothing else— just the elephants. That was all her five year old heart desired.

"Daddy, I will be real good and all we have to do is see the elephants and you can come home and go to sleep. I know ya are tired and I will be real quiet when we are on the bus ride back so you can sleep. Okay?" She promised.

Josh would smile and give her a half hearted hug and tell her it was okay. He was always thinking about work and not the treasure that was sitting next to him. He had been promoted to ambulance supervisor and in a period of three months had completely revamped the EMS service in Tremane. Morale was high, care was improved and response times were record breaking. He was a genius at work and a fool at home.

The day of the zoo trip came and Josh left work on time for a change. He had been run ragged with a full arrest and two transfers to intensive care units in Springdale. Josh was not looking forward to the bus trip from Tremane to St. Louis. He thought of ways to get out of it, feign illness or fatigue, but he did not. He couldn't after he arrived at St. Cloud Street to see little Alexis with her Strawberry Shortcake backpack in her little arms standing patiently on the front porch with a grin from ear to ear. She bounced a little as he pulled into the driveway.

She bounded toward the Ford Expedition to climb into the back seat. Josh helped her in.

"See Daddy, I got my seatbelt on and I am all ready, I told you I would be good!" She exclaimed, so proud that she was ready all by herself. She had even packed her lunch with a turkey sandwich, potato chips and grapes. The exuberant young lady had prepared a sack lunch for her father too.

"Daddy, I tried to make you coffee too, but I couldn't reach the cab'net." she said sounding sad.

"Don't worry, kiddo, I have coffee and thanks for the lunch, you are getting too big too fast" he said with rare warmth in his voice.

The bus ride was torture for Josh. He was surrounded by soccer moms continually gossiping about others and truly believing the issues in their lives were life and death situations. Josh stared down at his uniform pants that still had dried blood from two different people on them. Two people had died the night before and he was the last face they saw on this earth, so it was hard for him to relate to women that thought that the cable being out of service and the repair man that smelled like sweat and was rude, could ever be a "situation".

Alexis was quiet as she had promised and gently swung her legs back in forth as they dangled from the bus seat with a gentle contained excitement. She could not stop smiling. She kept looking at the elephant section of the zoo brochure.

"Kiddo, I promise we will see the elephants, before the day is over", Josh said with a tired smile and embraced her shoulders with his right arm.

"I know Daddy, you can do anything." Alexis said with a smile so large her face could barely contain it.

Alexis and Josh exited the bus at Forrest Park in St. Louis. They stood impatiently while the teachers gave pick up instructions. The bus was to leave at 1:00pm. Josh and Alexis began to walk hand in hand through the zoo; looking at the animals as they passed. Alexis would point and giggle then hug Josh's leg. She was short for her age, just like her father. The little redhead could barely contain her excitement and kept looking for the elephants.

Josh stopped at a souvenir stand and bought a plastic mold of an elephant for her. She clutched it so tightly her little knuckles were white from the pressure. They ate lunch together then continued their search. At last the signs pointed toward the elephant exhibit. It was nearing half past twelve. Josh was feeling the pain of the walk and dreaded the walk back. He had not been to sleep for thirty hours and he could tell.

The elephant exhibit came in to view and Josh's heart sank as he heard Alexis say,

"What does C-O-N-S-T-R-U-C-T-I-O-N spell Daddy?" she asked innocently.

Josh felt rage engulf his entire being and as he saw the sign that said *"Elephant exhibit closed for construction. Will open for viewing next month. Sorry for the inconvenience, please come again."*

Josh growled like a rabid dog.

"What is wrong Daddy?" Alexis asked noticing the tension in her father's demeanor.

Josh squatted and faced his daughter as her eyes widened with attention.

"Kiddo, the elephant exhibited is closed for repair; we cannot see the elephants today." He said as gently as he could.

Tears started to well in Alexis' eyes. Josh would not tolerate this because of some stupid construction. This was a zoo and there better be a fucking elephant here somewhere, he vented in his head.

"Don't cry kiddo, here is what we are gonna do; I need you to listen, Daddy is going to fix it okay. Are you ready, I need you to do something for me and we will see elephants", he instructed.

"Okay, what?" Alexis said with a sniffle.

"I am going to carry you 'cause we have to move fast and it will be a little bouncy, but don't be afraid, I won't drop you. Daddy has to run with you okay? Trust me." He said with a soothing voice.

"Okay Daddy", Alexis agreed.

Josh picked up her Strawberry shortcake backpack and loosened the straps to fit his shoulders and put it on cinching it tight. He put the model elephant in the side pocket and picked up Alexis, who reflexively wrapped her legs around his waist and embraced his neck with her arms.

He started to trot closer to the elephant exhibit and quickly spied his target. A zookeeper fixing a broken panel on the fence; he was the poor soul that had to encounter the enraged paramedic on that particular day.

Josh squatted and told Alexis to stand behind him and wait. He would be ready to run soon. Alexis obeyed as Josh approached the unwitting zookeeper, a small black man with a receding hairline.

He quickly moved and squatted immediately beside the zookeeper, startling him a bit. He was so close that the zookeeper's personal space was violated.

He stared at the surprised man in the eyes and did not give him a chance to speak.

"Sir, I have a broken hearted five year-old daughter over there", he said pointing at Alexis, "that all she wanted was to see a real live elephant. She has been waiting for two weeks and at five years old, two weeks is a lifetime. Now, I need to know where I can see an elephant for five minutes and don't bother spouting policy to me because I am no longer a rational human being, just tell me where I can see the elephants and I will disappear, but if you give me the wrong answer, I can tell you that the nearest call box is fifty yards from here and I am two inches away from you and I bet I can out run you. Now I will be civil if you give me the right answer. Choose your response carefully," Josh hissed with homicidal intent in his voice.

The zookeeper was so shocked at the speech of this wild eyed man in uniform that he said with fear in his voice.

"Go over the fence past the bridge, they are leading a mother and a calf into the pen, but hurry, they just left with them to be boarded up." The frightened zookeeper replied with fear in his voice.

Josh was gone before the man finished the sentence. He ran to his daughter noticing she was more wild-eyed than ever.

"Here we go kid, hang on", Josh said with urgency in his voice.

The deranged father ran full speed to the bridge with Alexis clinging to him for dear life. He made it quickly eyeing the fence that was partially torn down. He jumped the three feet from the bridge as he supported Alexis' head. When his combat boots hit the mud, he was already running. He scrambled up the hill and kicked the remainder of the fence down to allow his stride to clear it easily. He had twenty minutes before the bus left, which was nicely located at the other end of the zoo.

Josh ran further toward the storage rooms. He ran harder as his lungs breathed fire with Alexis clinging tight as he bounced through the uneven terrain. His eyes beheld a beautiful sight, at least to him, the back end of an African elephant lumbering in a large steel reinforced pen. As he came closer, he saw the baby elephant trailing slowly behind her mother.

Bonus, he thought.

Josh was covered in sweat by the time they arrived at the pen. Alexis shrieked with excitement as Josh stopped and lowered her to the ground pointing at the baby elephant.

Alexis craned her neck over the mounds of dirt that protected the site.

Josh wheezed a little as he hoisted her back up from the ground and placed her on his shoulders for a better view. He panted while Alexis cheered and pointed from her perch on his shoulders. Ten minutes until the bus leaves and Josh was already calculating the price of a cab ride back to Tremane and the impending war with Meridith about the cost.

Alexis clapped and laughed as the baby trumpeted back at her. She had her own private viewing of the two elephants as her father stood atop a mound of mud with her seated on his weary shoulders. He inhaled deeply though his nose as Alexis watched the elephants as long as she could. The mother elephant trumpeted too and the animals walked in a circle as if performing for the little girl with the insane father.

Alexis was giddy and could not stop clapping and pointing. Finally, after a few minutes the handler came to put them away. She was a tall tough looking woman that stared evilly at Josh and his daughter while she led the animals to the building. Josh grinned and stuck his tongue out. Alexis did not see her father's behavior and he was glad of it.

"Bye elephants, I am Alexis and this is my Daddy, he is a Paramedic!" she yelled as if they could hear. Josh held her until the door to the holding stall closed and latched.

"Okay kiddo we gotta run again okay, hang on", Josh said as he lifted Alexis from his shoulders and placed her on his hip as he had before.

"Go daddy, you can make it, you can, I know it!" Alexis rooted him on as he leaped from the mound and darted for the fence and the bridge. Josh ran full speed to the bus stop. Alexis clinging tightly to him as the Strawberry Shortcake backpack bounced on his back.

The bus doors were closing as Josh arrived. He thrust his arm in the door and the driver opened them again before they trapped him.

"I am late!" the bus driver said with contempt in his voice.

"That's what she said", Josh replied as he forced his way in and lowered Alexis to the bus floor. The duo found a seat and began the trip back to Tremane. Alexis curled up next to Josh and before falling asleep she said, "I love you Daddy, I am glad you are my Daddy."

She held the elephant model in her sleep as the bus rocked rhythmically down the interstate toward home. Josh stared out the window and smiled. At least he had done something right with his daughter. He would not take another trip with her for years to come.

Chapter 12

Josh continued to work ninety hours a week. He was always in debt and the credit card bills were mounting. He decided that he should attend college to get a better paying job. Halfway though Josh's first year of school at Kask University, Meridith decided it was time to have another child. The doctors told her to stop having children and Meridith heeded their advice for nearly twelve years. Now she decided she wanted another child. Josh was not enthusiastic about the idea.

He continually refused to have a child with her. He had Alexis and he wanted no more. He was working constantly to pay the bills and he had gained a whiskey drinking habit. The wars with Meridith over a baby were becoming more volatile

On a drunken evening Josh had told her the story of Kelly and Meaghan, he cried over the loss and Meridith pretended to console him. She knew deep down Josh felt he had suffered a severe loss due the uncertainty regarding Meaghan.

Meridith would say, "You are never here anyway and it is my body you are never here and you are so distant all the time. All you care about is work and some dream girl that fuckin' left you. I am here give me what I want and I will leave you alone!" Finally, Josh gave in and agreed to try to have a child in order to stop the fighting and tears.

"Okay, Meridith, I will try, but don't talk about Kelly. I trusted you with that story when you asked why I worked so much and I was a drunk, Okay? She is gone and I try to forget about it. It is better anyway. I suck as a dad and you want me to have another child. Fine! If it will get you off my back we will try", he snapped back.

Josh began drinking as much as he could when he was not at work or in school. He would arrive at class after working twelve hours and stay for another eight to attend the pre-med courses. He wanted to become a physician assistant and he was completing courses to attend a school in

Missouri after a couple of years. He worked to maintain a B average, even though he could have easily earned A's if he had been sober.

Meridith had two miscarriages in the first year of attempts, but she was undaunted in her goal to have another child. Josh could care less either way. He felt he was destined to be miserable. He thought being a physician assistant would eliminate the money problems and the insane work hours

Meridith drilled him on being more than a paramedic supervisor. She would constantly tell him he was not living up to his potential and if he really cared, he would make himself better. Her favorite speech to use that would cut to the quick of Josh's soul was,

"This "hero" thing you think you are doing is a delusion. You are just hauling old ladies to the ER. You are not superman and heroes do not exist, you could not save him and you have been a drunk ever since, so buck up boy and be a man for once and do the right thing for your family, be something for God's sake!"

She always brought up Josh's favorite teacher that had been diagnosed with lung cancer and died on Christmas day in nineteen ninety eight. Josh arrived as the paramedic when the teacher stopped breathing. The family requested that Josh do everything he could to save him. The cancer won the battle and Mr. Bardley lost his life and in a way Josh died a little that day too and Meridith always reminded him of it.

Eventually, Meridith became pregnant and the pregnancy seemed to be viable. After numerous ultrasounds Josh and Meridith discovered that triplets were on the way. Josh began to drink more and worry about how to afford three more children. Meridith was sick constantly then one day told Josh,

"I have to go to the doctor, something is wrong." Josh feared another miscarriage and found out shortly after that two of the three had spontaneously aborted, but the smallest one was still viable.

After a rough pregnancy and a great financial investment, little Sydnee was born. She was four pounds and four ounces at birth and remained in the NICU for three weeks. Josh named her as well. He gave her the name after a beautiful physician that he saw on television that was always saving the dying. Josh seemed to pattern his life after movies even though his life was more dramatic than most cinematic works.

As Sydnee grew into a small, but feisty, one year old; Josh and Meridith fought more and more with each other. Josh worked a second job at a liquor store to pay the bills while Meridith worked too.

Josh was planning to get out of this mess and take Alexis with him. He soon found the opportunity at Kask College. His school schedule allowed him a three hour break between classes. He was always up for twenty-four hours before his classes started due to his ambulance schedule and he used this time to get some much needed shut-eye in the student lounge next to the cafeteria.

He met Kimberly there. Their first experience together was at an old dump driveway in the country. Not what one would call a romantic environment, nothing about the situation had even a hint of romance.

Josh enjoyed the romp and considered it a one time thing. Kimberly had different plans. She wrote him an explicit letter describing the encounter and slipped it into his bag. Josh gave her his pager number in case she wanted a replay. She began calling him at work and eventually left her husband.

Josh continued the game and was not too surprised when Meridith found out. She read the note and the war began. In the fall of the year, Josh left Meridith with Alexis in tow. He began drinking more often and partying with Kimberly.

He was starting to fail courses and have trouble at work. Woody, his best friend had moved back to Illinois from the Carolina's and added to the party scene. Josh was still supervisor at the ambulance service and Woody, now a Paramedic, was riding along. Management was at war with Josh over some training programs and his desire to push the EMS service further than management wanted to go. His end was near and he knew it.

Josh had known Woody since he was two and they were best friends. Woody always followed Josh's lead which was the driving force behind his career choice and his becoming a paramedic. He wanted to be Josh. Woody was a short, fat, hairy black-haired man with no tact and poor social skills, especially around women. He was slower than and not nearly as intelligent as Josh. He clung to Josh as a mentor and idolized him. He would drool over Kimberly and how she looked when she wore her skimpy risqué clothes. Woody told Josh that he was so lucky to have a party girl like Kimberly to sleep with whenever he wanted.

Kimberly eventually moved in with Josh, bringing her pre-teen brat Lanna with her. She opted to leave her son, Zack, with his father, claiming it was better for him to stay in his home school district. Since, Kimberly left her son with his father and was satisfied seeing him on the weekends it was now another family of Josh, Alexis, Lanna and Kimberly.

The holiday season of two—thousand was quickly approaching and Josh was nearing the end of his time at Tremane. He had an opportunity to move to Booker, Illinois and small town in the southeast portion of the State and he was considering accepting it to get away from all of his troubles with Meridith and Tremane hospital. Christmas of two—thousand was life-altering for Josh. It started late on Christmas Eve.

He and his partner Bumble, he called her Bumble since her given name of Brenwonn was too hard to pronounce, were called to Route 185 a very icy road at eleven thirty in the evening, for an auto accident.

As they arrived on scene Josh saw his old roommate standing in the road. Tanner had seen the accident happen and stopped to help. She ran to the driver's door of the ambulance where Josh was seated.

"You better call Arch. He is trapped and has a very bad head and chest injury. It is a bad one Josh, real bad." She said in a professional almost somber tone. Tanner had been an EMT before becoming a radiology technician and Josh trusted her judgment.

Josh quickly keyed the microphone and radioed to dispatch,

"KRS, 4 Adam 18—dispatch ARCH to our location— head and chest trauma with entrapment—dispatch rescue and fire as soon as possible. Emergency traffic, road conditions poor and low ceiling."

"Roger 18, Contacting ARCH, Fire and Rescue" Sarah replied in confirmation over the static of the aging radio. Josh and Bumble ran to the vehicle that was wrapped completely around a power pole with the roof caved in with mangled metal littering the icy ground.

The vehicle had left the roadway and struck the pole nearly four feet above the ground. The car must have been airborne and moving at a rapid rate of speed to wrap around the pole in such a manner. Josh assumed that the vehicle had spun on the ice.

He found a small entrance at the rear window of the vehicle. He scrambled into the car to find his patient. Bumble was frantically assembling equipment as the winter wind blew harshly through her short blonde hair.

"Can you hear me?" Josh screamed over the whipping wind.

A feint groan was all that he heard from the patient. The young man in the car was crushed with torn metal trapping him from the chest down. He was barely visible in the darkness of the wrecked car. Josh could smell blood but no alcohol, which was odd in this type of crash this late at night. He pointed his flashlight at the man. He could barely see him with the limited light.

Josh was crammed into a space about two feet wide and three feet high. He was glad he had lost the fifty pounds after meeting Meridith. He had been so stressed that he did not eat and when he did he vomited or had stomach pains. He was thin and pale and his hair had grown past his shoulders. He truly looked like his namesake, Dracula. He was rarely out in the sun. He was at his best at night and this was his chance to do something heroic and save this young man's life.

"I'm gonna tube him Bumble!" He screamed.

"On it!" She replied handing him a laryngoscope, Ambu bag and a size 7.5 ET tube.

Josh inserted the tool into the man's mouth and visualized the vocal cords as he applied gentle upward pressure to open the airway. Immediately, a fountain of blood projected from the man's airway covering Josh from face to chest. He could taste the coppery blood as it entered his own mouth despite clenched teeth.

Josh waited in position for the blood to drain from the corners of the man's mouth and inserted the tube between the vocal cords. He attached the Ambu bag and squeezed. The man's chest rose but only slightly due to the weight of the metal on his chest. Josh listened for lung sounds with his stethoscope as he continued to ventilate the dying man. He heard the lungs inflate on the left, but not on the right.

Normally an endotracheal tube that is inserted to deeply will enter the right mainstem bronchus of the lungs causing air to be heard on the right side of the chest but not on the left, but in this case the tube was perfectly placed and still no sounds were heard on the right.

Josh knew what that meant. A collapsed lung on the right— a pneumothorax or a lung so filled with blood that no air can enter— a hemothorax; both conditions are deadly.

"Bumble! Got a hemo or pneumo you are gonna have to pop him, I can't reach his chest and his pulse is droppin', but I've got him tubed!"

"I have never done that Drac, but I will. You ready?" She screamed quickly

Josh squeezed the bag with his left hand to give the man air and, in the darkness, walked his fingers down the man's ribcage to find the placement for Bumble to insert the chest needle.

"Stick him right between my fingers!" he instructed over the howling of the December winds.

Bumble plunged the fourteen gauge needle into the man's chest and adjusted the catheter.

"He's bleeding bad, Drac! You want me to occlude it?" She screamed. A natural reaction for a trained EMT is to apply pressure to a bleeding wound but in the case of a hemothorax, it must bleed to make room for air to enter the lungs which results in a Catch 22 for the patient, you either drown on your own blood or you bleed to death.

"Let him bleed! I gotta get air in for now! Spike LR and give me another needle and an IV lock! I am going to put in an EJ!" He shouted with conviction in his voice.

Bumble quickly prepared the equipment and handed it to Josh. He had been in the car nearly twenty minutes when the helicopter arrived.

Josh plunged the IV needle into the man's neck hitting the external jugular vein then he expertly threaded the IV catheter into the vessel. Bumble opened the clamp and let the life saving fluid flow as she squeezed the bag with frozen fingers.

"Chopper's here!" She announced with relief in her voice.

"Good, tell them fuckers from the fire department to cut him outta here! I lost a pulse, throw me the epinephrine!" He ordered.

Josh pushed the drug into the IV and started compressions in the cramped space. He could only use one hand in that position, but one was better than nothing.

"Those chicken-shit bastards won't come near the car! The said it is not safe! The power is on and they can't shut it off. It is a main feed from the plant! They are calling CIPS to shut it down! The coroner is here too! He came as a firefighter and is ordering you out of the car!" Bumble screamed.

"Tell him to go fuck himself and get this guy outta here! I ain't leavin' this guy!

A firefighter arrived and tried to grab Josh's ankle to pull him out of the car. Bumble immediately pushed the man to the frozen ground and screamed,

"You touch my partner again, you mother fucker and I will shove this goddamn needle into your worthless brain, now get the fuck away!"

Bumble was tough, she had been raised on a dairy farm with four brothers and they were all afraid of her. So was the fire department after this little episode. Josh looked up to see blue shadows of the flight crew running toward him.

"Thank God!" He said to himself as he continued to pump on the man's chest.

"Whatcha got—oh shit!" The flight medic exclaimed as he shined a rescue light into the scene. He saw the man's body crushed beneath the metal and Josh covered in blood.

"How in the hell did you get him tubed and decompressed like that!" He asked.

"Talented, I guess now get us the fuck outta here!" Josh smarted back.

"Hang tight man, lemme see what they are dicking around about up there", he responded and left to run up the hill.

The flight nurse arrived and started to talk to Josh and dress the decompression site as best she could in the narrow space barely exposed from the wreckage. The flight medic came back to her side and began to scream in her ear over the wind and whirling sound of the helicopter blades.

Josh could not hear what they were saying but it did not look good. He saw the nurse open her jacket and retrieve a cell phone. He knew what that meant. Medical Control was going to call it and the man had no hope. He continued to perform CPR as he watched the man's blood cover the ground. It was starting to snow heavily now and the helicopter was taking a risk by remaining on scene with a futile resuscitation.

"Drac, they called it man, your done! Get the hell out of there before you get fried!" The medic ordered holding out his hand. Bumble dropped to her knees in the powdery snow that had begun to accumulate on the ground and buried her face in her bloody hands.

Josh squeezed the bag once more and stopped. He leaned his head forward and rested his forehead on the headrest near the corpse. He felt cold blood dripping on his head from the ceiling of the car.

"I am sorry. I tried. I couldn't do it." Josh said softly as if it was a prayer.

"Time of death 12:14 am December 25th", he heard the medic say. Josh hated Christmas from that day forward.

"Get outta there! The pole is broken!" a voice screamed from within the group of firefighters that were trouping toward the scene. Josh slowly emerged from the demolished vehicle. As he stood upright atop the wreckage he felt the icy wind strike his blood covered face. He felt the sticky viscous fluid begin to freeze on his face. At this moment the fire department powered on the flood lights to illuminate the scene. The blinding light revealed Josh's blood soaked figure towering over the crowd that had congregated beneath him.

His shoulder length hair was matted with blood and striking him in the face as the frigid wind whistled about the scene. The crowd looked up in horror at the sight. Aside from the whirl of the distant helicopter blades and the hum of the generator there was only silence—occasionally interrupted by a gust of whistling winter wind. Josh stood alone staring angrily down at the crowd that had refused to help him save this poor young man. Bumble was looking at him with tears in her eyes, but she said nothing.

Josh looked toward the heavens as if to ask for divine intervention. As he gazed into the black sky he saw the source of the danger. Eighteen feet above the vehicle, the power pole had broken in two pieces. Only the four crossing power lines were supporting the high voltage pole that was still swaying in the wind. Five hundred thousand volts of electricity dangled above Josh's head. He stood without fear watching it swing.

"Come on Drac! Get down. Let's go home." Bumble pleaded. She approached the car, disregarding her own safety.

Josh looked at Bumble. He saw the tears in her eyes as he gazed down on her wind-burnt face. He wanted to die with his patient. Josh hoped that the pole would break and end his worries. The only saving grace was Bumble. He never wanted any harm to come to her. Despite his own wishes for death, he obliged her request and jumped four feet to the ground.

He landed softly on the frozen ground and as he regained his balance and prepared to stand he saw the bear. On the ground a few feet from the vehicle, lay a white teddy bear with a Christmas ribbon wrapped around its center. The bear must have been a gift for someone. It was covered in dark frozen blood and the stuffing was protruding from the chest.

Josh felt fire fill his stomach and rage fill his chest. Bumble covered her mouth and gasped as she noticed the toy on the ground. Josh was already running toward the still speechless group of firemen.

"You worthless, bunch of chicken shit, beer drinkin', fat, lazy, sister-fuckin', inbred, morons! This kid just died because you bunch of bastards are too fat or afraid to work a wreck! You better pray to fuckin' God, that I never find a one of you wrapped in metal! You better fuckin' pray, you sons of bitches! I hope you fuckers sleep well tonight! You are all cowards and I am ashamed to know any of you!" Josh spat with vile and loathing in his voice, as he shook a bloody fist at them. He wanted to hit someone, but he could not decide which of the ten he wanted worst. In his opinion, they all deserved to be shot in the head.

No one said a word.

"Come on' lets go", Bumble said as she clasped her hand around his shoulder. She pushed just enough to cause Josh to turn toward the awaiting ambulance. He began to walk with clenched teeth toward the highway. Bumble turned and walked backward to face the stunned fire department. She extended her right arm and middle finger with enthusiasm and shook her head in disgust.

Josh came home covered in blood on Christmas morning. Kimberly was there and the children were asleep. She met him at the door.

"What happened, are you alright?" she asked with concern in her voice.

"Do I look alright?" he replied. "I lost him. I lost him no one would help, except Bumble, no one."

The uniform was so soaked with blood that Josh had to pull hard, just to remove his pants.

"Just burn 'em", Josh said as he stepped in the shower.

He felt tears filling his eyes as he saw the blood run down his body leaving pink trails behind as the hot water pelted his skin. The blooded encircled the drain and was washed away, but the memory of that Christmas morning would forever haunt him.

Josh did not celebrate Christmas that day; he slept while Kimberly and the children visited his parents. She came home alone around eight. Josh's parents had offered to keep the children after hearing of Josh's horrid night.

The sullen paramedic began drinking as soon as he woke up; bourbon straight out of the bottle. He told Kimberly the story in detail this time as tears streamed down his face he drank faster. Woody arrived at nearly nine in the evening. He had heard the story from the oncoming crew.

Woody said, "Arch helicopter called back to the hospital after you left. The crew is calling you a hero and you should be commended for your efforts, but the ER director wants to know if you need a debriefing", he said with a hint of fear in his voice. He knew how much Josh hated debriefings and he hated the director, Penny, even more.

He had been to several of these meetings where counselors, that have never had any EMS experience, sit in a room with you and relive the event and try to talk you through the "healing process". Josh attended these on a mandatory basis. He would never go of his own accord.

"Debriefs are for pussies, I ain't going. Penny can kiss my ass. She ain't much of a director anyway", he growled and took another swallow of *Jim Beam*. The bourbon was doing its job of making him numb.

"Figured as much. Hi Kimberly", Woody said as he helped himself to a beer.

"Hi", she replied with a half-hearted wave.

"Now we drink" Josh said with a slur in his voice as he poured shots of bourbon for Woody and Kimberly.

The hard drinking continued throughout the night. Idle chatter and an occasional cursing fit from Josh were the only sounds resonating from the small house. The trio drank until dawn and ended the evening with Woody and Josh passing out at the table and Kimberly asleep on the couch. This was the beginning of a pattern.

Chapter 13

It was the winter of two thousand and one when Josh quit working as a paramedic in Tremane and moved to Booker, Illinois to run EMS calls and work in the hospital there. Alexis, Kimberly and her children followed. Woody tagged along and rented a small apartment for himself, not too far from away from Josh. He always had to be near Josh for some reason.

Prior to making the move, Josh stayed at the hospital during call hours and Kimberly remained in town to handle the school changes and deal with the children while Josh was away. She would become depressed and call him at work, drunk out of her mind and cry. He would console her, hang up and go outside to talk with the nurses. He really had no concern about her drunken issues. He no longer had any loyalty to anyone, no one since Kelly.

In April of two thousand two they were married and Kimberly made the move to Booker in May. Josh purchased a small house that he could afford on his salary. He never seemed to have enough money to pay child support, for Sydnee, and clean up the mountain of debt left from the last divorce. He was working constantly and when he was not working he tried to deal with his depression by trying to drink it away. He tried to satiate himself by drinking hard with Kimberly. It was fun for the moment, but afterward the problems were still there.

He decided that he needed to start living harder. Pushing the limits of sex and alcohol helped him cope with the emptiness he held inside.

The children would play in there ten by ten bed room, while Josh and Kimberly drank hard alcohol and argued as the night wore on. It was not a healthy relationship and arguments finally gave way to stoicism, resentment and ultimately hatred.

Kimberly would scream and cry about the infidelity and Josh would retaliate about money and how she was not to be trusted and that he had made a mistake by letting her move in with him in the first place. The couple never came to blows, but the verbal confrontations were vicious and hurtful. Josh would sober up and pick up more work while Kimberly would continue to drink and ignore life. She was always depressed and would rarely talk unless she was drunk. She had been like this for the majority of her life.

To Josh, life was not worth living. He often had thoughts about suicide. His thoughts were amplified every time he opened a bottle of bourbon. Money was scarce, work hours were getting longer and the calls were getting worse.

In the dead of winter, Josh was dispatched to a field on the south side of town to retrieve a child that was found in a field wearing only a diaper for clothing. When Josh arrived, the child was wandering in the field delirious from hypothermia. He ran to the child and gathered her into his arms and ran quickly to the ambulance. Once inside, he removed his shirt and placed the frozen child next to his chest and wrapped himself and the child in blankets.

His body heat was the safest way to re-warm the child. In severe hypothermia the risk of cardiac complications is high and slow natural re-warming is the safest method to use in the pre-hospital setting. Josh was furious and immediately began asking questions of the police about the parents and how they could let this happen.

The police found the parents in a trailer nearly a mile away from where the child was found. They were brought to the hospital and questioned. They claimed to be asleep and the child must have opened the door alone. After several hours of questioning, the child was released into custody of the parents.

Josh was speechless; he hated the system and no longer wanted to be any part of it. He heard six months later that the same child had been stuck by an oncoming car and killed. His life was full of these stories and the memories began to taking toll on his mind.

He began to drink with Kimberly in silence. The fighting was not worth the effort; they sat and drank. Josh would occasionally tell a story about the latest tragedy at work. He would become angry and rant for hours. Often his verbal barrages about the world of paramedics would become nonsensical as the alcohol coursed through his veins.

The job was no longer his passion. The excitement of the job that had been there in the past had long sense left his heart and mind. The adrenaline rush was replaced by anger and apathy. He ached to get out of this profession before it killed him. He needed an outlet.

Shortly after the new year of two thousand and four, Josh received a card in the mail. The name on the return address was Kelly O'Hara. He quickly opened the card and read as fast as his eyes could move. It read:

> *Hope you are doing well, it has been a long time. It is no surprise how I found you considering what I do for a living. I hope you, and your family, are doing well and have a happy holiday season. I was digging through some old things and I found one of the letters that you wrote to me. It always makes me laugh and I still remember your smile. I put in the badge that I was wearing when we met. I thought you might like to have it. If you want to give me a call, my number is included.*
>
> *Take care,*
> *Kelly*

The expression on Josh's face must have spoken volumes. Kimberly noticed.

"Who is that from?" She asked as she munched on a potato chip.

"An old friend I haven't seen in years. It is a long story" he replied, his voice barely above a whisper.

"I got time" she answered innocently seeming interested.

"Not sober" he said. "I am going to get beer, I will explain when I get back and have one or two or eight." Kimberly giggled at the response. She was clueless most of the time.

"Get me vodka and *Red Bull*" she said as her eyes lit up at the thought of the alcohol she craved.

"Okay" he said as he walked out the door.

Those were the last civil words the two spoke the entire evening. Josh returned and the drinking began. He told Kimberly the entire story and how he was not sure about the child. He explained how much he had fallen for Kelly O'Hara when he was young. He cried, vomited and drank more.

"Ya know what," Kimberly slurred her speech as she always did after a few shots of vodka, "You should call her and just ask, as long as you don't run off with her and leave me sittin' here in this shit town.

"Fine, I will" he said "but later". The evening progressed, the alcohol consumption increased and eventually Kimberly stomped out off to bed shrieking,

"I wish you could remember everything about me! You make me feel like I'm never enough!" Kimberly stormed off to the bedroom slamming the door behind her. Josh said nothing in response. He sat on the sofa that was stained from many spilled beers, and continued to drink until he could no longer hold his eyes open.

It was nearly two o'clock in the afternoon when Josh finally opened his bloodshot eyes to the angry sunlight that he loathed so much. He started to rub his eyes when he noticed the badge. He must have fallen asleep with it in his hand. Sitting upright his eyes beginning to clear, he noticed the card on the floor. He struggled to make out the numbers written near the bottom in large print. He recognized Kelly's penmanship. She always printed in large, clear letters. His handwriting was atrocious and he always liked to read what she wrote. Her handwriting was beautiful to him, like everything else about her.

He gathered his composure and picked up his cell phone. His hands shook as he dialed the number. The phone rang twice and he heard the click of the answering receiver on the other end of the line. His heart nearly exploded and the pain in his head increased ten fold when he heard the familiar accent he had missed for so many years.

"Hello?" Kelly answered with an inquisitive tone in her voice.

"Hi Kelly, do you know who this is?" he asked expecting a *No*.

"Josh. Hi how are you?" Kelly asked as she swallowed hard.

"Great, things are going pretty good, how are things with you?" he lied. He did not want her to know he had become a suicidal drunk over the last ten years. "How is Meaghan?" he asked honestly trying not to sniffle as the words came out of his mouth.

"Just fine, she is ten now and loving life. She has horses and they are her little life", Kelly replied.

"So, did you ever get married", Josh couldn't believe he jumped straight to that question. He immediately began to scramble in his brain for something to lighten the mood.

"No, it is just me and Meaghan", Kelly answered truthfully.

"I'm on my third marriage, they won't keep me too long 'cuz I won't show them my balls" he joked remembering the comedy bit he had performed years before. That tag line had always made her laugh.

Kelly did not disappoint. She laughed heartily; her laugh was a welcome sound to Josh's ears. It had been so long and his heart still ached for her. Josh and Kelly continued with uncomfortable small talk for nearly thirty minutes pretending to be two long lost friends just trying to catch up on the events in each other's lives. Josh did most of the talking as he usually did when he was nervous. Kelly laughed in response to her own nervousness that had settled in the pit of her stomach and churned with each word that Josh spoke.

Josh spoke of his new passion for kickboxing and anything else he could think of to impress Kelly. He wanted to see her and Kelly gave him the opportunity.

"I may be coming down to see some friends in a few weeks and I would like to see you, if that is okay, I mean, I don't want to cause any trouble with your family. Just to catch up", she lied.

Kelly wanted more but she did not want to push her limits. She felt inside that she would be satisfied with just seeing him again. She hoped she could eventually convince herself that was all she wanted.

"Let me see when I can get off work and we will set up a time. It sounds great! I would love to see you again", he said quickly.

"I also have some pictures of Meaghan that I would like to send you if you want, I have some of her and the horses" Kelly offered.

"Please do, I would love to see them and I will call you as soon as I find out about work. Okay?" Josh said with enthusiasm in his voice.

"Okay, call anytime" Kelly said. "It was great to hear from you", she said.

"Okay, I will call you tomorrow", Josh promised.

"Okay, Bye", Kelly said as she held the phone in her hand refusing to hang up first.

This was odd for Kelly. She was not much of a telephone user and normally she would hang up quickly in most conversations, but not this one. This time Josh hung up first.

She gently placed the telephone on the receiver. She felt a tear roll down her cheek as she remembered his wily grin and the way he laughed as he embellished her with silly stories. Kelly prayed to herself that he would hold true to his word and call. *Josh would, he would not lie to her, she knew he would call; she just knew it!*

Later that evening the drinking began again and the same patterned emerged. This time the argument was over Kelly.

"You are gonna go meet her and leave me sitting here with the kids. I know you will sleep with her; you don't care about your kids or me—just this woman you slept with years ago and aren't man enough to get over her. Hell, you may even have a kid with her, if you go, don't expect any of us to be here when you get back! I will take Alexis to her mom's and tell her all of this shit and see how long it takes before you lose her again!"

Kimberly was so angry she spat when she spoke. Josh sat for a moment entertaining the idea of just walking out the door. He should have done so, but instead he stayed and continued to argue. Kimberly, in a fit of rage grabbed the badge out of Josh's briefcase and stormed out the door before Josh could catch her.

"You want your fucking memory then go get it!" She screamed as she threw the badge far into the weedy vacant lot next door.

"You bitch!" Josh replied as he ran across the street and was nearly hit by an oncoming car. He searched for an hour for the badge cursing Kimberly the entire time. He finally decided to return to the house to fight some more and hopefully find it in the morning when the sun came up.

He stared in shock as he saw the flames in the kitchen sink. Kimberly was standing there with a glass in her hand and smiling with contempt. She had burned Kelly's card. Josh was livid. This point was as close as he had ever come to striking Kimberly. Fortunately, he opted to leave. He started the Mercury Cougar and drove to the nearest motel for the evening. While he was gone, Kimberly continued her drinking to the point of poisoning. She did not tell him until the next morning.

The cell phone rang at the *Comfort Hotel* and Josh answered.

"I am so sick!" Kimberly's shaky voice said over the phone.

"I will be there," Josh said calmly as he sat up to dress. He drove quickly home to see Kimberly lying on the sofa, pale and covered in sweat. As she wished, he did not call the ambulance. He remained with her the entire day monitoring her vitals and caring for her as she wretched and vomited repeatedly. He knew that the amount was not enough to kill her, but it was enough to cause slow liver damage if she was not treated. She refused.

"Don't go, please, just stay" Kimberly said with tears welling up in her eyes. Josh knew he was being played, nonetheless, he called off the visit with Kelly; claiming it was not a good idea.

"Uh Okay, I guess" Kelly said as she heard the news, "I told you that I don't want to cause any problems. Goodbye." This time she hung up quickly. Josh wanted to be hit by a truck at that moment. At least he would not have to hurt as much with a truck smashing his body, as he did with the thought of hurting Kelly's feelings, if even for an instant.

He was right. If he knew Kimberly as well as he thought he did, he knew she would follow him and do something possibly more insane. Josh was about to crack, he needed to do something to get out of his own life.

The kickboxing seemed to help him vent his frustration. He trained constantly for two years with the local sensei.

He recruited a radiology technician named Amy into the sport. He affectionately nicknamed her Torch due to a mishap she had while working on her farm and accidentally set an old shed on fire. She was a fiery brunette that was an amateur weightlifter in the one—hundred— and—twenty—two pound weight class in high school.

Torch was a dedicated wife and mother. She had a right round kick that could separate your teeth from your head. She became his best friend and training partner. Again, Josh found something to obsess over that kept him away from home and family. He craved adrenaline and the liked the idea of the possibility of meeting his maker by kickboxing in the ring, though he never really believed there was a higher power. Since EMS held little chance of dying in the line of duty, he opted to compete with younger men with hopes he may just end his life in grand fashion by getting killed in the ring.

He fought his first fight in February of two thousand and four. He was beaten quickly by a fighter that later fought professionally and held a 43-0 record. Josh was devastated and still alive and embarrassed. He sought his chance to clear his name and heal his bruised ego. He found it in Joliet. He won a unanimous decision over a well skilled opponent. His winnings were two broken ribs and a broken nose. Torch his chief corner and a now a blackbelt told him in the beginning of the third round,

"You have to move your head or you are going to get killed!"

"Hopefully" Josh said as he bit down on the mouthpiece she offered to him. After the fight he decided he would give up on fighting. He was thirty years old, fighting more experienced men that were still in their twenties. Josh looked at it this way, he had not only been a fencer, but now a kickboxer too; and much to his dismay he was still alive in the same nowhere life.

As if life could not get any worse, Josh received another letter in the mail. It was from another friend from the past, Tanner. The letter was brief and to the point. It read,

Josh,

I hope all is going well with you, I am writing this letter to tell you that Harry, your little furry friend and mine died last week. He was nearly twenty and was not in pain.

I always made sure he was well cared for and I am crying as I write this. I know he was important to you.

All my love, your friend
Tanner

Josh read the note and felt tears start to fall. Everything that reminded him of Kelly was dying. Harry was his friend and as long as he was out there, there was a chance of him being with Kelly. Harry just knew things. It was like he could read Kelly's mind or something and he would tell Josh what to do with some odd gesture or expression. Harry was always sending Josh messages. It was odd, or maybe Josh had imagined it. He looked to the sky and under his breath he whispered,

"Goodbye, Harry, I will always miss you. I loved you buddy, I really did." Josh let the tears fall, he did not care who saw it as he sat on the porch with the letter already stained with Tanner's tears. He added a few of his own.

Josh was completely lost in his own head and as always he would bury himself in stress to avoid thinking. It was time for a new adventure, college—again. He signed up for management classed at SMC. He commuted for two hours per day, four days per week and within fourteen months he was awarded a bachelors degree in health care management with honors. He managed to accomplish this, work full time and hold an additional part-time job; all the while drinking whenever he could. Josh was offered a job in Springdale, Illinois in August of two thousand and seven.

He took the opportunity and moved to the city, with Alexis, Kimberly and Lanna in tow. Sydnee was now seven and refused to come and visit because Kimberly frightened her. Josh was simply ignoring life and letting it pass him by as he chased rainbows

Springdale was worse for him than any other place he had ever lived. He could drink every night and not worry about being on call and drink he did. He was ignoring everything; finances, children, family and everything else that was not work. Josh picked up a job at an ambulance service about forty miles south of the city to ensure that he had drinking money and he would not have to be around his own family. He wanted to either avoid life or find a way out of it. His chance came in May of two thousand and ten.

Kimberly began working at a bar and her drinking had gotten worse. She was no longer coming home until early morning and Josh was becoming more and more angry. She began to get to him and one night in early May; Josh having had too much Irish whiskey and too much of Kimberly in general, he decided to end everything.

After attempting to find the keys which Kimberly had hidden from him he left the house on foot. Two hours later he was standing on the train tracks waiting. He did not have to wait long. The bright oval light was announcing the arrival of freight train moving at a considerable rate of speed.

He stood his ground as the whistle blew and the form of the engine came into view. As the locomotive penetrated the darkness Josh waited for it to come closer. He felt no fear, which could probably be attributed to the fifth of *Jameson* that was floating in his brain. As the engineer applied the brakes attempting to stop he blew the whistle one last time before impact.

"*Move to the left son and run*" a voice said to Josh.

He listened. He stepped off the track the locomotive whistled by nearly knocking him to the ground as the sheer force of the train whipped past his body. He turned and ran.

Josh slept in a field that night to avoid the police that he knew were coming. He felt he could not live yet he could not die either. Something or someone was keeping him alive and he could not understand who or what that something or someone may be.

Kimberly found him sleeping by the car the next morning and screamed at him to go inside and go to bed. He listened and slept for twenty—four hours. He found out after he woke up that Kimberly had moved the majority of her things into a pile in the living room. She began to taunt him about the train episode and how this was all she could take and he was no longer worth any effort. He began to drink again. Josh was sinking deeper into depression with each passing day.

Mid-May had arrived and Kimberly was still in the house and the children were starting to fight with her. Lanna was constantly screaming at her when Kimberly would come home at four AM. Josh felt he was unable to control any part of his life anymore. He decided to eliminate the problem and do it right this time.

He calculated the correct number of medications he needed to cease breathing and one Friday in May after a screaming match with Kimberly, he decided he had had enough. He drove to the liquor store, bought a bottle of bourbon and a pack of cigarettes, returned home, casually locked the door to the garage and nonchalantly chewed up thirty Tramadol pills and began shooting shots. He wrote a note saying goodbye to Alexis and within thirty minutes Josh was unconscious.

Chapter 14

Kelly sat on her the front stoop of her home. It had been a rough week. Meaghan, now fifteen, was beginning to ask questions about her history. The teen wondered why she looked, acted and sounded different from any of her other family members. Meaghan's questions coupled with the day-to-day grind of running a horse ranch was starting to wear on Kelly.

She looked over her eight acres in Indiana and saw the silhouettes of her horses grazing in the pasture. The moonlight caused shadows to dance about their muscular equine forms. Kelly had retired from the police department and started selling ponies and quarter horses. She was an expert trainer and her small, but efficient stable, housed more than one champion show horse. Kelly always thought that Meaghan and the horses would make her complete.

She could not understand why she felt hollow inside. She lifted her coffee cup to her lips and she noticed her hand trembling and suddenly without warning tears began to stream down her face. Kelly hated keeping the truth from Meaghan about her true father. She was conflicted and had lost all sense of direction. Her emotions overtook her and she wept forcefully as her three small dogs stood at her side helpless, save an occasional nuzzle to her thigh.

Kelly knew she had to make a change and without guidance she had no idea which way to turn.

She did all she knew how to do, with her arms stretched toward the sky she said,

"God, please help me. I want to be happy. All I ever wanted was to be happy. If you can hear me and you will, please help me. What do I do?"

Kelly stood patiently waiting for an answer that did not come. She lowered her head and returned to the stoop and her dogs.

The next morning she looked at Meaghan, who was milling about the house, and noticed how much she looked like her father. She could not deny that the resemblance was eerie. Kelly felt a knot form in her stomach and she swallowed hard to avoid bursting into tears. She went to her room so Meaghan would not see her cry. She closed the door and after a few minutes of searching she removed the last letter that Josh had written to her. She gingerly removed it from the envelope and began to read.

"*Get up*" a voice said in the darkness. Josh opened his eyes. It was morning and he could not move. His body was covered in sweat and his head ached. He tried to stand but he could not. He fell back to the garage floor.

"Okay, this isn't good. I'm still here" Josh said to himself and passed out once again.

Kelly laughed as she read the letter over and over again. Josh was so silly at that age. His tone was light and carefree. She missed his touch and the stories he would always tell in his comedic tone. She looked out the window and wondered where he might be and what had happened to him. She had searched for him online several times over the past few months without results. She had all but given up hope. At least she had the letters that she had cherished all of these years.

"*Get up you son of a bitch, don't crap out on me you little bastard. I ain't done with you yet*", the voice said as if it were an echo in the garage. Josh opened his eyes and attempted to inhale; his lungs were shutting down and he was fully aware of it. This was not working. He had to be asleep when this happens or he would feel every molecule in his body dying slowly and painfully. He could not understand; he should be dead by now.

He lost consciousness again for a few moments.

"*I said fight you little fucker, don't be one of them lazy sons of bitches, get up dammit!*" the voice shouted.

Josh sat bolt upright on the garage floor. He was covered in sweat, his head and heart pounded as he forced himself to breath. He tried to hyperventilate to decrease the pain, but his lungs would not cooperate. He had to call; he had to call Bryan.

Bryan had been with Josh through all of the turmoil over the last few months and the two had become much closer friends than ever before. Bryan was always there to listen and was genuinely worried about Josh. Bryan was a hard-working man in his early forties that had raised a family, worked at the hospital and also raised small farm animals and puppies for a living.

He was a truly good man. He loved his wife and three boys dearly and would do anything for a friend. Josh called on Bryan after the train incident and as any good friend would, Bryan came to take Josh away from the stressors by offering him a ride through the countryside to allow Josh to vent and get things off his chest.

Bryan drove and quietly listened as Josh replayed his life for him to hear. He held nothing back and explained how he had grown into the man he was and how if he did not change something soon he may not be here for long.

Bryan smoked his menthol cigarettes and intently listened while he navigated the narrow roads of the country in the late hours of the evening. Bryan offered advice to the best of his ability, but what he offered that meant so much more to Josh was a trusting ear and no passing of judgment. He was the truest of friends that Josh was lucky enough to find. He was the type of man that would put himself at risk for the sake of a friend.

Josh told him everything. When Bryan learned of Josh's attitude toward life he put himself on call twenty—four—seven in case Josh needed to talk through anything. All of this was for naught until the moment that Josh called the ambulance shed hoping Bryan would answer the telephone.

The minutes that passed while Bryan and Al drove to the garage seemed like hours. Josh crawled across the concrete floor to unlock the door. Josh opened the door and crawled outside as he continued fighting for every breath. His head pounded. He was nauseated but he could not vomit, his vision was blurred and the kidneys had stopped working. He craned his neck to the sky as if it was easier to inhale from this position.

"I am gonna die", he said to himself. He was beginning to panic like a drowning victim with a mouthful of salt water. He tried to flail, but he did not have the energy. His heart was beating too fast to adequately circulate blood and oxygen. He felt his body temperature start to drop; his hands were only capable of gross motor movement.

"God, help them hurry or I am going to be dead when they get here!" He choked with a raspy voice. He fell forward, his face striking the sidewalk hard. He lifted his eyes and through blurry vision and half closed lids he saw his saviors, Al and Bryan were running toward him with the stretcher.

"Al, I gotta have Narcan, or I"m gonna stop…" Josh's voice trailed off as his head came to rest on the pillow.

"We got ya buddy, we got ya, we will help." Al said with unusual nervousness in his voice. As they loaded him into the ambulance Josh's arms began to contract, a signal of impending brain damage or death.

"Josh, you should have called man, you should have called," Bryan said with fear in his voice as he spiked a bag of normal saline.

Al started an IV and gave a dose of Narcan immediately; Josh felt the drug invade his system. It felt like a drink of cool water on a hot summer day. His veins were no longer on fire and he could breathe without fighting.

Josh relaxed and inhaled deeply. The oxygen flowing steadily through the mask that Bryan held for his friend felt like the first breath of air Josh had ever taken. Josh knew then he was going to make it, although he did not know why.

Al and Bryan rapidly transported Josh to the Level 1 trauma center. Josh was stable by the time they arrived. If it wasn't for the quick action of Al and Bryan, Josh would have died during the trip. Al and Bryan saved Josh's life that warm day in May.

Josh thanked them both by saying,

"I don't deserve it, but you two saved my life", he nearly broke down into tears.

Bryan came to the bedside and squeezed Josh hard on the shoulder and said,

"Always here for you, Josh, I will call and check on you." He turned quickly, to avoid breaking down and left the room with Al following quickly behind.

Josh was getting drowsy again and his vision was fading. He heard the nurse say,

"Medic, stop thinking about shit. Your pressure is 212 over 120. Stop it dammit or you're are gonna stroke! I am giving you Ativan. Now calm down in your head, you are not out of the woods yet!" she whispered just loud enough that he could hear.

"Now I am going to say the typical OD patient thing, 'nurse *I bet you have never done something this stupid before*?" Josh said with as much sarcasm as he could muster. He had heard this phase from overdosed patients more times that he could count. Now he was the one saying it. Life had come full circle.

She replied, "Not that anyone knows about, but I spent three days near death on my kitchen floor over a guy and my life, bourbon was my friend too."

Josh tried to be coy, "I guess the best things that come out of Kentucky is bourbon and racehorses."

"Sonny boy, stick to racehorses, just stick to the racehorses." She replied.

Josh fell asleep and was taken to the cardiac unit for observation. Kimberly arrived at the hospital for one reason. She did not care what happened to Josh, her plan was to have him committed. She had been a nurse's aide in the past and she was familiar with some of the hospital policies regarding suicide attempts. She hoped to have him committed, take custody of Alexis and have the house to herself to do as she pleased.

There was one problem with her plan; Josh knew the system better than she did and he used his experience and his natural way with words to talk himself out of an inpatient admission. He remembered how Tonya had helped Kelly out years before and he used the same technique. After three days of "cardiac" observation he was released on his own accord.

Kimberly moved out as soon as he returned home. He still had Alexis and that was all that mattered.

Josh divorced Kimberly in July of two thousand and ten. He had stopped drinking. He was lost and did not know how to attempt to recover his life. He turned to the people that cared for him, his daughters, Bill, Al and Bryan. He knew they were there for him. Al was a man in his mid-fifties that reminded him of a stereotypical fatherly type. He had been a paramedic for over twenty years and he felt the need to look after all of the "kids" in the department. He would always make sure they had time to rest, eat and enough equipment to do their job well.

Al was an intelligent man with a gentle nature and an all around family man that worked hard to pay the bills and send his children to school. He was truly a good man. Josh was glad to have him as a friend, a friend that had saved his life.

Bill was another interesting acquaintance that had unofficially appointed himself as Josh's sponsor. Bill was a hulk of a man, six feet and one inch tall and sported two hundred and thirty pound of solid muscle. He had short dark hair and deep set shadowy eyes that surely made him interesting to women. He was an athlete in the Celtic games and spent his weekends wearing a kilt and tossing hundred pound cabers and bags of rocks over metal bars that were suspended thirty feet in the air. Bill looked a lot like the celebrity comic and singer, *Henry Rollins*. Bill carried a similar attitude as Rollins. He was intelligent, comical and enjoyed satire immensely. Bill had been a hard-core drug addict and alcoholic for most of his young life, but by the age of forty he had been sober for nearly thirteen years.

His favorite piece of advice to offer when Josh was considering doing something volatile was,

"Play the rest of the tape, man. Think of it like a movie. What you do may make you feel better but fast forward to the consequences in your head and I bet you change your mind."

Bill was right and his words and discussions over the telephone were instrumental in Josh remaining sober and conscious of all that life really had to offer.

Josh was still empty inside. The alcohol was gone, Alexis was talking to him again, the bills were getting paid and work was going much better. He was amazed at how efficient he could be when he was not hung over.

Alexis and Josh cleaned house together, talked about her life and friends at school, spent time with her friends. Josh even met her boyfriend and invited him to visit and watch movies. Josh was becoming more of father than he had ever been. He still harbored dark thoughts in his head. When he felt like he was ready to give up, Bryan would call as if he knew things were bad, and Josh would feel better after they had spoken.

Josh was still working at the ambulance service on the weekends to keep busy and try to finish off paying for the debts that were still lingering. It was late in the evening on Saturday, July 25th, 2010 when his life changed again.

Due to Alexis' prompting, he finally obtained a Facebook account to reunite with old friends. One friend request sent a shock through his heart. He stared in disbelief at the message that read,

Kelly O'Hara wants to be friends: Accept or Decline?

Josh clicked *Accept* immediately and began to view her profile. Kelly was still so beautiful after all of these years. He felt the same heat inside his chest when he looked at pictures of her. She had many photos of her with her friends and horses which in some cases were one and the same.

She looked happy in all of the pictures and she was always surrounded by people. Josh always knew that Kelly had the uncanny ability to attract people. She enjoyed spending time walking the fence lines with her horses trailing behind her. The horses knew Kelly was their caretaker and maybe even viewed her as their permanent mother; they followed her everywhere like large loyal puppies that would never let her leave their sight.

Time seemed to have no effect on Kelly; she had not aged over the years. Josh lowered his eyes in despair as he saw the hint of his reflection in the computer screen. His hair was thinning with age and lines on his face had deepened drastically over the years, especially about the corners of the eyes and the center of his forehead. He could tell he had spent too may hours frowning and squinting.

His face was weathered and rough, too rough for a man in his mid-thirties. The trauma from kickboxing had taken its toll as well. His left eye held a puffy appearance that had not been their seventeen years ago. He was always sucker for a right hook and the appearance of his left eye proved it.

He could not look at Kelly's page without thinking of Meaghan. They were linked in his mind. He looked at pictures of Meaghan. She was pretty and had a strong look about her. She had a round Irish face with dark hair and eyes that appeared to change color. Her cheekbones were high and pronounced; she had a smile that looked familiar. Her nose was straight and thin in the middle and pointed slightly upward at the tip.

She looked almost angelic in his eyes. In one photo, she was making a face and had her nose crinkled and her eyes wide open. He thought for a moment that he had seen that photo before, but he couldn't have. Then reality hit and struck him with the force of a sledgehammer to the chest. Meaghan looked like Alexis! Josh swallowed hard. He accessed Alexis' profile and set Meaghan and Alexis' pictures side by side. The resemblance was undeniable. He nearly fainted.

He began to chain smoke and pace. He could not believe that Kelly wanted to talk to him after all of this time. *Why would she want him now?* He was not the perky teenager he was when they met all those years before.

Josh decided to send her an email and take his chances. If anything it would be nice to hear her voice and more importantly her infectious laughter. He prepared to click the "Compose" button and the computer lit up with an alert. He was too late. Kelly had already sent a message to his inbox. It read,

Hi Josh,

I feel really stupid emailing you even though I have to admit I've been looking on here for you, forever. I've been reading your posts and I am sorry to hear about your divorce though

of course I never knew you got married. It's been so long since I saw you or talked to you. I know we spoke for while and I still can't figure out what happened. I remember I wanted to see you, but for some reason you decided against it. I have never stopped thinking about you and wondering how you are. I apologize if I have hurt you in any way, it was not my intentions if I did. You are still and will always be in my heart and why that is I don't know. My feelings for you will never change I suppose.

I still would very much like to hear from you and would love to talk to you and perhaps meet up again. This is really awkward for me as I just can't seem to express what I am feeling. I am hoping I will hear from you soon.

Kelly

Josh clicked reply before he finished reading the words. He sent a single simple message, *"Call me"*, with his cell phone number listed at the bottom. He stood up and took a deep breath as he felt his hands start to shake again and his stomach churn. He lit another cigarette. Within five minutes his phone began to ring. Josh nearly tripped over his own feet trying to reach for it. He answered on the second ring. His voice trembled as he choked on the word *Hello.*

A soft voice with a north Chicagoan accent said, "Hello."

Chapter 15

"Kelly! I have one thing to say to you," he said trying to sound angry

"Show me your balls!" he joked.

Kelly began to laugh hysterically on the other end.

"I can't believe after all of these years, you still remember that!" she said in disbelief.

Josh's voice softened to a whisper as he said with more honesty in his tone than he hoped she would notice, "I remember everything about you Kelly. I always will."

"How have you been?" Kelly asked trying to sound nonchalant.

"Not good babe, but I am better now that you called", he said quietly with a hint of despair buried in his words.

"What has been going on?" Kelly asked, fearing what he might say. She hoped his health was not in danger.

"I know what has happened, because I lived it. Why it all happened I cannot tell you. Life got really crazy for me since I saw you last. Things just kept getting worse and I was usually the cause of it, I think. I don't know", he was stumbling over his words. He had never done that before when he spoke to Kelly. He could tell her anything without fear and she always looked back at him with those gentle brown eyes.

"Talk to me, Josh, it is okay, I have the rest of my life," Kelly winced on the other end of the phone. She could not believe that those words came out of her mouth. It was too much, too early, it sounded like commitment in her head.

Although her heart designed the words her mind rebutted and informed her she should be committing herself, for even hinting about interest in anything long-term with a man she had not seen in years that may have turned into an axe murderer for all she knew. Kelly fell silent hoping Josh did not notice the underlying feeling in such a simple statement.

"I don't know. I feel like I have been locked up in this box my whole life and I have been trying to drink and fight my way out of it. Feels like I can see through the keyhole, but I can't get out. Crazy, huh?" Josh said.

"No, tell me about what is going on" she asked with intent in her voice.

Josh told Kelly everything. He was brutally honest about how he had been drunk, suicidal and depressed for most of his life. Josh felt like he was trapped in his own life and there was no way to get out. The conversation lasted with Josh explaining in explicit detail every sin he had committed and how he was at the end of the proverbial rope.

Kelly was silent throughout Josh's review of the last sixteen years. She was conflicted in her heart and soul. She listened in disbelief as Josh rolled out the stories of the wives, the bad calls, the sex episodes, fighting in the ring and eventually the night of the overdose that nearly claimed his life. A logical woman would have ended the call with a *"Well, nice talking to you, have a good one—I have to go"*, but Kelly could not.

She felt differently. Her heart ached as he told the story of what had happened to him since she saw him last. She felt in some strange way that she could have prevented all of this and given him the love he desperately craved and never received. She knew there was more to him than what he had become. In the same thought, she was impressed that he had succeeded in college and had done so many things in his career, all the while living through a personal turmoil at home. She wanted nothing more than to hold his injured body and heal his broken heart.

Josh finished his tale by saying, "So, that is pretty much it and how have you been?"

"I have a headache" Kelly replied. He was always the talker and Kelly was always reserved and quiet which worked out nicely.

She continued, "I guess my life is pretty boring compared to that", she admitted. She spared Josh the details of the abusive relationships and the constant stresses of her job at the police department. She planned to tell him of the most frightening time of her life, but Kelly put herself second to Josh. She felt that she needed to be strong for him and not add additional burden to his situation by telling him how she had feared for her life at several times over the years. Kelly feared for Josh's safety as well all those years before. She knew if she allowed Josh to become part of her life he may end up killed.

Kelly was never a paranoid person. Her grandmother had made her strong. Her name alone had sealed her destiny. Kelly means "Warrior Woman" and she truly was. She rarely harbored fear of death for too long.

The only true terror she had experience was when Meaghan was nearly killed by a rampaging stallion.

Meaghan was around four years of age when Kelly brought home a stud pony. Kelly sent him to the university to be gelded but something went wrong. The surgery was botched and the pony was only partially gelded and still had the raging episodes of a stallion.

Little Meaghan was in the pasture with a Beau and Fanny, two gentle mini-horses, while Kelly was bringing supplies from the house. The minis held a special spot in Meaghan's tender heart because they were little like she was and loved to play. One mini-horse in particular was very special to Meaghan. He was her first pony. His name was Charlie. He was nearly ten years old when Kelly brought him home; Meaghan was at the tender age of two when she gave Charlie his first loving hug. Her little arms could barely reach his neck and Charlie, feeling the gentleness of the child, lowered his head to receive the embrace. A friendship that would last a life time was born.

He quickly became Meaghan's best friend. He was light grey in color and had a long silver mane that fell neatly about his withers and a matching silver tail that barely missed the ground when he stood. He was barely thirty one inches tall. Charlie was docile and would wander around the pasture with Meaghan, like a family dog. Charlie was not just a horse; he was part of the family and Kelly and little Meaghan would make sure that he lived his life surrounded by the love only a family can give.

When Meaghan would run and giggle through the pasture Charlie would prance and kick his back legs in the air to entertain her. He would run in circles, then run back to little Meaghan, turn quickly and stamp his hooves playfully then run away again while looking at her and tossing his head with a cheerful whinny as if to say,

"Tag, your it, come and catch me!"

Meaghan would run after him laughing the entire time. Charlie loved Meaghan and she loved him too.

One spring day, Meaghan was out in the pasture petting the newest addition to their family, Beau, two-week old mini-horse that had been born to Fannie and Charlie. Charlie was grazing near the fence keeping a watchful eye on the young girl and his new family as he always did. The scene was peaceful as the gentle spring breeze wafted through pasture carrying the sound of a child's giggles and the feint whinny of an infant mini-horse into the abyss.

Kelly secured the stallion in the barn after she learned of the error that had occurred during surgery. She knew he could become hostile and dangerous; she did not want to take the chance of Meaghan or any of her treasured minis being harmed by this insane pony.

He breeding was as a Pony of the Americas and he had an attitude that mimicked a bull. Kelly was taking no chances as she double checked the soundness of the gate. Feeling confident that the pony was adequately penned, Kelly walked to the house to gather some equipment to care for the rest of the horses. She smiled as she saw Meaghan playing her peek-a-boo game with the willing baby horse. She patted Charlie on the neck as she passed by.

The stallion was becoming restless in the stall as he spied Meaghan and the Fannie in the pasture. He wanted out and he was not going to be contained as long as he breathed. He kicked hard and the immovable gate frustrated him further. His eyes went white with rage as he kicked violently and reared. The gate gave just enough for him to topple over the barrier. He was at a dead run in an instant as he eyed his target, the little Fannie, Baby Beau and the smaller Meaghan.

Kelly was exiting the house with her arms full of equipment when she saw the charging pony. He had his ears pinned back and his mouth open baring his teeth, while shaking his head violently as he ran. Fannie, Beau and Meaghan were directly in his path. Kelly dropped everything and ran as fast as her lean legs could carry her. She screamed loudly,

"Meg! Get to the tree! Hug the tree! Hurry, Run!" she screamed.

Her only hope was that Meaghan could make it to the tree near the edge of the pasture and hide behind it as the crazed pony rampaged thru the pasture. Kelly hoped it would give her time to get to Meaghan before the pony did. He was nearly four feet tall at the shoulder which made him more than large enough to easily kill Meaghan and any of the minis.

Meaghan ran to the tree. The pony continued his charge his heavy breathing filled his lungs and blasted from his open mouth as he ran. Meaghan was losing the race the pony was covering the distance too fast. Kelly ran harder but sheer distance determined that she was not going to make it. She screamed again, this time at the pony.

At the last moment like a bolt of angry lightning, Charlie interrupted the charge by colliding with the rampaging pony. His launch from the ground was so quick, it appeared as though he had been shot out of a cannon. Charlie struck the pony in the hindquarters and clamped his strong jaws down on the pony's tail.

The pony slammed to a halt due to the weight of Charlie, now completely suspended by the stallion's tail, with all four hooves dangling above the ground. Charlie released his grip and spun with the speed of a cat and began violently kicking at the stallion, striking any portion of the pony's body that his miniature legs could reach.

The pony retaliated kicking hard, striking Charlie's right eye with his concrete-like hooves. Charlie, in pain and blinded, refused to go down as he continued to attack the bewildered pony until Kelly arrived. Charlie backed away as Kelly restrained the pony forcefully locking him back in the barn. Kelly looked at Meaghan who was crying still hugging the tree. Fannie and Beau had retreated to the fence line and stood quivering in fear. Charlie limped toward the fence to check on his own family.

Kelly ran to Meaghan and scooped her into her arms and covered her with kisses.

"Meg, baby, are you all right?" she cried. "I ought to shoot that damn idiot!" she vented.

"Charlie, got hurt mom, is Charlie okay? He saved me!" Meaghan cried loudly, tears streaming down her soiled reddened round face. Kelly felt tears coming to her eyes and a lump swelling in her throat. She carried Meaghan to the wounded Charlie.

"Down!" Meaghan ordered, kicking to get to the ground to check on the welfare of her savior. Charlie's eye was badly swollen and draining clear fluid. Kelly placed her on the ground and followed as Meaghan ran to the injured animal. Meaghan embraced Charlie and covered him with kisses. She thought that would make it, "*all better*".

"Mommy! Help him" Meaghan pleaded as the tears continued to flow.

"I will baby. I am going to call right now", Kelly promised as she examined the damage to Charlie's right eye. She knew it was serious. She would have to call the university to see if anything could be done for her beloved Charlie.

Kelly took Charlie to the veterinarian and the news was grim. He would never regain the sight of his right eye. The veterinarian treated the wounds and gave little Charlie pain medication and antibiotics, but as for the use of his right eye—no treatment was possible. Charlie would be blind in his right eye for the rest of his life. Kelly felt sick. She would have given her own eye if it meant restoring sight to Charlie. Kelly treated Charlie with tender care and slowly he returned to his old playful self acting as if nothing had happened when he played once again in the pasture with Meaghan and baby Beau.

Kelly took the crazed pony to the auction and sold him. She made sure that he would never set a hoof on her land again. Although he was a crazed animal, Kelly opted not to put him down; maybe someone could work it out of him and Kelly considered euthanasia as a last resort for any animal.

From that point forward, Meaghan always approached Charlie from the left to give him her daily hug and thank you. Charlie never had to fight after that day, he lived in peace with his equine and human family that loved him equally so.

Kelly opted to wait and tell the story of Charlie and Meaghan to Josh, when she had time to decide where this conversation was going. Kelly preferred to be silent and choose her words carefully, unlike Josh who would simply say what was on his mind and deal with the consequences later.

Josh came to his senses and decided to ask why she wanted to see him.

"So, what is up with you, I guess things are okay then?" He could not bear to ask directly for fear she may not want to see him or may change her mind.

"I just wanted too – see how you— felt…" her voice trailed off. She was afraid to ask what she really wanted to know. She feared that he was angry with her for leaving so abruptly sixteen, nearly seventeen years ago.

Josh waited for this and had played this conversation over and over again in his mind. He had always wondered what he would say if Kelly wanted him back. He thought he would have a grand statement that would steal her heart and make her his forever. He was a writer, a poet and now nearing academic professional status in his career. Josh was bright and was never at a loss for words, so this part should be easy. A no-brainer.

He took a deep breath and stopped. He said nothing; a weird sensation tingled through his body. He felt as though he knew what she was thinking. When he met Kelly he could never tell what she wanted or was thinking. She was able to conceal even the most intense emotions inside her. She had developed this skill as a result of years of abuse and tragedy.

Being a police officer helped develop the guardedness that she depended on to protect her physically and emotionally. The only time Josh truly knew what she was feeling was when she chose to let him, such as with laughter and love. The rest of the time she was a blank slate to Josh. He never knew what she was really thinking or feeling, until now.

A familiar voice whispered in his head,
"*She wants a life with you and the children; don't screw it up, be careful, I have let you go as far as you need to, now focus on her, just pay attention and think before you speak*". Josh blinked and shook his head as he held the cell phone to his ear.

"You still there?" Kelly asked, noticing silence that was uncharacteristic of Josh.

Josh inhaled quietly to calm his nerves and focus his voice in a softer serious tone as he said,

"Kelly, I feel the same way about you now as I did then. I care about you. I love you Kelly, no one else could ever compete with you. Everyone else in my life was competing with a ghost. No one was ever going to be enough for me—no one. All I ever really wanted was Kelly J. O'Hara; that is all I ever wanted." He said with a voice that was not his own.

He continued, "When can I see you? I mean if you still want to." He said already knowing she would meet him.

This little mind reading thing with Kelly was a nice gift to have, he wondered if he was imagining the newly found skill. He would wait for her response and see if he was close in his opinion as to what she was thinking.

"Tomorrow?" She replied her voice cracking as she held back the tears. Josh could not help but feel satisfied that he was right. He was excited as he looked at the clock. It was two AM and he was exhausted. He could sleep through the morning and then have just enough time to prepare to meet Kelly, for the first time in sixteen years.

"Meet me in town at the *Dairy Queen* at one. I will be there." Josh said trying not to jump up and down like a kid with an entire plate of ice cream to themselves.

"Okay." Kelly agreed inhaling deeply with a hint of a shudder.

"See you then." Josh said as his phone beeped alerting him that the battery was nearly dead.

Josh put his phone on the table as the screen went dark from lack of power. He finished off a cigarette in two puffs and retired for the evening. He closed his eyes and smiled. As he drifted off to sleep he envisioned the smiles of Kelly all those years before on the dock of the hospital. He slept without dreaming. Josh enjoyed a restful sleep of tranquility that he had not experienced in years.

For the moment, Josh was at peace with himself and the world around him. The chains that restricted his soul were beginning to loosen allowing him to take the first deep breath of freedom in what seemed like a lifetime. Freedom felt good and his body responded and allowed the tensions of his past life to fade, if only for a few hours in the darkness of night surrounded by snoring paramedics.

Kelly planned for the visit all night in her head. She awoke around five am. She had not slept well considering she was talking to him until two. She felt nervous, excited and scared all at the same time. She could not decide whether to scream, dance, cry, sing or vomit. Her emotions were a wreck. She began to ask herself questions;

"What if he doesn't want me when I get there?
What if he doesn't like the way I look?
What if he thinks I am too old?
What if he doesn't show?
What if he thinks I am fat?
What if he thinks I am too boring?
What if he asks about Meaghan?
What do I do if he wants more?
What do I do if he runs away?
What am I going to do or say when I see him?

Kelly was near breakdown when a voice entered her head that could not have possibly been her own.

"Quit whinin' and just get down there. Do you need a swift kick in the ass? Dammit girl, get up there and get what you want."

A sudden calm enveloped Kelly's heart and mind. Immediately, she dressed and planned her trip. The three hour ride was painful, it seemed to take days. The highway seemed to crawl by, even as she sped quickly in her red Monte Carlo to her destination and hopefully Josh.

She arrived early at *Dairy Queen* and no sign of Josh. Josh was on his way to the post office to mail the signed divorce papers to Kimberly as if to put a rubber stamp of *Closed* on that part of his life. He was, as usual, running late but just a few minutes. He hoped she would still be there, if not he would chase her down. He was not letting her go again; he had grown more stubborn with age.

"*Great! This is the ultimate screw you!*" Kelly thought, remembering what her friend Lea had said the last time she tried to meet Josh. "You hurt him so bad he probably doesn't want anything to do with you." Lea said coldly.

Kelly sat for ten more minutes staring at the dashboard. She finally picked up the phone.

"Josh? Where are you?" She asked nervously.

"Be there in one minute," he said with cheerfulness in his voice.

She began to sweat. Her heart was pounding as she saw the 2007 gray Dodge Caliber pull into the DQ driveway. Josh smiled like a child at Christmas when he saw Kelly's silhouette in the driver's side of the red coupe, parked facing north as if to make a quick getaway. He grinned at the thought of her running and him chasing with the police behind. He grinned wider as the scene from *The Blues Brothers* flashed through his head.

He was wearing a suit and Kelly had never seen him in one, he bet that the sight would throw her for a loop. He noticed how she had not aged over the years. She looked as young and beautiful as she had that fateful Thanksgiving.

"She ain't getting away again, no way", he said as he loosened the tie.

He pulled up next to her car and exited the vehicle quickly. He gave himself a quick glance in the window of his car to check his appearance. He hated that his hair had gotten thinner over the years. Maybe if he made her laugh hard enough she would not notice so much.

He walked toward her and said nothing. Kelly's cinnamon brown eyes met his gaze and he immediately embraced her. The couple held each other tightly in silence for what seemed to be a lifetime. Josh cupped the back of Kelly's head in his palm as he had done so many years before when they made love and cradled his head against hers. He felt her shudder as the tears silently fell from her eyes. He hated to see her cry, even if they were tears of joy and release.

All of the emotions that Kelly had tucked deep inside of her soul were pouring out like bursting water, long held captive by a constraining dam. She hoped her nose did not run as she felt the tears fall freely onto Josh's nice suit. She was shocked to say the least that he looked like a man now and no longer a ruddy faced boy.

"*Take her to the park*", a voice said in Josh's head. Another voice immediately followed saying, "*She needs you to make her laugh. She doesn't like feeling so emotional. It just makes her feel weird.*" The second voice said.

Josh looked up a bit into the blue sky, dotted with few clouds, and thought, "*I must really be schizophrenic now, I have two voices in my head*".

"*Shut up and do it!*" the voices said in unison.

"Come on let's go to the park" he said softly. Kelly followed him to the car just as she had the day he rescued her from the hospital. She felt safer than she had in sixteen years.

The park was nearby and empty in the middle of the day. Josh joked, made faces and told stories to make Kelly laugh until her sides hurt. Josh told stories of his kickboxing, sword fighting, crazy professors in college and made light of everything he could to make Kelly smile. He was showing off again for her. He felt like he was that goofy eighteen year old kid that had to ramble on with comedy to conceal his own nervousness. Catching up was an exhilarating experience for the both of them. Josh finally stopped to inhale much needed oxygen and Kelly leaned back on the park table and breathed heavily while holding her sides that were aching from too much laughter.

The conversation, as it had to, turned to a more serious note.

"Meaghan?" Josh asked, as he looked into Kelly's receptive eyes. His inquisitive look was all Kelly needed to know. The words need not be spoken. Josh needed to hear from her that Meaghan was his child. The confirmation had to come from Kelly's lips.

"Yes, the answer is yes, you always knew but I ..." Kelly could not finish the sentence.

She started to feel guilt rushing in. She had to keep it together; she did not want Josh, who appeared to have his life back together, to think she was a blubbering fool that could not handle telling the truth without breaking down.

Josh, as always being quick to jump ahead in a conversation, inquired,

"Are you going to tell her? Do you want me to meet her?" This alleviated the pressure on Kelly. Her eyes revealed relief that he seemed willing. It was like he had read her mind and was planning to finish her responses all on his own. It was like he had a plan already.

"Do you want to? What do you want to do?" She asked knowing he had already decided to meet Meaghan. Kelly supposed she should at least ask.

"Does he already know what I am thinking?" she thought without speaking.

Josh had years to think about how to answer this question and now was not the time to waste thinking. He responded with as much certainty as he had ever possessed in response to a single question.

"Here is what I want to do; I want to kiss you, hold you, make love to you, meet Meaghan, be a good father and get old with you and the kids. Period. Sometimes you gotta say "Fuck it".

Kelly was shocked at how quick he answered and she could reply only one way.

"Okay!" She said bluntly. She wanted to laugh, cry and scream with release simultaneously. She embraced Josh. He held the embrace for a moment then with the zeal of a teenage hormone ridden boy, he pulled her away cupping her head in his hands again and kissed her hard on the lips. The kiss sent lightning through both of them. The pressed harder into each other, pulling their bodies close as if attempting to close a gap that spanned not miles but years.

The lightning turned to intense fire as the kiss lasted and the embrace tightened. He ran his fingers through her hair as she gripped his torso that had thickened with muscle over the years. Kelly felt his firm chest press against her breasts as he kissed her hard and repeatedly, his tongue dancing around hers as they pressed closer together. She was tingling everywhere and she felt the heat between her legs alert her that she must have him.

Josh was faring no better he was aching for her body. He did not care if it was right there on the park bench. He needed her more than the air that cascaded over them in the warm summer day. He had left her in the summer heat and now he was winning her back in the same way. Life had come full circle for the two lovers that apparently God himself had planned all along.

Later that night, Josh met Kelly in a hotel. He knocked on the door and Kelly opened it before her could wrap again. She embraced him at the threshold. He kissed her with the same intent and desire that he had on the park bench earlier that day. The two kissed and pulled at each other's clothes leaving a trail of garments across the hotel room floor.

He remembered her scent, the taste of her lips and the warmth of her body that surrounded his heart like no other could ever do. He felt whole as he entered her body and looked deeply into her wide open eyes. Kelly pulled him deeper into her and moaned as he kissed her lips again.

"I love you Josh, I love you", Kelly said as she felt him move rhythmically inside her. The longing for his body was replaced by release and gratification as she reached climax more forcefully than ever before. She screamed without realizing her actions. She had never lost complete control before, even with him.

Josh was on fire. Every pore in his skin was burning; he could not stop pressing himself deeper into her body. She relaxed after allowing her body to feel every movement of her lover. She waited for his release as she looked into his eyes. She wanted to feel everything in her heart and mind as well as her body. His sweat dripping down on her body sent shockwaves through her soul. Each droplet held love and power; to Kelly they were angel's tears covering her chest and abdomen. She grasped his face hard and kissed him harder as she felt him thicken inside her. Kelly's eyes widened and she gasped as he released. Josh collapsed onto her inviting chest. She stroked his hair as the breathing of the two became one.

For the first time in his life Josh felt his life had meaning. The reason, for being on this earth, the woman that opened his eyes to the wonderful world of what a family could be and true honest wholesome love, was wrapped in his arms and longingly gazing at him with sweet cinnamon eyes.

He felt as though the prison that had enslaved him was nothing more than an empty box that had been opened with love and simply discarded as a useless object, not worth remembering. He was now bathed in love enforced by the lean muscular thighs of Kelly, the only woman that could ever make him whole. She had given him a reason to live, to love, to exist. Kelly had opened his eyes to the meaning of true love and devil be damned if she was ever going to let him imprison himself again.

Kelly began to weep as Josh held her close and cupped her head as he had always done.

"I am so sorry for what I did to you and Meaghan, I should have…" she started to say through the tears.

Josh interrupted, "You did what was right for the both of you, you let me go to try to save the world and the world nearly killed me. You came back to save me again. I was lost without you. All of these years; I have been chasing rainbows and running in the dark, all the while locking myself and my children into a box full of pain and despair that from which I could never escape. You opened my life to me again. I remember what it feels like to be happy, truly and honestly happy. Kelly, you are all I want and all I have ever needed."

Josh brushed the tears away from Kelly's cheek. He kissed her softly and strengthened his embrace. He made love to her again slowly all the while, never breaking his penetrating gaze into her soft brown eyes.

"I love you, Josh", she said as she nestled her face into his chest.

"I love you, Kelly, I always have.

The hours passed quickly. Josh was dreading the return trip home. He wanted nothing more than to stay with Kelly until dawn. Alexis was home asleep and he had to get home before she awoke for school.

"I have to go soon— so what do we do now?" Josh asked.

"I guess— I go back home and tell Meaghan. Are you sure this is what you want? It has to be forever. I can't bear it if it is not." Kelly said with sternness in her voice.

"I don't want anything else, I will tell Alexis the story and we will go from there. I will tell her tomorrow" Josh said with intent.

Josh left a few hours before dawn and spent the morning and early afternoon drinking coffee to stay awake at work. He wondered if Kelly had told Meaghan and how that conversation had turned out. Four thirty could not come soon enough. He would be on his way home and able to talk to Kelly and see where his life was going. He really did not care where he ended up as long as it was with Kelly.

Kelly was steeling herself for the conversation with Meaghan. She poured herself a cup of coffee, which she never intended to drink, as she asked Meaghan to join her.

"What's up Mom?" Meaghan asked.

"I have something to tell you." Kelly swallowed hard as she tried to formulate the words in her head.

"Ok?" Meaghan asked her eyes becoming wide with anticipation of something serious.

"Yes?" Meaghan said quickly to encourage Kelly to continue.

"A long time ago, when I was in Tremane, I met a man. He was young and funny and made me laugh. He was there at the worst time in my life and I needed a friend." Kelly inhaled again to prepare for the rest of the conversation. She hoped she could explain the rest of the story to the wide-eyed teenager sitting before her.

The perceptive Meaghan was already ahead of the story.

"Are you telling me that I have a father?" Meaghan said as Kelly tried to spit out the rest of the story.

"Yes, Meaghan, your real father was a man I met nearly seventeen years ago. I didn't know how to tell you." Kelly said as Meaghan burst into tears.

"Wait, Meaghan!" Kelly said in an attempt to console the sobbing girl.

"Mom that is all I ever wanted was a real dad and a real family! Why did you wait to tell me until now?" Meaghan said sniffing with tears rolling down her face.

Kelly could not respond quickly enough. "Meaghan, I thought it was the right thing to do, I am so sorry, can you forgive me?" Kelly asked with tears in her eyes. Meaghan replied,

"Mom, does he know about me?" She asked with anxiousness emanating from her entire body.

"Yes, he was there when you were born." Kelly said and began to tell the story again of how Josh was the EMT that drove Kelly and to the hospital. She continued to explain the rest of the story as Meaghan cried and smiled.

"I am happy Mom, this is all I want; does he want to see me?" She asked with anticipation.

"Yes, I spoke to him last night and he wants to meet you and introduce you to your sisters." Kelly said with relief.

"I have sisters too!" Meaghan nearly squealed. "Can I meet them too!" she asked.

"Yes, how would you like that for your birthday? It is coming up" Kelly said happily.

"Yes, Mom, more than anything!" Meaghan exclaimed.

"I will be calling your Dad, when he gets home from work; I will let you talk to him", Kelly said with a warm feeling entering her chest making it a little hard to breathe. She was on the verge of bringing a family together once and for all.

"When does he get off?" Meaghan asked.

"Four thirty, I think. I will call about five" Kelly said quickly.

Meaghan sat with Kelly and continued to ask about Josh and how Kelly had managed to find him again. At that moment, sitting around the kitchen table in Indiana the mother and daughter bond between Kelly and Meaghan grew stronger.

In Illinois, Josh nearly ran out of the door of his office as the clock stuck half past four. He hurried home and as if it was perfectly timed, the phone rang as he pulled into the drive. It was Kelly.

"Well, I told her everything." She said with a sigh of relief

"And?" Josh asked.

"She burst into tears and cried through the whole thing. I tried to just get it all out there." Kelly said.

"She has been waiting for me to call you ever since. She is more excited than I have ever seen her. She cried a lot, but it was a good cry I think. This is all she ever wanted and it has made her very happy." Kelly said with what sounded like a smile in her voice.

"Is she okay" Josh asked with concern.

"She is more than okay, she is very happy" Kelly answered.

"Is she there? Can I talk to her?" Josh asked.

"Yeah, here she is" Kelly replied as she handed the telephone to Meaghan's shaking hands.

"Uh, Hello?" Meaghan spoke into the receiver.

"Meaghan, as you know this is your Dad. Your real Dad and I want to start off by saying, I love your mother very much and I was there on the day you came into this world. I will do anything I can to make you both very happy." Josh had to get to the point quickly in case he lost his composure and started to cry.

"So, what are you like? And I have a sister?" Meaghan asked to confirm.

Josh told Meaghan about her two sisters and how Alexis looked so much like her that it was uncanny. He told the story of the trip to the hospital, with Kelly in labor in a comical tone to make Meaghan laugh. The laugh sounded so familiar, at times he would forget it was Meaghan and swear he was talking to Alexis. The conversation lasted for an hour with Josh telling Meaghan, how he had come to meet Kelly and what he had been doing, censored of course, over the past sixteen years. He asked about school, her friends and her life with the horses. He was becoming a typical father, a thought that had frightened him terribly in the past was now an act that was as natural as breathing. He felt free in his heart.

He finished the conversation with Meaghan, with an "I love you" that nearly made he and Meaghan cry. She responded with the same phrase and gave the phone to Kelly who was also wiping the tears from her eyes.

Josh spoke with Kelly about the plan to meet the day before Meaghan's birthday and spend a few days together at Josh's house. He knew time was running short and he would need to have a similar conversation with Alexis. It was his turn to tell Alexis about Meaghan, he hoped he had the strength to do so. He said goodbye to Kelly as she wished him, "Good luck" with the conversation with Alexis. He clicked the phone closed and called for his daughter.

"Lex?" Josh called into the living room.

"Yeah, Dad." she answered.

"Can you come outside? I need to talk to you." He said nervously.

"Uh, Okay?" She said expecting the worst. She was used to major issues, since Josh's recent breakdown she could only imagine it was something worse. She could not take anymore. She gritted her teeth together as she walked out to the porch swing. A technique Josh and his sensei had taught her during the time they spent learning Tae Kwon Do together during Josh's martial arts phase. She would do this to prepare for being hit in a sparring match to avoid being knocked out. The technique worked similarly for her when she was preparing for bad news.

Her father always seemed to have bad news. She would like, once, just once for her father to have some happy news for her.

She expected nothing good when she sat on the swing uneasily looking at her father who was chain smoking, also not a good sign. Alexis, like Meaghan, was very perceptive.

"Lex, I do not know how to say this so I am just going to spit it out." He began as Alexis sat down on the porch swing.

"A long time ago, I met a woman named Kelly when I was working in Tremane. I was just young kid, only four years older than you. We started seeing each other. I loved her, but she thought I was too young and well she decided it was best that we did not see each other anymore", he stammered.

"And?" Alexis said folding her arms across her chest an action that later Josh would notice that Meaghan performed when she was irritated. Josh continued,

"She had a daughter. Her name is Meaghan. This happened two years before you were born, even before I met your mom, I did not know until Monday, you see, I transported Kelly to the hospital when she was pregnant.

I thought the baby may be mine, but I was not sure and Kelly for her own reasons told me that she was not. She thought it was the right thing to do at the right time. I was really young and I was not sure what the right thing to do was, so I did what Kelly asked. I stayed away— then I met your mother and you know the rest." Josh exhaled and stared at the floor of the porch on Dean Street.

Alexis' hazel green eyes were already welling with tears as she covered her eyes with her hands she cried,

"I have a sister, you never told me about! You know I don't get to see my other sisters!" she said referring to Terri's other children.

"All I ever wanted was a sister like me. Not stupid like some of the ones that pretended to be my sisters! They never liked me. Dad, I don't know how much more I can take! Mom gets in trouble and now I can't see her or my sisters, you get drunk and go crazy and almost die; now I have a sister, come on! I can't do this!" She cried in anguish.

Josh felt tears rolling down his face. He could not say anything, she was right and all of her statements were painfully true. He could barely look into the eyes of his daughter; he had wronged her in so many ways. He prayed silently that this long shot at a true family could, in part, make amends for so many dark years that had passed into eternity.

"I know I was a bad father, Alexis and I can never ask you to forgive me, but Meaghan wants to meet you and her mother Kelly, too. Can you be okay with this, you are so important to me and to them, would you be willing to meet them?" he asked, forgetting that he had already set the date.

Alexis, knowing her father too well, expected they were coming, whether she liked it or not said,

"When do they get here?"

"Tomorrow" Josh said feeling sheepish that Alexis had already busted him out.

"I guess I will have to be", she said as she stared down the street at nothing in particular.

Josh sat with Alexis in silence for an hour. He did not know what else to say except, "Good night and I love you", as Alexis passed to retire for the night.

"Love you too, Dad", she said and disappeared into the house.

Work was terrible the next day. The minutes felt like days and Josh could not focus on anything. He was relieved when the four thirty mark arrived. Kelly and Meaghan were to arrive at his home at nine.

Josh and Alexis were standing outside when the red Monte Carlo stopped in the driveway. Josh walked toward the car as Meaghan opened the passenger side door and stepped out into the driveway. Alexis stood near her father not sure how to react to this meeting.

The two girls walked toward each other slowly. The girls were nearly mirroring images of each other and they, along with Kelly and Josh, both new it. The only difference was hair color and Meaghan was about two inches taller. They embraced each other.

"Hi, Alexis, I am Meaghan, your sister", Meaghan said as tears again entered her hazel green eyes.

Alexis replied, "I am Lexie, your sister", tears glistened in her eyes as well. The two were silent as they hugged each other firmly.

Kelly stood at the rear of the car with her hand over her mouth, crying softly, as the two girls stood locked in an embrace, rocking gently side to side.

Josh embraced Kelly then stared into her dark eyes and said,

"Those are our girls, smiling", Josh said with happiness swelling deep within his heart. He had never felt so complete.

"I know, baby, I know", Kelly said with a smile.

Josh escorted them all into the house. The group spent the night telling stories of their lives while Josh entertained, making them all laugh mostly at his own expense. For the first time in years, he heard Alexis truly laugh; however this time the laugh was in stereo.

Meaghan's laughter was exactly the same. Meaghan did have a bit of the northern accent, similar to Kelly, but her mannerisms were all Alexis and Josh. She had his eyes, his smile and his nose. He stood dumbfounded as he eyed each similarity between girls with equal zeal. It was too eerie.

The way they stood, walked and laughed confirmed that the two girls were linked by more than history, pure genetics. The girls chattered and laughed about comical experiences in their young lived as Josh and Kelly watched proudly from across the kitchen table. Josh joined in the comedy and described the last time he had been pulled over by a very rural police officer in a small town near them. He pulled his pants up high and spoke with a nasally twang and imitated the small town peace officer with enthusiasm. Kelly and the girls laughed until they cried. Alexis had never seen her father act so silly. She was enjoying the carefree evening at home.

Meaghan spoke about her horses and the shows that she had won with her ponies and quarter horses. Alexis sat with her hand supporting her chin as Meaghan embellished the story of how *awesome* it was. She was an avid storyteller, often sending herself into fits of laughter with her own comedic routine. Alexis suffered the same fate. She would describe her grandfather, Josh's dad, and become so tickled with her own description she would burst into laughter.

She would laugh until she cried. Her laughter would spark Meaghan into a fit of giggles and the two would laugh together and wave their arms in the same pattern. It appeared as though they had spent their entire lives together and were constantly sharing a private joke that only the two of them were privy to the punch line.

Later that evening, Josh and Kelly asked the girls to join them on the front porch to talk. Both girls looked at each other with raised eyebrows. They were used to these types of conversations. It usually meant for Meaghan that she may be moving and for Alexis it usually meant that her father was leaving and she had to go with him.

The girls followed single file out into the evening breeze. Josh and Kelly greeted them and asked them to sit. Both girls let out a sigh as they sat down. Kelly grinned and shook her head as she observed the similar mannerisms. She looked at Josh, who had noticed it too. He chuckled and nodded.

Kelly began the conversation.

"Girls, now that you know the whole story, we have to make some decisions. Josh and I want to be together, but it is not all about us. You must be part of the decision; we want to make a family and you both have equal say in the matter." Kelly said as the girls both stared at the cement steps upon which they sat.

"We can move to my farm; in which case Alexis would have to change schools and Josh would need to find another job. If we stay in this house, Meaghan would have to switch schools and I would sell all of the horses." Kelly said as she swallowed hard. Josh heard her gulp and looked at the sky thinking, "If I let her do that, they will all hate me and probably tie me, covered in honey, to an ant hill."

Both girls in unison, the synchronized actions were becoming more evident with every minute, turned and shook their heads saying,

"No!"

Kelly seemed relieved with the response as she let out a long breath that she had been holding tight since making the comment.

"I don't want to lose this, Mom, All I ever wanted was a family and switching schools is not that big of a deal to me. We can move down here and maybe board the horses", Meaghan said hoping her solution would work for everyone.

"Dad, you promised that we would never move and I could finish high school here. You promised and I don't want to leave!" Alexis snarled.

"I don't care about this house though, but I want the horses, can we find another place?" she asked offering a solution of her own.

Kelly and Josh looked at each other and smiled.

"It's possible", Josh said, "Why don't you girls talk it over without us interrupting and we will wait for you inside. When you come to a decision, come and talk to us."

Kelly added, "Your dad and I want to be together and we will make that happen, but we need you girls to talk it over and help us decide exactly how we do this so everyone is as comfortable with the decision, okay?"

"Okay", both girls mumbled under their breath as they looked down again. This time they were unconsciously twirling their hair at the same time. The mannerisms were becoming almost comical. Kelly walked quickly into the house to avoid laughing.

Kelly and Josh joked in the kitchen about funny things that had happened in their lives in the years past. Josh was playing the comedian again to keep Kelly from fretting about the emotional conversation occurring just outside. He knew she was worried about how the girls felt about this life altering event. Against his better judgment, he continued to make her laugh.

After nearly an hour, the girls came in. Meaghan had been selected as the spokesman, while Alexis stood, arms folded, as if she was working a protection detail for the President.

"We want to live here and keep the horses. I will switch schools and Alexis said she will do what ever it takes to keep the horses." Meaghan said in a matter-of-fact tone.

"Are you sure?" Josh asked, "Alexis horses are a lot of hard work."

Kelly nodded her head in agreement.

"Yes, that is what we want", Alexis confirmed as Meaghan now stood in a defensive posture.

Kelly and Josh looked at each other while the girls waited.

"I guess we have had all of the decision-making we can handle for a night, I am going to get ice cream, girls let's go." Kelly said as she picked up the car keys.

"Best decision we have made so far", Alexis said with a nod of the head that Meaghan mimicked immediately after. The rest of the evening was filled with more laughter and stories. As the girls left for their bedroom, Josh said, "I love you, goodnight".

"Love you too," the girls said in stereo. This time they noticed the harmony in their voices and laughed as the topped the staircase to their bedroom.

Kelly and the girls spent the next day together prepping for Meaghan's birthday. Josh was working and counting the hours. As the afternoon arrived, Josh realized he had no gift for Meaghan. She turned sixteen today and he would not come home empty handed.

He drove to the nearest mall in search for a gift that had to be perfect. He found a jewelry store that had a beautiful necklace with a ruby pendant attached. It was a perfect gift for Meaghan; it had her birthstone and would look wonderful on her. Josh bought it immediately and had it wrapped.

His cell was continually alerting him to new text messages from his awaiting family. He was preparing to respond when his eyes focused in on two necklaces that were on display; that had two beautiful and identical, diamond encrusted keys as pendants on each chain. He heard a familiar voice in his head that was not his own say softly,

"Kelly's keys are there, don't not leave without them; I put them there for you. She opened your heart and gave you your life back, now open hers and bring those girls together, don't be an ass, do what I tell you." A voice in his head instructed. It was the same voice that was there with him on that dark day in the garage.

Josh had to have them. He approached the counter and a motherly looking woman with short blonde hair approached the counter.

"Can I help you?" She said with a warm smile.

"I have to have those keys, both of them", he said urgently.

"Sir, tomorrow they will be twenty percent off, I can hold them for you if you want to save a little. I know how hard it is out there these days and I try to help my customers.

"Nope, gotta have them today", Josh said handing over his debit card.

"What is the special occasion?" She asked with a smile, "By the way my name is Sandi, Sandi Beach, I know it is weird but my parents had a sense of humor."

Sandi scanned the card while Josh said, "Let me tell you a story about those keys", he began.

"I met a wonderful woman when I was eighteen and I lost her sixteen years ago. I have missed her ever since." He began and continued to spell out the story of Kelly, Meaghan and Alexis and how the two girls acted so much like sisters, even though they had only known about each other for a single day. He added that the keys were special to him, they meant freedom and they alone could unlock the chains of time that had kept a family apart.

Sandi forgot about the printing receipt as she listened intently to him. She began to cry as he told the story with all of the emotion he held within his heart. Josh leaned on the counter to point at the keys and say,

"Kelly opened my heart and I think my girls should always be reminded of how she brought us all together, those are Kelly's keys.

"My god, that is a beautiful story, you just wait honey, I am giving you tomorrow's discount anyway and these keys are blessed. I swear they are blessed by God. Now, get home to those girls and that woman that is waiting for you!" She said as she quickly wrapped the keys.

Josh smiled as he walked around the counter, he could hear Sandi telling the story to several of her co-workers, sniffling between sentences. He hurried home as instructed.

Kelly was waiting, along with the girls as Josh gave Meaghan the ruby necklace. She thanked him and admired it in the box. She held it up to her chest while Alexis whistled and nodded in approval.

"You didn't have to do that, Josh." Kelly said concerned he had spent too much money. She always said a family was the best gift anyone could ask for in this world.

Josh didn't miss a beat as he produced two more boxes from his pocket.

"Now, I have something special for my two oldest girls", he said proudly as he placed the boxes on the table. The girls opened the gifts and gasped at the sight of the prize inside. Meaghan forgot about the ruby necklace and quickly put the key around her neck. Alexis did the same. Kelly stood silent with her hand covering her mouth with tears trying to emerge from her eyes.

"Dad, now we really look alike!" Alexis said.

"Oh yeah! I am never taking this off, except to shower of course." Meaghan said.

"Me either, thanks Dad!" Alexis said gleefully.

"Thank you, Dad", Meaghan said. She looked up at him with her bright eyes and for the first time she was staring at her real father, a man that truly loved her with all that he was.

"Keys for my girls, to unlock any dream you may have," he said, hoping no one would think he was being melodramatic. If they did, they did not show it in their faces.

The girls examined every detail of the keys, while Josh and Kelly went to their spot on the porch.

"Now we gotta find a house", Kelly said.

"That is your department. You find it and I will try to work it out with the bank, I don't know how, but I will", he said, already worrying about the cost. The two sat and stared at the sky while smoking an occasional cigarette; wondering, each in their own way, how in the world they were going to accomplish this and move a herd of horses across two states by winter.

Kelly began searching for a farm and after a couple of set-backs she found the perfect place. She discovered ten acre farm with two barns, two ponds and a drive that wound through the property effectively separating the ground into perfect pastures for her horses. The barns were green and since they were an Irish family it must have been an omen. Kelly already had a name for the place, a little pun on the horse business, *Little Road Apples, Pony Farm*. She giggled as she had to explain to Josh what "road apples" were and how they ended up there. He thought it was perfect.

This farm would have gone unnoticed had Josh not found the perfect realtor, Kari. She was a transplant to the Midwest from Manhattan Beach, California and she had the perfect tan to prove it. Her gentle appearance and dark auburn hair that fell neatly about the shoulder may have fooled some folks about her business worth, but not for long,

Kari was a firecracker in the realty world. She was attractive and had facial features that mirrored the actress, *Sandra Bullock*. She had an athletic build; possibly from years of playing beach volleyball as a teenager in California, and she was always well dressed. It would be easy to imagine Kari at a local softball game gently giving athletic advice to the young girls, while simultaneously consoling a player with a sprained ankle and applying an ice bag to relieve the pain. She was kind in her personal life, but in business she was a wildcat and heaven help the fool that crossed her in a business deal.

Kari wore her business suit like a uniform. She had philosophy;

"Get the job done and do it right now", which made her perfect for the needs of Josh and Kelly. Winter was rapidly approaching and the horses had to be moved from Indiana to Illinois and fast.

One realtor broke confidentiality rules and was deliberately delaying the return of Josh and Kelly's earnest money. Kari would have none of that, nor would Kelly. Between the two redheads this man did not have a chance. The money was quickly returned after the two marched into his office like they were on a mission to save Christendom. The man gave Kelly the check and she gave him a piece of her mind, while Kari spouted potential litigation action if he caused any problems with them again.

Kari worked tirelessly and beat the bank and the sellers into submission. She even forfeited her commission at closing to make the deal and ensure Josh and Kelly would have home and a place with plenty of room and pasture that was needed to save the horses. Kari was napalm in heels.

It would be beneficial for any businessperson to stay on her good side. Kari was the best in the business and she succeeded where others would have failed. After the sale, Kari sent a gift card to the new family and wished them the best, she was off to frighten another banker and she would do it decked to the hilt.

Chapter 16

Josh and Kelly were married in May on Kentucky Derby day. The wedding was held on horseback at the *Little Road Apples Pony Farm*. Mama D, a paramedic friend of Josh's was in charge of coordinating the festivities for the day. Her real name was Donna, a country girl at heart that enjoyed horses, family, the country and hometown cooking. She was an excellent cook and a better friend. She warmed up to Kelly and the girls and was always bringing them little identical gifts, such as bracelets, shirts, hats and the like. Mama D continued the tradition of identical gifts that Josh had started.

Mama D was a self appointed auntie for the new family. Bryan, Bill and Al attended with their families; awaiting the moment when Josh would probably be tossed into the cake by an ornery pony or quarter horse. Kelly had stocked the farm with both over the last year. She was selling ponies and training racehorses; an odd combination, but it worked well considering Josh and Kelly were the oddest of combinations themselves.

Kelly even had mystical-looking goat, named Weezer, trained to be the ring bearer. He was a chubby little goat with a bluish undercoat and black spots and sapphire blue eyes that you would think glowed in the dark. He looked like a magical creature from a fantasy novel. Charlie was there too, he was stationed on the bride's side of the platform with Beau and Fannie standing with him. Kelly said she would like to have Charlie be there at the happiest moment of her life, since he had given her and Meaghan so much happiness over the years. Charlie looked as proud as horse can with his head held high in the air as though he was in the middle of a show arena.

The wedding was a big hit, ending with Millie, a quarterhorse running Josh off into the pond immediately after the ceremony had ended. The horse nearly trampled Bill, Bryan and Kari as she galloped by with the flailing Josh hanging on for dear life. Everyone was laughing, especially

Meaghan and Alexis who had swatted Millie on the hip to cause the horse to bolt. Even Josh was laughing in his wet tuxedo. Millie may have even smiled a bit too since she was still dry having stopped just short of the water before flinging Josh into it.

The farm on Deer Creek Road was always filled with laughter.

After the wedding festivities had long since passed, the girls had gone to college and the farm had grown into a ranch, Josh sat on his back porch sipping coffee with Kelly on a cool summer afternoon. They sat in silence as they watched the trainers working the horses, children learning to ride and old men learning to drive ponies.

"You still having that damn bassett hound do the "Show me your balls trick?" The aging Josh asked with a grin.

"Yup, when in doubt ya have to say fuck it!" Kelly answered with a smile as the wind blew her silver hair into her face.

"Quarter horse trainers think we have two or three good prospects this year." Josh said as he took a drink of the black coffee. He ran his hand over his head as if he still had hair there.

"Yea, maybe Congress this year, been five since we have been to one, maybe will go this time instead of letting the girls handle it. What, do you think old man?" Kelly said with orneriness in her tone.

"Old man my ass!" Josh said as he tossed the coffee over the rail and ran after Kelly, who darted toward the door, laughing as she ran. A grind in his hip quickly reminded him of hip surgery he had several years before after being thrown through the barn by a quarter horse with an attitude. He limped as he tried to run after Kelly, who was coughing a bit as she entered the kitchen.

"You old geezer, I still love you" she said smiling causing the wrinkles in her face to deepen a bit.

"Could a geezer, do this?" Josh said as he stepped forward on his good leg and swung her about into a dip, like a slow ballroom dancer, planting a passionate kiss on her lips.

A trainer was walking by the bay window with a champion quarter horse named *Am I Close*. He was so named because Josh would always recite what he thought Kelly was thinking and ask,

"Am I Close?" He still maintained the talent of reading her expressions, just as Harry had all those years before. That furry feline always knew what was on her mind and of course had to relay the information to the dim-witted teenage Josh.

The trainer, Bobby, and Am I Close spied Josh kissing Kelly passionately as they passed by the windows.

"Boy, from what I tell ya, I would not have given them two 80 to 1 odds of makin' it. Shows what I know. I always bet on the favorites" Bobby said as he shook his head in dismay. The horse whinnied in agreement as they walked to the practice track. Josh and Kelly continued to kiss, until Josh lost his footing and they both fell laughing to the floor.

"Medic!" Josh screamed in jest.

"Oh hush, you'll scare the horses, now kiss me before you break something else", Kelly said pulling his lips to hers on the hardwood kitchen floor of their home.

Harry was here first, waiting patiently as always,

"I've been looking for you. I have a story to tell you", he purred as he began to tell me the story of how Josh came to know Kelly.

It was then that I knew why Kelly had certain behaviors over the years, the distant looks, the sadness she held in her eyes when she thought no one was watching, the way she obsessed and guarded Meaghan as if she was the most precious gift she had ever received. It all fell into place as Harry began the tale.

"Well, Harry", I sighed, "I suppose now we just watch and wait."

And wait we did. I watched them both struggle over the years; I saw Kelly buy her first home but she wasn't happy. I watched Josh continue his destructive path of alcoholism, depression and finally the suicide attempt.

I thought, *"Okay, here is where I step in. Josh you saved Kelly once, now someone needs to save you."* It was my voice that spoke to him that day in the garage.

I told him, *"Don't give up yet. You need to fight, now get up!"*

During this time I witnessed the most peculiar thing; Kelly would sit on her front porch late at night and talk to me. She would ask me all kinds of questions such as,

How should I handle this?
What should I say in this situation?
Grandma what do I do, can you help me?

One night in particular when Kelly was crying and feeling utterly depressed she did the most uncharacteristic thing; she walked out into the middle of her lawn, raising her hands to the sky she began to pray. She said with a weakened voice and tears streaming down her face,

"Please God, tell me what I did wrong? Tell me why I have worked so hard for everything and although I have everything I ever needed, I am still not happy? What am I doing wrong?"

"*Good grief,*" I thought, "*I have got my work cut out for me once again.*" This time I answered her prayer. As a familiar voice in her head, I told her,

"*Find him, it is time.*"

As Kelly began her search, I was already busy working on Josh. I sent the nurses to him and told them what to say on that fateful day in the ER. Feeling confident that the little shit would survive, I helped Kelly find him again. I enjoyed watching the two of them come together once again, but my work was not complete. The two estranged lovers were not yet a family.

I thought,

"*Okay, one more thing and then I have to go and the rest is up to you.*"

I sent Josh those keys and a blessing that would free them from the prisons of darkness that had contained them both for many years. These keys were not mere pieces of metal and stone. They held the blessings from God that would open the hearts of Kelly, Josh and most importantly the two young, beautiful girls, to a life filled with happiness and love and most importantly, family.

I knew it would not be easy for them at first. When it comes down to it, they really did not know each other at all and the feelings of guilt and unspoken regrets made the reunion trying at times. It must have been difficult for two families to collide and try to make things work, but for some strange reason Harry and I knew they would survive. Kelly and Josh were simply too stubborn to fail.

Harry and I believe true love does exist and we are fortunate to have had the opportunity to see it materialize, as we watched from beyond the grave. I met Harry shortly after my death and we shared the stories of the two most important people in our lives.

"*Well, just look at those two old geezers on the floor down there, they are just happy they can get out of bed in the morning and make it to their rockers on the front porch. You have to admit that it is heartwarming to see them hold hands. I expect to see them soon."*

"Harry, my little fur-ball friend, I am gonna grab a beer and sit in the recliner and watch the game going on down there. Would you like to curl up in my lap? I think our work here is finished."

"By the way, my name is Virginia, but you can call me Grandma Honey."